JACK FLINT
AND THE
SPELLBINDER'S CURSE

JOE DONNELLY

Illustrated by Geoff Taylor

Orion
Children's Books

First published in Great Britain in 2008
by Orion Children's Books
a division of the Orion Publishing Group Ltd
Orion House
5 Upper St Martin's Lane
London WC2H 9EA
An Hachette Livre UK Company

1 3 5 7 9 10 8 6 4 2

A catalogue record for this book is
available from the British Library

ISBN – 978 1 84255 703 7

Typeset by Input Data Services Ltd, Bridgwater, Somerset

Printed in Great Britain by Clays Ltd, St Ives plc

www.orionbooks.co.uk

For Linda Young, Gavin Docherty and
Chick Young, for years of fun.

ONE

Corriwen Redthorn had vanished.

She had tumbled, *was thrown*, through the space between the standing stones and she disappeared.

Jack Flint lurched from the far side of the ring of stones with Kerry Malone taking most of his weight. But for his friend's help, he'd have dropped to his knees.

They were hurt, bruised and bloodied. Jack felt as if every inch of his body had been beaten. Blood matted on Kerry's shoulder where *She* had hit him, slammed him into the air.

The *Morrigan*.

As old as time, as foul as sin, the Goddess of Death.

She had harried them across the dead lands, rending the rocks with her fury. They had made it to the gateway – the ring of stones so close to home – so nearly safe, but she had come sweeping after them, a shade within shadow.

She had almost killed them both. But they had survived and had sent her, screeching, down into the infinity of dark.

Kerry groaned. Jack could see the bruise swelling across his cheek, but his eyes were still bright and somehow fierce.

'We beat her,' he said.

'We did. And I think I got us back to *before*. I mean, before it all went crazy.' Jack paused. 'Where is she?'

'I told you. She's gone.'

'No,' Jack said. 'Where's Corriwen?'

They both turned round quickly.

'She was . . .' Kerry started, then stopped. 'I think she was here. I was running with that thing coming on like a train. Then I threw the heartstone to you and she hit me such a wallop I went ass for elbow.'

'Corriwen was hit too,' Jack said. His heart lurched. 'She was hit. I saw it.' He started to walk, ignoring the pain.

'She went flying.' He took a slow step and then another in the direction Corriwen had tumbled when the Morrigan had flipped her away, expecting to find her broken body against one of the standing stones. That final blow must have been devastating.

He moved from one stone to another – then he saw it. On the soft earth, where Corriwen had landed and rolled, scuff marks in the thin grass.

They continued towards the space between two standing stones.

Then they vanished.

Jack looked at Kerry.

'She must have gone through,' Kerry said. Regret and relief were struggling in his expression. 'Back home to Temair.'

Jack shook his head. 'No,' he said. 'That's not the gate to Temair. The *Farward Gate*. She was thrown through the *wrong* one. They were all open at the same time. I saw different places out there.'

They locked eyes. 'Kerry. I don't know *where* she's gone.'

'Oh Jack,' Kerry whispered.

Jack picked up the amberhorn bow and hefted his backpack. His jacket was in rags. One shoe was torn from sole to heel. He was hurting from head to toe. The standing stones towered above them.

Beyond them, Cromwath Blackwood's trees crowded close. Beyond them, some distance away was the tall wall that was built to keep people out. Now he and Kerry knew the astonishing secret of the wall and the stones. The *gates*.

On the other side of the wall was a world back to normal. One without creeping darkness, or whispering shade.

Perhaps the Major's telescope would still be focused on the woods, Jack thought. Everything back the way it was. *Home*.

He itched to get back there, ask the Major all the questions about who his father really was and where he came from. He'd surely have the answers.

Jack paused, heart aching with the need for that knowledge. He walked across the ring, to the space between the stones through which they had run, panicked, on that first night.

Jack leaned against the stone, utterly worn. Utterly torn.

Corriwen Redthorn had saved his life. She had helped both of them survive all the odds in her strange world and helped them get back again.

In a rush, he recalled all their travels in Temair. Their

battles; her bravery. Jack Flint owed a debt of life to Corriwen Redthorn. A debt he would repay come what may, no matter the cost; no matter the sacrifice.

He turned back and faced across the capstone to the gateway through which she had disappeared.

Kerry's eyes followed him, sensing the fight going on inside Jack's mind.

'What do you want to do?'

Jack slammed both fists against the great stone, venting his frustration and despair.

Unsteadily, but very deliberately he limped across the ring of stones.

'She's lost somewhere. Lost and alone. I've got the key to open the gate.'

He turned to face Kerry, looked him straight in the eye. He held up the black heartstone on its silver chain.

'I'm going to find her,' he said.

Kerry nodded. Understanding was clear on his face. He clapped Jack on the back. They both winced.

'Not on your own, you're not.'

'I can't ask you . . .' Jack began.

Kerry held up a hand. 'You're not asking. And you don't have to. We're not going to let a girl come between us, are we?'

'Cross my heart,' Jack said.

'And hope to die.'

And together they walked forward into the unknown.

4

TWO

They passed between the standing stones, turning their backs on the world they knew and everything that was familiar.

The obsidian heartstone suddenly began to vibrate against Jack's chest, so fast it sang a clear high note that sounded like glass on the verge of shattering. He gripped Kerry by the arm as the light of the moon vanished behind them and they waded into a darkness that seemed solid.

Kerry said something, but his voice sounded stretched and far away. Brilliant colours spangled and sparkled all around them. Jack's skin puckered, every hair standing on end as stings of a thousand nettles prickled all over him.

He tried to call Kerry's name but the words were snatched away. His ears popped and pressure pounded behind his eyes.

And then they were stumbling in daylight, pitched forward on short cropped grass. Kerry tripped and his arm pulled from Jack's grip. He went down with a cry and Jack sank to his knees.

Kerry shook his head. 'My ears are still ringing.'

Jack breathed clean cold air. A hard frost rimed the ground and a bitter wind blew.

Somewhere in the distance a lone curlew piped.

'Winter,' Jack finally said. 'Or autumn. Wherever we are.'

'Just brilliant,' Kerry muttered. ' Couldn't she have picked somewhere warm? Like the Bahamas.'

'She didn't have a choice,' Jack replied.

'Only kidding, Jack. Let's find her and get out of here.'

Jack got to his feet, still hurting all over, and helped Kerry up. Both of them looked around, almost as if expecting Corriwen to be sitting on the grass, but there was no sign of her, no footprints, no trodden leaves. No marks in the rime of frost.

The ring of stones had vanished. Only two great pillars of the gateway stood. The stone was eroded with age, but they could still make out the worn carvings on each of their four faces.

'Look,' Kerry said. 'It's a harp. Maybe we're in our own time.'

A harp was etched in great detail into the south face. The others depicted what looked like a great sword, a witch's cauldron, and a club of some sort; its head shaped like a skull.

Down the slope, a stream wound its way through rushes and over shingle shallows. Together they started down the hill towards the water. Jack dropped his pack and the amber-horn bow. Kerry dug his sword into the turf and together they waded in, side by side until the water came up to their thighs, to let its icy cold ease their hurt.

The flow cleansed the cuts and scratches and sucked the heat from their bruises until they began to feel numb from the cold. They clambered up the bank and lay gasping under a leaden sky that threatened rain or snow.

Kerry propped himself up on one elbow.

'You look like you've been hit by a bus.'

'Thanks. You don't look so good yourself.'

'I've felt a whole lot better,' Kerry admitted. 'And I've lost half a shoe.' He held it up. The sole flapped like a fish mouth.

Jack raised a dripping foot. 'Mine are torn to ribbons.'

'I could use some fresh undies. Maybe there's a charity shop.'

'Somehow I doubt it.' Jack levered himself to his feet. 'Come on, she's here somewhere.'

'You sure you got the right gate?'

'Pretty sure.' Jack *hoped*. 'You saw where she hit the ground.'

'Was she hurt?'

'I don't know. Maybe. *It* hit her pretty hard. Swiped her off her feet.'

'I know what that feels like,' Kerry said. The water had washed most of the blood from his rabbit-skin tunic. Jack hoped the cold had closed the wound. He would have to look at it, check the damage.

They made it back up the hill and stood next to the stones,

scanned the land around them. The slope gentled down on all sides, short grass and clover for a hundred yards. A hedge of some sort beyond the stream; a pine coppice further on. Hills in the distance.

Jack rummaged in the backpack and drew out the Major's binoculars, fingered the focus ring and the coppice snapped into close-up clarity. A flock of snow buntings broke cover and whirred out of sight. Jack scanned the trees and saw nothing, then panned around, searching beyond the hedgerow and the stream. There was still nothing to be seen. He had hoped to catch a flash of Corriwen's red hair.

Kerry kept his eyes on the ground. If there was any trace, anything to see, he'd find it. He might have had trouble with books at school, but he could read the ground the way Jack could read stories.

After a while he came back, shaking his head.

'Not a thing,' he said. 'Nobody's been here in a while.'

'That doesn't mean she wasn't here. Or that she won't be.'

'I don't get you.'

'I think time runs differently on the other side. She could be in the past ... or the future.'

'You're taking the mick!'

'I wish I was.'

Jack was holding the heartstone in one hand. It was warm from the contact with his skin, but now no pulsing beat warned him of danger. Finbar the Bard had told him it was a key, and Jack knew now how true that was. He sensed it was much more than just a key. It had saved him from the hellish heat when the ground in Temair had split into bubbling fissures. What else this stone could do, he didn't know. But it had been his father's, and it was the only link he had to a parent he'd never known. He held it tight and tried to think what to do next.

'This links all the worlds,' he finally said. 'And it opens the gates. That's why the Major gave it to me. My father must have been the keeper.'

'So how did the Major have it?' Kerry asked.

'I don't know. He didn't have time to tell me, remember?'

They'd had no time at all, when they ran from the foul darkness that oozed through the big house. It had happened so deadly fast on their way home from the Halloween party. The darkness had flowed up the walls into the Major's house.

Nightshade. That's what he'd called it. Something profoundly bad that had broken through a thin place in the fabric of their world. The Major had stayed to fight it and had told them to run. Down the dark stairwell, along a tunnel Jack had never seen before and they had found themselves in Cromwath Blackwood, then through the mysterious ring of standing stones to Corriwen's world.

Temair. A world Jack had only read about in the Celtic Legends in the Major's library, but a world as real as his own, and for a time, infinitely more terrifying. Yet it was a world, Jack discovered, where his father had already travelled, and even as they journeyed through its dangers, he had found cryptic clues about John Cullian Flint. They had fought their way across Temair, hunted and harried all the way and they had faced the ancient Morrigan that Corriwen's uncle had resurrected in the Black Barrow. They had faced her, fought her and survived.

Jack raised the heartstone, catching the sunlight and sending a prism of purplish light across Kerry's cheek.

'So where are we now?' Kerry asked.

'Only one way to find out.'

Jack took the backpack and pulled out the old Book of Ways which had guided them through the perils of Temair.

He opened it and again, as if by magic, words slowly appeared on the blank page. The script was different, more rounded and ornate than that which had scrolled on the old vellum pages in Temair. On either side of the lines, more faintly etched, the massive stones stood alone on the small hill.

Together they read:

> The Farward Gate of Fair Eirinn
> Journeyman, a quest begin
> The green sward turns to winter Waste
> And famine spreads in evil Haste.
> Traveller be southway bound
> Ere a friend now lost is found.
> Yet journeyman be well aware
> This Eirinn now is serpent lair.
> The quest is now to find the song
> To find a king, to right a wrong
> To fight for right, to face the fate
> Before you find the Homeward gate.

'Clear as mud, as usual,' Kerry remarked.

'Some of it.' Jack's expression was troubled.

'So where are we?' Kerry repeated.

'Eirinn. It's another name for the Celtic world.'

'So it's Temair again?'

'No. The writing's different. This isn't like where we arrived before.'

'Too right. That was totally creepy. Remember the hand that grabbed me?'

'That wasn't the worst of it. *She* was. The Morrigan. Whatever's going on here can't be as bad as that.'

Jack examined the script again. It had taken them a while, back in Temair, to realise the Book of Ways gave warnings as well as directions.

'It says we go south, to find a lost friend.'

'Does that mean Corrie's here already?' Kerry asked.

'I think so. Probably. Or the Homeward Gate is south of here.' Jack closed his eyes, got his bearings, and pointed beyond the coppice. 'It's that way.'

'Okay,' Kerry said, rising to his feet. 'We'd better get moving.'

Jack grabbed his wrist and tugged him back down to the grass.

'But there's more to it than that. It says we have to do something else before we reach the Homeward Gate. I think I worked that out on Temair. You have to *earn* your way home.'

'Are you kidding?'

Jack shook his head. 'I think that's what the Book of Ways is all about.'

'To hell with that,' Kerry said. 'I've had enough quests to last a lifetime. The last one nearly got us killed about ten times. No. We've done our bit. Now we find Corrie and then get our backsides out of here.'

'I wish it was as simple as that,' Jack sighed. 'Somehow I don't think that's how it works.'

He could tell Kerry was itching to be up and off, despite the exhaustion of the past days. Jack squeezed his wrist.

'If we don't get some rest, we won't be any use to Corriwen,' he said. 'And it's getting dark.'

Kerry finally nodded and leaned back against the big stone.

'Maybe you're right. I'm done in.' He closed his eyes for a moment, but a moment was all it took for sleep to take him and soon after that, night crept its way over the hill, casting long shadows that thickened to dusk and then to a starless night. As the last of the light faded, a huge wedge of geese, flying high, arrowed west towards the set sun.

Sometime in the night, their honking woke Jack from a troubled slumber in which the Morrigan screamed after him in dreams. He could barely see the flock, but now they were flying east. He couldn't figure that out. Maybe the geese were just as confused as he was.

It was colder now, much colder, and he huddled inside the old leather jacket in the shelter of the stone, leaning against Kerry to share their warmth, two boys in the dark of a strange world. Above, the sky was black and he scanned it from north to south, searching for the corona that had shone in Temair, but there were no stars and no moon.

Eirinn, the book had said. *Eirinn*. A name from the books

in the Major's library, the tales of mythic heroes that he'd read cover to cover, losing himself in their quests and glory. There's a kernel of truth in every legend, the Major had told him. The universe is stranger than we *can* imagine.

How right he'd been on both counts. But what else did the Major know? Finbar the Bard said he was the last in a long line of *guardians*. Guardians of the Ways.

Now Jack Flint and Kerry Malone were travellers of the Ways. *Journeymen*, like the book said. That first time, they had stumbled through the gate to escape the nightshade pursuit.

This time they had leapt into the unknown to find Corriwen Redthorn.

Jack pulled the jacket closer. He dozed fitfully, wondering if they would ever find Corriwen and the next thing he knew Kerry had clamped a hand over his mouth and pressed him against the stone.

Jack tried to speak, but couldn't make a sound.

'Shhhh!'

Kerry's eyes were shadows, his face turned to look down the hill. Jack nodded.

'You were snoring,' Kerry whispered. 'I heard something.' He took his hand away. 'Out there.'

Jack twisted and peered into the night.

A low rumble like far-off thunder came from beyond the hedge. Kerry tensed beside him.

'What is it?'

The ground vibrated under them, rattling their teeth.

'Can't see, but it's *huge*.'

Heavy footsteps thudded and they heard the hoarse rasp

of slow breathing. They huddled tighter, holding their breath so as to make no sound. Kerry's hand was on his sword-hilt. Jack reached for the amberhorn bow. They stayed still as mice, until the giant footsteps faded.

'I never saw it,' Kerry finally whispered.

'I don't *want* to see it,' Jack replied sincerely. 'Maybe this place isn't as quiet as it looks.'

It certainly wasn't as nice in the morning when they woke, still huddled together, hungry and stiff and frozen.

When Jack opened his eyes, the ground was white with snow, and a snell wind blew sharp spindrift crystals of ice against his cheek.

THREE

They were so numb they could hardly move. Jack roused Kerry who had curled tight against him like a sleeping husky. His shoulders were dusted with ice and his skin was blue.

The snow glistened in the morning sunlight.

'Come on,' Jack said. He scanned the land for any sign of the monstrous creature that had lumbered so close in the night. 'We'd better move before we freeze to death. And I want a look at you. Maybe you broke a rib.'

'Feels more like half a dozen,' Kerry said. 'Lucky she hardly touched me or I'd be dead meat.'

They moved upstream until they came to the thorn hedge, spiked with icicles. Along its length, something had smashed straight through.

'Just as well it never saw us,' Kerry said. 'It would have flattened us for sure.'

The coppice tinkled like fairy bells, frosted pine needles sparkled in the dawn light.

'Weirdest weather I ever saw,' Jack said, recalling the line from their Book of Ways.

*The green sward turns to winter Waste
And famine spreads in evil Haste.*

Before he could ponder that any further, Kerry broke in.

'We have to find something to eat. My stomach thinks my throat's been cut. I could eat a scabby horse.'

'Me too. I'd give anything for bacon and eggs.'

'Sausage and mash. Steak pie.'

'Burgers and beans.'

Kerry grimaced. 'Enough. My belly's rumbling loud enough to hear a mile away.'

'We'll find something,' Jack said. ' I'm sure we will.'

But he wondered what there could be that was edible. They finally stopped beside an upturned root big enough to give them some shelter. Jack made a fire while Kerry got his fishing line and scouted around for good places to lay snares. When he came back, Jack had a billycan boiling over a small fire and a tin mug steaming with thick tea.

'No milk, no sugar, but it tastes fine.'

Kerry picked up the mug and drank with relish. 'Best I ever tasted,' he said. 'I found rabbit runs. There's mushrooms, but I don't know if they're safe. And I nearly hit a pigeon.'

The heat of the fire warmed them up and their damp, ripped clothes began to dry. Jack got Kerry to loosen the rabbit skin tunic he'd made himself for the Halloween party that now seemed a lifetime away. A ragged cut ran from Kerry's armpit across his ribs and his skin was bruised purple.

'I don't like the look of that,' Jack said.

'I don't like the feel of it,' Kerry said. 'But at least we're still walking and talking.'

Jack tore the sleeve of his own shirt, soaked it in the hot water, dabbed it against the cut and winced as Kerry took a sharp intake of breath.

'I think it needs stitches,' Jack said.

'Phone for an ambulance,' Kerry deadpanned. 'I don't trust you with needles.'

He gritted his teeth as Jack made a pad and clamped it against the wound, then fastened Kerry's tunic to hold it in place. It was the best they could do.

'We have to head south,' Jack said. 'That's what the book says.'

Kerry was about to reply when a sharp cry pierced the air. It startled both of them, but Kerry recovered quickly and got to his feet.

'That sounds like dinner,' he said, leading the way from the campfire through a tangle of holly to a narrow track. He'd laid snares here, little loops of fishing line close to the ground. The first three, carefully planted in the centre of a rabbit-run, were still intact, but when they came to the final one, close to the edge of the coppice, it was clear something had been caught.

What was clearer still was that the snare had been cut through, and whatever Kerry's poaching skills had earned them for dinner, was gone.

'I don't believe it,' he hissed. 'Somebody's stolen my catch.' His hand went to the hilt of his sword and he drew it out, turning slowly to scan the trees around them. Jack did the same, amberhorn bow at the ready. The only sound they heard was the growl of their empty stomachs.

'See anything?' Jack said under his breath.

Kerry shook his head. A few leaves had been scattered. A few yards away there was a small depression in the soil.

Slow and stealthy, they followed the near-invisible trail, pausing every now and again to listen, but the forest was silent, except for the distant tap-tap-tap of a lazy woodpecker. As they moved on the pecking got louder. Jack wondered if woodpeckers were edible.

Kerry paused, one hand raised. Jack pushed beside him and they peered into a clearing, and as soon as they did, they smelt wood smoke and then the mouth-watering smell of meat cooking.

A good fire was going in a circle of stones and an old black pot was bubbling away on the coals.

Kerry pointed to the centre of the clearing and a small figure sprang into focus. It was wearing a brown hooded garment and was hunched, close to the fire, working at something they couldn't see.

'Freakin' thief,' Kerry grated. 'He's cooking our rabbit. Let's get it back.'

He wriggled forward, eyes fixed on the hooded figure.

He got to within four paces then lunged and grabbed it by the neck.

The creature squealed like a piglet as Kerry's hand clamped round its throat. Jack ran forward and snatched at the hood.

Kerry yelled in fright as a hairy face loomed at him, mouth lined with long, black teeth as sharp as needles. He got such a start he lost his grip and the creature squirmed away. But Jack grabbed both arms. The creature howled and wriggled but Jack held it tight and then, amazingly, all the black teeth tumbled out of its mouth onto the grass.

'Take your hands off me, you great big oaf!'

Jack froze, as startled as Kerry.

A small whiskery face grimaced up at him. 'If it's gold you're after, that girl's got it,' yelled the little man. 'Her over there.'

Kerry turned to look and the little fellow tried to pull free, but Jack hadn't been fooled. He held tight until eventually the struggling stopped.

'Who are you?' the man demanded. 'Sneaking up on a fellow at work.'

'You stole our food!'

'Oh, yours was it?' His elaborate whiskers shivered like antennae as he spoke. 'And here was me thinking all game's fair game.'

'It was ours. I trapped it myself.'

'Well you should keep an eye on your snares. You never know who's about.'

'We know that now,' Jack retorted. 'Who are you?'

'I'm a leprechaun. Jack of all trades, and master of most. So it's gold you're after, is it?'

'We just want our dinner,' Kerry said. 'And anyway, you're no leprechaun. We've seen them. They live in trees.'

'In trees, eh? That must be the Sappelings you're thinking of. Distant relations, so I believe. Third cousins thrice removed, something like that. A different branch of the family.'

He chuckled, nudged Kerry in the ribs. 'Different *branch*. I must remember that one.'

Kerry rolled his eyes. 'Sure. We twigged the first time.'

'Twigged. *Twigged*? That's even better. You're a sharp one for a thieving poacher.'

'Who are you?' Jack demanded again.

'I'm a Cluricaun. Different family of the leprechauns, so to speak. Who wants to live in an old tree when you've got the open road ahead of you?'

He patted himself down. 'And you've caught me unawares, square and fair, so I suppose it'll have to be the gold I give you.'

'We don't want gold,' Jack said. 'We just want our dinner.'

The little fellow snatched his arm away. He lifted his red cap and showed a bald dome of head, tufted at the ears with white hair. He had sparkling blue eyes.

'Well then, if you had just told me that in the first place, we could have saved all this fuss and bother. Here. I've a fine rabbit stewing. Too much for me, so you're welcome to share.'

'Thanks a million for sharing *our* food,' Kerry snorted.

'Don't you mention it, young feller. And no need to thank

me. I always enjoy a spot of company over a rabbit stew. Sit down and we'll share and share alike and you can tell me what you're doing in this neck of these woods.'

'What happened to your teeth?' Kerry asked.

The leprechaun smiled, pulled his lip down and showed a fine lower set. 'Still got every one, so I have.'

'They were black and spiky,' Kerry said. 'Gave me a heck of a fright.'

The leprechaun burst into laughter.

'Teeth? That weren't no teeth. Those were my hob-nails, for making shoes. Shoes. That's what we're best at, us Cluricauns, cobblers to kings and princes.

He winked. 'And cobblers to them all, say I.'

FOUR

The rabbit stew was simply miraculous. It was thick and spicy, mixed with wild mushrooms and other things that neither of them could identify even if they cared to. They were so hungry they could have spooned it from the bubbling pot.

'You can call me Rune,' the little man said. 'Lately of old Skiboreen. You know the place?'

'I've heard the name somewhere,' Jack said.

'Beautiful place, it is. *The grass it grows green down in old Skiboreen; the porter is flowing and free. The song and the laughter rise up to the rafters, and herrings leap out on the quay.*'

He leaned back, rummaged in a leather pouch and produced a long clay pipe. Jack did a double take as it emerged, surely too long to have been encompassed by

22

the small bag, but Rune didn't seem to notice.

He looked them up and down.

'I can tell from the look of you that you don't hail from these parts,' he said.

'We don't,' Kerry said, wiping his mouth with the back of his hand. Jack frowned, warning him to give nothing away, at least until they knew more.

'Well, if I was a guessing man, I'd guess the pair of you have been in the wars. And by the dress of you, I'd guess that you're from someplace I've never been, and I've been many a place.'

He sat back, blue eyes twinkling. 'So, if I'm not mistaken, I'd say you travellers just came through yonder Fairy Gate on the hill.'

Jack and Kerry's jaws dropped simultaneously. They looked at each other, taken completely by surprise.

'But what I can't guess is whether you just stumbled through by mistake, or was it a deliberate step?' He lit the pipe, blew a smoke ring. 'You know about the Sappelings. And you,' he nodded to Kerry, 'wield a big man's sword. So I'm guessing you're here on a mission, am I right?'

Before Jack could stop him, Kerry blurted out, 'We're looking for a girl.'

'Aren't we all? You should try Skiboreen.'

'How do you know about the gate?' Jack demanded. They had trusted people in Temair and had been sadly disappointed, not to mention almost killed.

'The gate?' Rune repeated. He chuckled. 'I'm a Cluricaun, and I travel all the roads. Tinker, tailor, cobbler, nailer, and much else besides. A traveller's got to keep

23

an ear to the ground he walks, and that way you learn the *ways*.'

And from what you've just said, you *did* come through the gate, so I imagine then that you're looking not just for any girl. You're looking for a girl in particular. One that you've maybe lost, hmm?'

Jack nodded before he was even aware of it.

'And tell me some more, Jack. This girl, she wouldn't happen to have red hair, would she? And can she fight like a cornered badger?'

'You've seen her?' Kerry cried. 'She's here?'

Rune shook his head.

'So how do you know about her?' Jack wanted to know.

'Oh, half of Eirinn knows about her, the fighting girl with fiery hair.'

The Cluricaun gave a mischievous smile. 'I did hear a whisper about a girl on foot in these parts a day or so past. No, what I'm telling you is that Dermott the Wolf, he's got hunters out scouring for her all over. Looking for a fighting woman with red hair.'

'That's Corrie,' Jack said. 'But who's this Dermott, and what does he want with her?'

Rune took another puff and crossed his legs. He closed his eyes and, for a moment, Jack and Kerry thought he'd fallen asleep, but after a while, he began to speak.

'Dermott's the lord of Wolfen Castle, way in the west. A bad lot, both him and his dark spellbinder. Dermott stole the throne from good king Conovar's widow and killed his baby boy.

'You might have noticed that things are not at all well in

24

Eirinn. Last night there was a hard chill in the air, and this close to midsummer. Crops are failing all over, since spring never turned its face this past while. Other places were bad-blighted by ice before the corn was knee-high to a Cluricaun.'

'It snowed last night,' Jack said. 'We almost froze to death on the hill.'

'Ice in summer. That's never a good sign.'

'So what's gone wrong?'

'That's the question. Some say Dermott's stolen the Golden Harp of Tara Hill.'

Jack caught his breath. 'The Harp of the Seasons!'

'What's that?' Kerry asked.

Rune looked at Jack, motioned him to explain.

'I read it in the Major's library. This king called the Dagda had three magic things: a huge club that could wipe out lots of people at one swipe; a silver cauldron that was never empty, and a golden harp that made the seasons come in the right order. It's a legend.'

'Legend?' Rune interrupted. 'So says you. But everybody knows the harp has kept harmony in Eirinn since the Dagda and the Sky Queen sailed to the stars long, long ago. And now there's only discord and famine.'

'That's what the book said,' Kerry said.

Jack shot him another warning look. Kerry realised his mistake, but it was too late to bite back the words.

'And other things,' Rune said, ignoring Kerry. 'There's been Fell Runners seen on the Mourning Mountains, and Bogrim in the mists of CorNamara and more besides.'

'What are they?' Jack asked.

'Things you don't want to meet on a lonely road,' Rune said. 'Old, bad things have woken hungry in dark places, too. So, you've come here at a time of trouble, and here you are, looking as if trouble has already found you.'

'We've had a couple of . . . er . . . accidents.'

'Can't be as bad as the last place,' Kerry said. He lifted a foot, showing the tattered trainer.

'Well, seeing you kindly let me cook your coney, and were good enough to catch a Cluricaun without claiming the gold, maybe I can help you there.' Rune stood up, grabbed his bag and beckoned them to follow round the base of a tree, past a couple of big rocks that looked as if they'd been rolled there long ago, until they came to a green mound, covered in trees. An arched passageway, made from cut stone, led inside.

'I stay here when I'm passing. It's a Drumlin.'

'What is that?' Kerry asked the obvious question.

'It's where they buried one of the old kings, an awful long time ago. In the battles with the Fir Bolg. Empty now, all mouldered to dust, whoever he was, so don't fret. You might see a thing or two in the dark, but there's nothing to worry about. Wraiths never harmed a soul who didn't deserve it.'

Kerry and Jack exchanged a glance, but Rune sat down on a stone by the entrance and reached for a three-legged object that Jack saw had been elaborately and cleverly carved from a single piece of wood. Its legs were at right angles to each other, and each ended in a small, perfectly carved foot.

'Slip a foot on there,' Rune instructed Kerry, who shucked off the useless trainer and placed his own foot on the wooden one.

Jack did a double-take, at first unsure anything had happened, but then he saw it. As soon as Kerry's foot touched the wooden last, the carved foot immediately swelled and buckled as if alive, and in a smooth, flowing motion, stretched to match Kerry's own foot exactly.

Rune turned to Jack, flipping the cobbler's last over, and instructed him to do the same. Under his sole, Jack felt the polished wood buckle and stretch to fit him.

The Cluricaun picked up Kerry's trainer and examined it.

'Flimsy thing,' he stated, shaking his head. 'And made with neither love nor skill. I see children slaving over this. Not a good shoe, at all, at all.'

He picked at the Velcro band that crossed over the tongue, peeled it back with a small rip.

'But this is clever. Never saw a shoe fasten like this.'

He tugged Kerry down to his height. 'Now let me look at that cut.' Kerry let him examine the long weeping gash where the skin was a florid red, as if infection was setting in.

'Nasty,' Rune said. He delved into his bag, drew out a smooth stone jar and applied a sticky black ointment to the cut. Kerry closed his eyes and let out a slow breath as the ache instantly subsided, and then, in front of Jack's incredulous eyes, the red faded and the long gash closed itself over from bottom to top, like a zip fastener.

'Closewort, we call it.' Rune patted Kerry on the shoulder. 'That'll be fine in the morning. Go on and get some sleep, and you'll be on your way to find your girl, and may the road always rise up to meet your feet.'

He led them inside the Drumlin, lit an oil lamp made from a single sea-shell, and as soon as the boys sat down on the dry earth, tiredness overtook them. In minutes, they were asleep.

FIVE

A sharp crack of sound startled her from troubled sleep. She was instantly awake, but it took her a few seconds to remember where she was, as awful images faded; Jack Flint tumbling into the searing brimstone; the Morrigan swooping on them.

Corriwen Redthorn shook her head, trying to banish them. Beyond the trees, an animal yelped in pain.

She rolled on the dry leaves, got to her knees, feeling in the gloom for her knives. In a hole under the spreading roots of a beech tree, she'd found a shelter of sorts, out of the rain that had drenched the forest last night.

Hooves thudded in the distance and she peered out into a sparkling morning, fearful of the sound of horses and the cries of men. She had been alone and hunted before, and she knew how to hide.

The high cry came again and she got to her feet, sore and hungry. Beyond the beech, a wall of juniper hid her from view from the open field at the edge of the forest. She approached it cautiously, paring back the dense leaves to peer out.

The field ran down from left to right, curled tight against the trees at the north end. Clumps of gorse and broom dotted the grass where animals had grazed once upon a time, but there were no cattle or sheep here now.

Two men on horseback rode through the brushwood, flattening it under heavy hooves. One of them shouted, deep and hoarse. His arm raised, flashed down, and the sharp crack jarred her ears. On his flank, another man in helmet and greaves wielded a lance. As he brought it down in an arc its tip flashed in the sun.

Something darted from one gorse bush to another, avoiding the spike by a hair. All Corriwen saw was a blur of grey, and it was gone.

The man shouted again, spun his horse and crashed through the bush in pursuit.

Hunters, she thought. They had not trailed her here. Just two men out for sport, probably flushed a boar from a thicket. They would eat well tonight, while she scrabbled for berries and set spike-traps for small coneys.

Corriwen was about to turn back to her hide when the whiplash cracked again followed by another cry. For a confusing moment she saw the animal lurch under the horse's belly and scamper between two thorny bushes. The lance swung and almost impaled it as it twisted and came dashing towards her.

Her first thought was to wish the men had killed it, stopped it racing for the trees, where they would no doubt follow. She didn't want to be seen again, not since the first time when horsemen had veered from the road and hunted her like a fox before she'd lost them in thick trees. That had been a week ago and miles away, but it was enough to make her want to stay hidden.

The creature came on in a lurching run and she pulled behind the trunk, just in case it snicked her in the passing with its tusks.

The whip-man turned his horse fast and came powering after it, trying to reach it before it made the trees.

And that was when Corriwen saw it was no boar, no animal at all.

It was a boy, running fast as he could, face pale with fear. He was running for his life. Running, but limping badly as if he'd already been hurt.

The whip lashed, fast as a snake, and curled tight round the boy's ankle. The horseman hauled the reins and his horse skidded to a halt. The boy was jerked backwards, only a yard or so from the forest edge. His feet went up in the air and his body came down with such a thud she heard all the air whoosh out of his lungs.

'Got him,' the man growled.

'My turn now,' the other cried. The lance tucked under his arm glinted once again, sharp and deadly, set to spear the boy where he lay, but he twisted, shoved out with one foot and rolled out of danger. The man cursed, swung the lance high, and stabbed it down.

The boy yelped as the whip dragged him back.

'Lie still and take it like a man,' the lancer grated.

He stabbed again.

'No!' Corriwen's scream rang out.

The nearest horse reared, startled by her voice. Its rider stayed fixed in the saddle, but the motion dragged the boy further along the ground, scraping his face through the thorns.

She was in full view now, running fast, despite all her senses urging her to stay out of trouble.

Her hackles were up, knife in her left hand, a staff in her right. The horseman wheeled again, turned to face her. In a moment of confusion she darted in between him and the fallen boy and with one swift swipe, sliced through the fine end of the whip. The boy scrambled on all fours, desperate to get away.

The lancer turned towards her. 'What do you think you're doing?'

She jinked to the side, grabbed the boy's arm, dragged him to his feet as the lance came swinging round. She ducked, still hauling the boy through the gorse towards the trees.

The lance snagged in the briar, giving her a vital second, and they were off, the boy hobbling but still able to make headway.

'Run,' he gasped. 'They'll take you too.'

'Get them,' the man roared. The trees were twenty yards away, fifteen running paces, but even this close she realised it was too far. Instinct made her push the boy to the left, a hard shove which sent him out of the path of the horses she knew were right on her heels, and just as instinctively she threw herself to the right, as the lance raked a line across her shoulder, enough to tear her hood, but not enough to wound.

Corriwen swivelled as the lash curled through the air, aimed straight at her face. She thrust the staff up to save her eyes, spun away as the whip curled around it and the horse went bulleting past in a flurry of hooves and mud. She fell back, putting all her weight into it. The sudden jolt on his whip arm dragged the horseman out of the saddle. He hit the ground with a thump.

Corriwen spun again as the lancer drove in.

'Now you pay, outlaw,' he bawled.

Corriwen stood her ground, feet planted apart, forcing her breath to be slow, eyes fixed only on the lance-point.

Then, like a cat, she twisted on her feet and slammed the staff down just behind the spear-head. The horseman yelped as his weapon jarred into his armpit. Corriwen used the staff as a brace, as she swung her feet up to take her assailant square in the ribs with such force he was slammed off the horse.

'I'll kill you,' the fallen lancer bawled, trying to free himself from thorns which clung like hooks. 'Obstructing a Wolf's Man in pursuit of a felon. You'll hang for this. Hang and bleed!'

Without a word, Corriwen turned away and ran for the woods, just as the stumbling boy pushed through the juniper cover and disappeared from view.

In seconds she was on his heels and both of them ran deep into the trees where they grew thick and close and where a horse could never follow. Her only regret was that she'd lost a good walking stick.

SIX

Rune had placed Jack's bare foot on the wooden last and both boys had watched as the carved foot had buckled, stretching out until it mirrored Jack's own, just a little bit bigger than Kerry's.

'My, the pair of you must leave big tracks in the mud.'

He bent to his bottomless bag and began to remove strips of what looked like leather of different textures and colours.

'The trick is, you use thirteen hides. Coney, wolf, all the fast ones. And shoe horn from the four-horn goat. Best climber ever there was.'

With that he bent to the task, tip-tapping, hunched over the last, and after a while the soft and steady beat of the little hammer on leather lulled them into sleep in the warmth of the cavern ...

Until Jack awoke suddenly in the darkness, his senses all on edge.

The tapping had changed tone. Beside him, in the wan light of the fire at the cave mouth, Kerry was curled on a bed of leaves, snoring, both hands around the hilt of his sword.

At Jack's throat, the heartstone was vibrating, fast as a tuning fork, its note so high it was almost inaudible. Jack clamped his hand over it and the vibration surged through his hand, through flesh and bone.

Jack heard the other sound again, a steady pulse, not a tapping sound, but a far-off beat that seemed to shiver the stones under him. He sat up, straining to see, straining to hear. There was no sign of the Cluricaun.

The beat grew louder, like footsteps. Jack stood up in the gloom, trying to work out the direction, and as he did, he felt his feet move him towards the deeper darkness at the back of the cave.

Doom-*doom*. It *did* sound like footsteps, getting louder as they approached. He remembered what Rune had said about the drumlin.

'*Where they buried one of the old kings, an awful long time ago. You might see a thing or two in the dark, but there's nothing to worry about. Wraiths never harmed a soul that didn't deserve it.*'

Jack felt no fear, only curiosity. He moved forward, one hand touching the stone walls, breathing in the fine dust of centuries past, while the footsteps echoed from wall to wall.

A shimmer of pale blue light, at first hardly visible, grew stronger.

'What do you want?' he asked. 'Who are you?'

A shuddery sigh was the only response, like an autumn wind through brown leaves.

The blue glimmer began to take shape, walking as if exhausted. It was a man-shape. Head bent low. Jack heard the clink of armour, but still, he was not afraid. He took a step forward and the light coalesced, became a figure that stood tall and broad, head still bowed.

He could see through it, as if it was smoke; see the cracks in the stones beyond.

'Who disturbs my rest?' The voice was a whisper. 'Who calls me awake?'

The shape wavered in the air, somehow solid, yet insubstantial. The shield it carried was round, scarred from many a battle. It bore a sign that Jack Flint had seen before; five bright stars in a perfect semi-circle. They glistened like precious stones.

'The Corona,' he whispered.

The free arm raised and Jack saw the great sword, blue as a gas flame, the blade pitted and chipped from hard use.

Jack took a step back. On his chest the heartstone pulsed, but he felt no fear.

'No peace,' the spectre sighed. 'No harmony.' The apparition held him with its empty gaze. 'Heroes, long gone to rest. We fight no more.'

Then, very slowly, parchment fingers reached out, touched him on the neck then closed around the heartstone. Jack tried to protest, to pull away, but his feet were welded to the ground, his muscles frozen.

The spectre raised the heartstone in front of Jack's eyes. It gleamed in the blue light. Suddenly he *saw*.

Through its transclucent sheen, the spectre's face was transformed.

Blue eyes held his in a steady gaze. Fair hair hung in braids beneath the gleaming helmet. Scars ran in clefts across a cheek.

'You come to reclaim harmony. Our fight is over. Your battle just begun.'

The voice was no longer dry as dead leaves. It echoed from distant walls with strength and regal power.

Something gleamed in the corner of Jack's vision, a flash of gold.

Its other hand held a torque, almost a complete ring of gold.

'Talisman for a king. For peace and harmony and an end to wicked ways.'

The torque touched Jack's forehead. He felt it cold and smooth.

Then it was gone, and the heartstone dropped and settled against his chest.

The spectre turned and walked away, fading as it went. Doom-*doom-doom*.

Jack was left alone in the dark.

In the morning, two pairs of leather boots sat side by side on the flattened grass beside the ring of stones where the embers still smouldered. Rune must have tapped away all night.

Beside the shoes, two pairs of leggings in greenish leather, and tunics with hoods. And with each, a belt in braided hide that gleamed as if burnished with spit and polish. Kerry's sword was now held in a sturdy sheath.

Jack had woken first and sat beside Rune. He held up the torque.

'I saw your wraith,' he said. 'He spoke to me.'

'A good king from long ago. That's a king's torque.'

'Why did he give it to me?'

Rune shrugged. 'Who would know a king's mind?'

'Not a coincidence,' Jack said. 'And neither are you, I think. You were waiting for us here, weren't you?'

Rune chuckled. 'Maybe I was hoping a traveller would come again.'

Jack's heart stuttered. 'There's been one before?'

'Oh, long ago. In the Dagda's days. A traveller helped him save the harp for Eirinn in its hour of need. Maybe Eirinn now needs another such.'

'What was his name? Do you know?'

The Cluricaun shook his head. 'All I know is Eirinn's in his debt.'

And he would be drawn no further, despite Jack's questions.

Kerry was delighted to cast off his dirty clothes, the ones he had stitched together for the Halloween party.

He bounced up and down. 'I never had a pair of shoes that fit first time. Never had a new pair in my life.'

'Well, you look just the part for sure,' Rune said, 'And you won't stick out like a boil on the backside neither.'

'That's really kind,' Jack said.

'Well, you wouldn't take the gold, as you've a right to ask.'

'We never believed you anyway,' Kerry chuckled.

'Well believe this. You've some travellin' to do. So you can't get distracted.'

At that he flicked his hand up and they heard a thin metallic jangle. Something gold whirled up above their heads, caught the light. It was a coin. It made a small whirring sound as it reached the apex of its travel, then started to fall towards them.

Jack raised his hand to catch it, but when his fingers closed around it, there was nothing there. The coin, whatever it was, winked out of existence, leaving his hand empty.

And when he turned to Rune, the Cluricaun was gone.

'We look like a pair of garden gnomes,' Kerry said. 'I'm like something out of *Snow White and the Seven Dwarfs*.'

'Which one are you? Dopey?'

'Yeah, well you must be Grumpy,' Kerry grinned. 'As usual.'

Jack chuckled for the first time since they had stepped from their world into this one.

'Hi-*ho*, hi-*ho*!' Jack pulled the hood over his head, and got another laugh from Kerry.

They walked on in fine morning sunlight, food in their bellies and more rested now after the strange night in Rune's drumlin.

'Hi-ho, *hi-ho*.' Jack quickened his steps to match the beat. He had cut a sapling for a walking stick and swiped a thistle-head, sending it tumbling in the fresh air.

'Shhh ...' Kerry froze. 'I hear something.'

Jack held his breath, listening, then he too heard it. The sound of horses. They cautiously climbed a rise, staying low.

A group of horsemen were coming fast along a rutted road. Even in the distance, it was clear they were armed.

'Some kind of patrol,' Jack said. 'Let's stay out of sight.'

Moving quickly, they ran down the lee of the hill towards a stand of trees and reached shelter before the horsemen arrived and within a few yards they were hidden from view.

'Rune said there's patrols all over,' Kerry said. 'We'd best stay off the roads.'

As the horsemen clattered past, Jack and Kerry pushed deeper into the trees and the forest darkened around them. Soon they were well away from the edge of the forest and the sounds of the riders faded.

'It's a bit like Sappeling Wood,' Kerry said, brushing a gauzy spiderweb from his face. He pulled his hood up.

'But there's no sign of the little people,' Jack replied. 'And the trees don't move.'

Over a rise beside a runnel clogged with rotting leaves and down the far side they found themselves descending into a dell where so little light managed to break through that it was like damp twilight. Here it smelt of decay and wet and no birds sang. They paused for a moment before moving down the slope into the shadowed basin when Kerry stopped.

'Did you hear something?' He spoke in a whisper.

Jack shook his head. Kerry stood stock still, listening. Finally he shrugged.

'Just my imagination,' he said.

'I hope so. It's kind of creepy here.'

'How far do we have to go?'

'I don't know.' Jack looked around him. This forest could go on for miles, but he thought it best to keep going in the same direction, bearing south.

They moved on down into the basin and the air of strangeness hung heavy. Birds or bats fluttered in the branches above. Beside a runnel, a big warty toad eyed them, expanding its wattled gullet in slow gulps.

'It *is* kind of creepy here,' Kerry finally agreed. He still had his hood up, but now he had drawn his sword. They had seen nothing, but the trees crowded closer, causing them to edge together until their shoulders touched. It made Jack and Kerry feel a little more comfortable, but not much. A low wind moaned, and Jack took that as a hopeful sign that they would soon be out in the open, in sunlight.

The dell continued downslope. Underfoot, years of fallen leaves left a thick dark brown carpet. Spiderwebs stretched from trunk to bough like silvery nets, festooned with packets of silk-bound insects. In one web, a bat fluttered helplessly until a black spider, big and shiny as a snooker-ball pinioned across its web and snatched the creature in a flicker of motion.

'Spiders,' Jack grimaced. 'I hate them.'

'Big wimp,' Kerry said. 'They're only bugs.'

'Never seen bugs that size.'

The spider scuttled across its rigging, carrying the cocooned bat like a prize. Jack walked carefully around it, making sure he didn't disturb the web. Behind him Kerry bent and picked up a thin frond of fern and as he followed, he lightly flicked Jack's ear with it.

Jack visibly jumped and Kerry let out a whoop.

'Gotcha!'

Jack whirled and Kerry's laughter stopped dead.

'Very funny.'

'*Suh* . . .'

'What?'

Kerry's eyes were wide. At first, in the gloom, Jack thought he was looking straight at him. But then he realised Kerry's gaze was fixed beyond Jack's head.

'Okay, very good,' he said. 'I'm not falling for *that* again.'

'Suh-*suh* . . . *SUH!*'

'Suh *what?*'

'Suh . . . *SNAKE!*'

'Oh really?' Jack shook his head. 'You can think of something better than that. You don't get snakes in . . .'

A black streak launched itself at him, fast as a lightning strike.

All Jack caught was a glimpse of a mouth gaping open,

a wide red mouth. He got an impression of two insanely long teeth lunging for his face.

SEVEN

Corriwen pushed the boy ahead of her, following a trail she already knew through the trees, putting as much distance as they could between themselves and the felled men.

Even as she ran, Corriwen wondered what trouble she had got herself into.

'Probably a runaway servant,' she thought. And now she had brought herself to the wrong kind of attention.

Yet it had been impossible to sit and watch. There was nothing else a Redthorn could have done.

Jack and Kerry would think she was crazy for taking on two armed men, but she thought even they might have approved in the end.

The boy hobbled on and she could tell he had run before, away from people maybe. Through trees certainly. He had fair hair that had been cut with a knife, rough and patchy, and two braids hung down his back.

She pulled beside him, tugged at his arm.

'This way.'

He looked at her, hazel eyes bright, chest hitching.

'No,' he said. 'This way. I know a place.'

He stopped and favoured his twisted leg, leaning hip-shot on the straight one. The raggedy cape was slit twice across the back where the whip had caught him. Blood seeped through.

Corriwen paused. The way she knew would take them along by a narrow river to where they could cross on the boulders at the falls.

'I really do know a place. They won't follow.'

She shrugged agreement. This was not her forest, not her world. After what she had seen in the gorse field, he surely wouldn't want to get caught again.

'All right,' she agreed. 'But make it fast.'

'I'm doing my best.' He grinned. 'But I'm no deerhound, for sure.'

As he led the way Corriwen could see that his leg was bent and twisted so that his foot curved in towards the other. It looked much shorter than his left leg, giving him a *tip-thud*, *tip-thud* sound effect as he ran, clutching a tattered deerhide bag under his arm.

He followed the bank downstream until the river forked round an island and pulled to the right, up a little gully. He climbed through the water to a flat spot where a fire had been lit before. The boy slung his bag down on the grass and lowered himself to sit on a stone.

Corriwen used the little Swiss Army knife Jack had given her to cut a strip from her own cape and soaked it before dabbing at the cuts on the boy's back. He gritted his teeth and let her work.

'You shouldn't have helped me,' he said. His face was grubby and his tattered cape was held together by a small brass pin-brooch. 'Now they'll come hunting you.'

Corriwen cocked her head. 'Well, I appreciate your gratitude.'

He grinned again, quite a mischievous grin and his eyes crinkled up.

'I'd have got into the trees.'

'You'd never have made it,' she said flatly. 'He had you caught with the whip. They'd have stuck you like a boar in a thicket.'

'Fine, if you say so. Allow me to picture a happier result for myself. But now you're in trouble. You can't fight Dermott's men and get away with it. He'll want his revenge.'

'I've heard that kind of talk before.' Corriwen snorted. 'And I'm still walking. Anyway, why were they trying to kill you?'

He looked at her, as if she was stupid.

'Because we were hungry,' he said. 'Because the crops failed again. Because I went into the forest and got something to eat.'

'And they'd kill you for that?'

'You can't steal Dermott's deer, or his salmon, or his rabbits. He's a jealous lord, as you must know.'

'I don't know,' she said. 'Because I don't know who Dermott is.'

'You must have come from far away then.'

'Further than you could ever imagine.'

'Must be somewhere in Eirinn. There's nowhere else, far as I know. So who are you and what brings you skulking in these trees?'

'Skulking? I came to *your* aid,' Corriwen said. 'I don't know who you are, poacher boy.'

He laughed again, as if none of the chase or whiplashing had happened.

'I'm Connor. They call me Connor Twist. Sometimes Connor Hobble.'

'Because of your leg?'

'What else? I can see I'm going to have to watch out for that sharp mind of yours.'

She took no offence. 'You'd best do just that. Anyway, what happened to your leg?'

'Don't know.' He slapped his crooked calf. 'Faerie touched, some of the old wives say. Spell-bound at birth. I was only little at the time, so I can't remember.'

He opened the ragged bag and pulled out a little piglet with some kind of cord wrapped round its back legs. Three round stones clacked together.

'What's that?' she asked.

'A throw snare,' he said, untying the cords. He held it up and showed the smooth stones joined together by short lengths of string. 'A Cluricaun showed me how to use it. It tangles round their feet.'

'What's a Cluricaun?'

'Don't you know anything? One of the little folk. They can be kindly to the unfortunate.'

She watched as he lit a fire then skinned the animal and expertly jointed the hams.

'Didn't your mother tell you what happened?' she asked.

'Probably would have, if I ever met her. I was found half drowned in the sea and taken in by Lugan the Woodman and Mereg his wife. I pay my way. You don't need fast legs to herd the cows. All you need is a good dog and a big stick.'

He spoke very matter-of-factly, as if his affliction was a minor inconvenience.

'And when the harvest fails and the cows fall, then you don't even need a dog.' The piglet dripped crackling fat into the hot coals and the delicious aroma made Corriwen ravenous.

Connor turned over the roasting meat. 'We ate the dog, poor thing. Pig's much better, I can tell you.'

Corriwen agreed. 'I've eaten some ugly things.'

'When you're hungry, they look a whole lot better.'

The pig hams smelt only half as good as they tasted.

Grey dawn found Corriwen recalling the previous night, waking from the best sleep she'd had since she'd been thrown into this unfamiliar world.

At least now she knew the name of the place. Connor could talk, most of it round a bone he gnawed until it was shiny white, licking his fingers loudly in between sentences.

'And Dermott, ever since he became king in the west and the seasons went awry, he's been overlording everybody else. Some say his warlock, Fainn, put a curse on the sky so now it doesn't know summer from winter. They say the sun still shines along the northern shore, but here we haven't seen the Corona for a long time. People are hungry, and they're afraid the Sky Queen has turned away.'

'I haven't seen stars since I came here,' Corriwen agreed. 'Nor the moon.'

'There's a shadow over Eirinn, but it's been to Dermott's good. Somehow there's food in CorNamara, where he's the landholder. He's been buying the chiefs from Munster to Leinster and even down to MacGillicuddy's Reeks. He'll have the whole of Eirinn under his hand.'

Corriwen understood the pattern. Mandrake had used his wealth to buy treachery in Temair, and used his own sorcery for much worse.

Connor finished his food, yawned, curled himself up on the grass by the fire and went to sleep. Corriwen had time to think.

It had been seven days since she tumbled between the stones, to find herself in a cold puddle with hailstones beating down like pebbles.

She had drawn her knives and rushed back to help them fight the she-devil, but when she ran between the stones, there was nothing there but more hailstones.

The ring had vanished.

She had waited for two days until hunger and cold drove her out beyond the hill to find something to eat and light a fire before she froze to her marrow, her hope whittled to virtually nothing.

Jack and Kerry did not come.

Somewhere, she hoped, on this world there was a homeward gate that would take her back to Jack's world. She would have to find it.

She roused Connor and they made their way out of the forest.

And only a few miles down the road, a troop of horsemen came galloping from behind a thicket and ran them down.

EIGHT

On the very edge of a sheer cliff pounded by an angry ocean, Wolfen Castle stands alone, a pile of stone with turrets and battlements on the landward side; no need for them on the seaward because the rock drops straight down 500 feet and more to jagged rocks frothing the surf.

Wolfen Castle, the westernmost stronghold in CorNamara has a huge drawbridge that bridges a crevasse in the bare rock, eaten in on either side by the ocean's hunger so that even from the landward side, it is all but impregnable. It has not been breached in a thousand years.

On this morning, dank cloud scraped around the turrets and wind whipped the pennants that bore Dermott's wolf-head crest. A lone horn blew on the wood-covered crags a mile away. High in the castle a bell clanged and the drawbridge began to lower across the crevasse.

Some time later, a band of horsemen came along the road at a gallop, shod hooves sending up sparks as they clattered on the cobbles. They reached the drawbridge as its edge thudded home and without pause, the horsemen, led by an immense man in black furs, rumbled across the timbers.

Dermott the Wolf was back.

He reined his stallion by the stone steps and leapt from the saddle while servants unhitched the livery and tended to the panting steed. Dermott swaggered down the steps, chest out, chin high, a big man in all ways. Thick, black, shaggy beard; wide bull shoulders; arms knotted with muscle; fists like mallets.

He wore a broadsword in a shoulder-scabbard so that its hilt stuck up behind him, ready for a fast and deadly draw should the need arise; a dagger on each hip, and a studded mace in a loop on his belt. In one hand he carried a thick braided leather whip.

The shaggy tunic belted at his waist was spattered with red. When he drew the sword, it was streaked crimson. He handed it to a boy who stood within arm's reach, shrugged himself out of the tunic and let it fall to the ground.

'Both clean by supper,' he said. 'And strop the edge. I might have blunted it.'

Fainn the warlock was deep in the bowels of Wolfen Castle.

He had heard neither horns, nor thundering hooves, nor

even the thud of the drawbridge, but he knew the Lord Dermott had arrived. He always knew.

The room had a high arched ceiling supported by stone pillars. The walls were festooned with jars and bottles and all manner of strange things whose importance would only be relevant to a sorcerer. Fainn knew. He had been steeped in such black arts since before anyone living could recall.

He was tall, as tall as Dermott, but slender, almost gaunt, his nose thin as a blade. His hooded cloak at first seemed ragged and torn, but on closer inspection – and few took the chance to get so close to Fainn – it could be seen that it was fashioned from bats' wings; black bat wings sewn together with such craft that no seam was apparent. It fluttered when he moved.

On his head he wore a leather cap moulded to his skull like a second skin, and no one knew what kind of hide that might be, though a few who guessed correctly shuddered at the thought.

His pallid skin bore blue-black tattoos. He pushed the wings of his cloak back to reveal a snake coiled around a wrist. Weasels chased each other towards his elbows. Spiders hunched in the centre of webs. Bats fluttered with every flex of knotty muscles. Flies crawled on his knuckles between tufts of black hair.

Barely an inch of his skin was unadorned by creatures, some of them living, some never seen by man, so artfully created that they looked as if they could crawl off his skin and slink into the dark corners to hunt.

Fainn lowered himself into the chair beside the vast table that was like none other in the whole of Eirinn. Cut from a single great tree, across its surface, in high relief, was carved a map of Middle Eirinn, the hills, the rivers, the moors and boglands; east to west, north to south, sea to sea. The nine kingdoms of Eirinn dwelt in miniature on the tabletop.

Close to the Eirinn Table, a fire glowed deep red. Every now and then Fainn sprinkled a powder into the flames. Orange and green flared, sending up clouds of dense smoke that joined the pall hovering over the Eirinn Table, roiling in the hot updraughts, but never clearing to allow sight of the ceiling.

The shadow over Eirinn had been there for a long time. Fainn made sure it remained so. It was part of his plan.

Fainn the Spellbinder set out the tools of his dark trade, eyes moving constantly over the fine map of this land. From his cloak he drew a pouch made from the same leather as his skull-cap, and from it produced what at first appeared to be a crystal ball.

From inside the clear crystal, an eye, an unblinking human eye, stared out, its pupil contracted to a tiny dot. Other strange artifacts came out of the pouch. One was made of bone, another looked like a shrivelled piece of leather. Fainn set them in a circle, and waited.

Dermott was coming. Fainn kept his eyes closed, knowing the exact moment when Wolfen's Lord would turn the handle and push the door wide.

It slammed back against the wall, sending a draught through the room to stir the flames yet again.

'Good hunting, my Lord?' Fainn had not turned. Dermott was used to that. Fainn could see without looking.

'Fair,' Dermott stood in the doorway, his shoulders

55

blocking out the torchlight beyond. 'Kellen of Dennegoll needs to be taught a lesson. I killed his son anyway. He'll see sense soon enough.'

Kellen of Dennegoll lorded the lands north of CorNamara, on the borders of Middle Eirinn beyond which the mountains grew high enough to form a barrier against the wild lands beyond. So far, despite the fact that in Dennegoll, spring and summer had not arrived for so long that the people were close to starving, Kellen had refused to cede power to Dermott.

'They will all see sense,' Fainn agreed.

'Kellen thinks his boats can feed his people with fish and live out hard times. Stubborn as stone, so he is.'

'Stone wears. Stone cracks.'

'Let's crack him.' Dermott strode across to the Eirinn Table and bent over it, pointing a calloused finger in the direction of Dennegoll, where long fjords gave protection to Kellen's fleet.

'Give him a chill. Make him shiver. Lock the stubborn fool in.'

'As you wish, my Lord,' Fainn said. 'I'll deepen his winter.'

He stretched over the table, thin hands curled into fists. Dermott's were hooked on his sword-belt, black fur on his shoulders bristling.

Fainn opened his fingers, muttering secret words, and a fine dust shimmered down, slow as feathers, sparkling as it descended on to the carved surface where Dennegoll's harbours huddled on the very edge of Eirinn.

The dust blanketed the whole little kingdom and as they

watched it settled, solidified, became as clear as ice. Dermott could feel the sudden cold from where he stood.

'That should cool a hothead,' he rumbled. 'A few weeks of that and he'll give me everything he has.'

Fainn's eyes glittered. He loved his work.

'Now,' Dermott said. 'I got the message on the return ride. What did you want to show me?'

'Tell you, my lord, not show you,' Fainn said. 'Though I would if I could see for myself.'

'You and riddles,' Dermott said. 'Never get your sword-arm straight, do you?'

Fainn allowed a thin smile. Dermott was a man of action. But action needed vision, and as a Seer, a Spellbinder, none was better than Fainn.

'Something has . . . *transpired*.'

'Transpired? What do you mean?'

'I sense a change. Something *new*.'

'So what is it, Warlock? Something to concern me?'

'That I cannot see yet. Though I will search. All is ready.'

'Is it to do with this damned woman? The one who's supposed to be coming to kill me?'

Fainn shook his head. 'The runes cannot lie, my Lord. Nor can I change what they say. I have cast them many times and they tell the same doom. A fighting woman with fire-hair will be your bane.'

'Unless we find her first. I have hunters scouring every kingdom. When we find her, she'll raise no army against me, that I can promise.'

Fainn gave a small bow. 'What I sense is different. A *difference*. A change in the way of things.'

'Change is good. Haven't we changed most of Eirinn? Bent it to our way?'

'This change I cannot yet perceive. But I will keep searching.'

'Do that,' Dermott commanded. 'Do it now.'

Fainn first arranged his ghastly collection on the table then held the staring crystal eye against his forehead. He began to speak in a hissing whisper.

> Blind man's eye from socket torn
> Cry of boy-child never born
> Lip of maiden, kiss of mother
> Skin of sister, heart of brother
> Blood and bone, tooth and nail
> Sense and search where living fail.

Fainn moaned. A shiver ran through him, making the bat-wings flutter. Dermott watched as the eye swivelled, strangely alive, somehow *scanning* the long table carvings. The collection of mysterious objects writhed, like living creatures trying to escape. As the eye swung, left and right, the air stilled and segments of the carved map stood out clearly.

Dermott saw the forest, etched near the far end of the table, beyond Lennister, far from CorNamara, close to the north border where man's knowledge ended.

Yet, even as he looked, his eyes could not quite focus on that section of the Eirinn Map. It seemed to waver and blur. He knuckled his eyes and looked again, but still it eluded his gaze. As if it refused him admission.

All of a sudden, the eye clouded. Dermott sensed that its sight had failed.

'Well?'

Fainn's face was gaunt with the strain of searching all across Eirinn. 'Something I cannot see, or touch, or hear. Not with any of the shade-senses. Not yet.'

'But there has been a *change* in the world.'

'It's the woman, am I right? The red-haired warrior?'

Fainn shook his head.

'A new threat. One I don't understand. From far away someone comes. But I sense he has been here before.'

'Who can threaten me? I control the seasons. I possess the Harp.'

'Indeed, my Lord. And with the seasons in your grasp, so is all Eirinn. But I would fail my oath if I ignored what my art tells me.'

Dermott drummed his fingers on the table.

'You tell me there's a new threat and then say you don't know what it is? Could it be that you're wrong with those damned runes?'

'Some things take time to come clear. I will discover what you need. But, I swear, the runes cannot lie.'

'Damn your runes! Fighting woman *indeed*. I'll roast her hams and pickle her hide.' He looked up. 'So what now? Should I send a column? An army?'

Fainn shrugged. 'Not until I see what there is to see. There might just be another way.'

He rose, stalked to the far side of the table and leaned over the surface. He drew his sleeve back and like a conjurer, produced a knife, its blade so sharp it whispered as it parted the air. Fainn stretched his arm and touched the blade to a coiled black snake tattoo. A drop of blood fell on the table-top. Dermott thought he heard a sizzle as it seeped into the wood.

'Now we might see what hides in the trees,' Fainn said.

'If you do,' Dermott boomed, 'I'll send hunters to bring it to me, whatever it is. Then we'll have some sport!'

'Indeed, my Lord. Indeed we shall.'

NINE

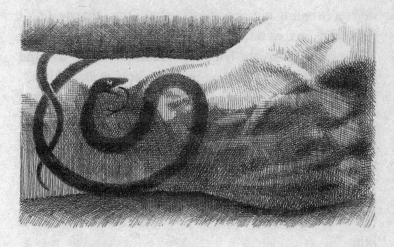

The snake lunged, a blur of black. Jack lifted his hands to defend himself.

Then he disappeared.

Kerry saw it strike. And Jack simply vanished.

Venom spurted and the snake rolled in a tangle of shiny coils. Kerry leapt back as its tail slapped his shin.

'Jack?'

'Over here.'

'Where?'

He saw a movement. Jack was somehow about ten feet away, lowering himself from the branch of a tree. Kerry moved cautiously towards him, eyes alert for any other snakes which might be lying in ambush.

'Did you see that?'

'Couldn't keep my eyes off it. What happened to you?'

The snake hissed and twisted.

'Kill it,' Jack said. 'There's something badly wrong with this.'

'You're telling me. See the size of it? I thought you didn't get snakes in Ireland.'

Just as he spoke, the tail coiled around Kerry's ankle and suddenly the serpent was on him, winding itself up his leg. Kerry's hand clamped just under the head as it drew back to strike again and Jack saw long hinged fangs swing forward.

Kerry tripped, tangled in the coils, desperately trying to hold those teeth away from his face. The snake lunged again, forcing his arm back and the fangs missed his cheek by a whisker. Kerry's free hand was trying for his sword, but he had fallen on top of it and couldn't reach to grab the hilt.

Without a pause, Jack pulled an arrow from his quiver, the last of them from the Major's study. He held it like a dagger and slashed down with all his strength.

The barb dug right between the snake's eyes and pinned it to a root. Immediately its coils opened and it went into a spasm, poison drooling from its fangs until it went suddenly rigid.

Kerry got to his feet, drew the sword and swiped its head clean off.

'Nearly had me, Jack,' he said. 'That was too close. I hate snakes. *Really* hate them. They give me the heebie-jeebies.'

He checked his blade, wiped it clean on a fern. 'And anyway, what happened to you? One second you were there, and then you disappeared.'

Jack shook his head. 'I don't know. I jumped back and

then I found myself up in that tree. It was all a blur.'

'Never saw anything move that fast.'

'I know. I never even saw it coming.'

'Not the snake, Jack. *You!* Like greased freaking lightning, you were.'

Before Jack could reply, leaves rustled at their feet. Kerry's eyes swung down and for a second he saw nothing at all. Then, without warning, he shoved Jack with his free hand, pushing him back.

A second snake raised its blunt head from the leaf scatter. A forked tongue flicked. A yard away, another one uncoiled, perfectly camouflaged. A third oozed silently from a hollow log.

In mere seconds, the forest floor was alive with snakes, dozens of beady eyes fixed on the two boys. They all hissed, a strange sound like venting steam. Kerry shuddered.

'Jack, I think we better . . .'

Jack grabbed him by the sleeve and they were running.

Underfoot, snakes struck at their legs, almost too fast to see.

But Jack and Kerry were faster still, jinking right and left, so fast that everything else seemed to go in slow motion, until they were beyond the clearing and into the dense centre of the forest. Finally Jack slowed to a halt.

Kerry swept a hand across his brow. His nerves were jittering.

'Did you get bitten?' Jack asked.

Kerry shook his head. 'I was going a mile a minute. I squashed a couple I think, but none of them got their teeth in.'

He scratched his head. 'I've never run as fast as that in my life. Being scared makes you go faster.'

'It wasn't being scared,' Jack said. He sat on a log, scanning all round first to make sure there were no unpleasant surprises, then raised his foot.

'It's these boots. I think Rune was trying to tell us something. When that snake came at me, I didn't even think. Next thing I knew, I was up in a tree. I must have jumped.'

'That was some jump. Ten feet at least. More, even.'

'And then,' Jack continued, 'when we made a run for it, I could see all these snakes coming for us, but they looked like they were going slow. And we were going *fast*.'

Kerry looked down at his own new boots. 'Much better than the charity shop. I wish I'd had them every time Billy Robbins chased me at school. And when those Scree were after us.'

'Just as well we never took the gold,' Jack said, beginning to relax. 'It wouldn't have done us any good.' He looked around, trying to work out which way to go. They'd been heading south, but he wasn't quite sure which direction they'd taken when they ran from the snake-glade. Here in the forest, the trunks crowded like hoary old men, with barely room for the two of them to walk side by side. Above them, the canopy was dense enough to block out the day.

'That way, I think,' Jack pointed. Kerry didn't question his sense of direction.

The forest was even darker here, with only a winding trail between the trees. The only sound was the murmur of insects and the slither of creatures under fallen leaves. They moved warily, apprehensive, eyes wide. Kerry had his sword out, just in case.

After half a mile, Jack knew they were heading in the wrong direction, as the narrow trail wound around trunks and mossy banks, but for the moment, it was the only way to go.

He stopped and touched Kerry's arm.

'I heard something.'

Kerry nodded silently.

The sound was almost below the hearing threshold, more of a sensation than actual sound. Like a deep vibration, somehow as oppressive as the dark wood itself.

'What is it?'

'Dunno, but we have to keep moving.'

Jack felt the heartstone squeeze against his chest and immediately his hackles crawled. It was always a warning, as if the heart could sense danger. He had learned, with good reason, to trust it.

'Something's wrong again.'

'I know that already. We need to get out of here.'

'But we're going in the wrong direction. It's the trees, and the track itself. And those sounds we heard. It's as if we were being led the wrong way.' He brushed a cobweb away and the spider at its centre scuttled up its drag-line. The web parted with an audible snap.

And still that low pervasive sound shivered through them.

'Jack, I really think ...'

But Jack had halted. Behind them, the leaves were stirring, moving in slow waves.

Ahead of them, a shaft of light managed to pierce the canopy. Jack saw a stone wall.

'Maybe it's the edge,' he said. 'Like Cromwath Blackwood.' Jack felt a shudder run through him, though whether it was a tremor in the earth or something inside him, he couldn't quite tell.

Then they saw it was no boundary wall.

It was a house. Old, sagging, built from crumbling stone festooned with ivy. A swayback roof could have been mildewed thatch, or it could have simply been covered by years of falling leaves and twigs.

A doorway gaped. Two slit windows on either side were like blind eyes.

'We could hide here until morning,' Kerry said. 'I think it's getting late, and I sure don't want to be wandering around when it gets really dark.'

'Maybe we could light a fire,' Jack said.

Very cautiously they made their way across the clearing.

They were only ten yards from the little stone house when a sudden inexplicable smell of crisp hot bacon made Jack's mouth water. His stomach rumbled involuntarily.

'Oh, man,' Kerry said. 'That smells like pure heaven.'

He almost ran towards the doorway. Jack thought he could make out the flicker of an open fire reflecting on a wall inside.

But then he saw a movement that made his heart lurch.

The doorway gaped *wider*.

It was just a small motion, barely perceptible to anyone

who wasn't completely alert. But the heartstone on his chest was pulsing fast, and Jack was totally alert.

From somewhere in his memory, from a nature programme he'd seen on TV, the image of a lion in the Serengeti – stretching and yawning just before a hunt – flashed across his mind.

In that instant, the mouth-watering smell of bacon turned into the reek of rotting flesh.

Without even thinking, Jack snatched at Kerry's hood and dragged him back with such force Kerry landed with a thump on his backside.

'What in the name . . .' he started to say, scrambling to his feet, before he too caught the gagging stench and clapped a hand over his mouth.

Jack grabbed his arm, eyes fixed on the doorway where the lintel was now rough and jagged, like a row of teeth ready to crunch down.

A voice spoke inside his head.

'Come in. *Come in!*'

Jack shook his head, hauling on Kerry who was bent over, retching.

'*Boyssss. Tasssty boysss.*'

The voice sounded ancient and dirty and very, very hungry.

Jack suddenly remembered what Rune the Cluricaun had told them: old, bad things have woken hungry in the dark places. He sensed an awesome hunger inside the strange house.

'Move,' he cried. Out of the corner of his eye he saw the windows close to black slits and the gaping maw extend towards them, as the air was sucked back, dragging at them and sending leaves and twigs whipping past them into the depths of the house.

Jack bent to minimise the suction as they struggled through the dark glade, snapping the spiders' webs, fending off trailing branches.

Jack risked a glance over his shoulder and saw that the house had changed.

It no longer looked anything like a house. It was no more than a rocky mound slowly subsiding into the forest floor.

They kept running, on and on, through the trees until eventually they saw daylight ahead. Another hundred yards of flight and then they were out into the clear.

Jack let out a long breath. 'We were dead lucky.'

'I'll never eat bacon again as long as I live,' Kerry gasped. 'Cross my heart.'

'Rule number one,' Jack said. 'Stay out of the woods.'

Kerry agreed wholeheartedly.

Before them a hardpack road wound south, between low hedgerows. A few moments later they were on their way, thorn-scratched and jittery, but in one piece.

And they had walked only half a mile when a snarling beast as big as a pony came crashing out of the hedge, opened its jaws and snatched Kerry into the air.

TEN

Corriwen swam up out of unconsciousness, bloodied and sore and motion-sick. She felt as if she'd been thrown from a horse and trampled in a stampede.

She and Connor had been put in some sort of cage on wheels, which was now trundling along a rutted road. It was night and no stars shone. A cold wind moaned through the cage bars, almost perfectly matching the sound that Connor was making, slumped in the corner, arms bound behind him.

The men had come out of nowhere, so it seemed. Corriwen and Connor had skirted a small town, keeping tight to the hedgerows. In the distance they could see armed horsemen scouring the fields and it would have been easy to sneak past them, but then a pair of mistle thrushes set up a squawking ruckus as they crept under the thorns and gave them away.

Two riders peeled away to investigate and Connor was just not fast enough crawling through the hedge. In an instant the whole troop had surrounded them, including one man with a lance and a tightly bandaged and splinted arm. It was fair to say he was mightily pleased to have found them.

They dragged Connor out by the ankles and began to lay into him with fists and a horsewhip. His cries of pain made Corriwen turn back, knives at the ready, and she scored a couple of cuts in the thrust and parry until a fist knocked her flat.

When she came round, both of them were bound and bruised, but, she assured herself, there was nothing broken, and while they were on the move, there was a chance of escape.

After a few miles, the horsemen called a halt and drew the wagon close to a tree where they lit a fire and set reed torches around, which gave Corriwen and Connor some light, but little heat. The smell of cooking food was mouth-watering at first, and later it became simply maddening.

'We're in for it now,' Connor whispered. 'Dermott will hunt us.'

'I'd say he'd caught us,' Corriwen said.

'No. What he does with poachers and the like, he sets them loose and sets the hounds after them. He likes the hunt. And the kill.'

'Sounds like a sweet man.'

'None worse,' he agreed. 'The whole of Eirinn's turned inside out all because of him. Everybody knows.'

'Everybody knows what?'

70

'Him and his warlock, Fainn, they've worked evil spells to turn the seasons upside down, and that's why there's little food. We have to poach to live.'

'How can he change the seasons? They're surely fixed for ever.'

'Ah, but they say he stole the Dagda Harp from Tara Hill. That's the cause of it all.'

'I don't know anything about that.'

'Where have you been? The whole land is abuzz with it.'

'I'm from ...' Corriwen paused. She didn't want to get into long explanation. 'I'm from the north. I'm waiting for my friends.'

'Up north is just bogs and badlands. Fell runners and the like. Bogrim from the tarns.'

'I never met any of them.'

'And not likely to either,' Connor said. 'Not unless we can get out of here.'

Corriwen edged across to him. 'I'm working on that,' she said. Their captors had taken her knives, but they hadn't found the little Swiss Army knife which she used now to cut through her bonds. In moments she had freed Connor. He stretched his stiff arms and groaned softly.

'That's a good trick,' he told her. She crossed to the bars of the door, solid wood staves bound with rawhide and tied shut with a knot of thick rope. Very carefully Corriwen sawed through the rope, pushed the gate open and they both crept into the shadows.

The hobbled horses snickered as they approached. Corriwen made Connor pause. They were only a few yards from the circle of men.

'We'll get a big reward for her,' one said.

'You think she's the one?'

'Red hair and a pair of knives. Fights like a wildcat. Who else?'

'We were looking for a woman, not a slip of a girl.'

One laughed. 'Unhorsed you, she did. And broke your arm. Can't get a better fighter than that. She's the one Dermott wants, for sure.'

Corriwen listened intently, hardly daring to breathe, and what she heard shocked her. They had been hunting for her, even though she had met no one in this place until yesterday. Did they know who she was, or where she was from? Did they have Jack and Kerry as well?

By the fire, another man spoke up.

'What does he want with her?'

'I just follow orders, how should I know?'

'He'll take her for a wife and fight side by side,' another said. 'They say Fainn has something to do with it, but it's none of our business.'

Corriwen was completely mystified.

She and Connor crawled, quiet as mice, behind the tree. Cautiously she reached round the bole and felt for her knife-belt. She felt much better with her own weapons. Then they moved beyond the shadow of the tree to where the horses were hobbled.

'We'll take two and scatter the rest,' she said.

'I can't do that,' Connor said.

'Why not? Stay and they'll hunt you down again. You don't owe them anything.'

'It's not that. It's just ... well, I never sat a horse before in my life. We only had pigs and a cow.'

He said it with such sincerity that Corriwen almost burst out laughing, but she held it in as she led the way to the horses. They were all loose-saddled, but still had their reins. She tightened the girths, then using both hands, boosted Connor on to the furthest horse. Quickly she untied the rest, climbed on a big black stallion and, yelling like a banshee, slapped its rump hard.

The horse bucked, reared high and then all of them stampeded together through the brush.

Behind them total confusion erupted.

At first the men thought they were being attacked. They jumped to their feet, drawing swords, spinning to face the enemy. Then they saw their horses gallop away.

They cursed. An arrow whined past Corriwen's ear, but she held tight to the reins and the tether on Connor's mount. He gripped its mane like a drowning man, eyes wide with either excitement or terror, but he managed to keep his seat and they were gone in a thunder of hooves.

In Wolfen Castle, Fainn shuddered.

This was out of his control. He felt it like a twist in his cold heart and pains shot up and down his arm.

'What's the matter?' Dermott the Wolf leaned over the table. Fainn's expression was a grimace, showing long, yellowing teeth. They ground like gravel underfoot.

Fainn wrenched back his sleeve.

'Something ... something *touched* me.' Even Dermott could hear his surprise mingled with absolute fury.

On Fainn's arm, the snake tattoo writhed and then went suddenly still.

'I saw something,' he said. 'Deep in the forest. A glimpse ...'

'What did you see?'

Fainn frowned.

'Men. Boys perhaps. But strange. Like ghosts.'

'Boys? Ghosts?' Dermott demanded. 'Talk sense to me, Spellbinder!'

'Not of this world,' Fainn insisted. 'From elsewhere. Far beyond Eirinn. I must ponder this.'

On his arm, where the snake's ferocious head lay on its own coils, a drop of blood appeared, swelled quickly, then trickled towards his hand in a dark stream, more purple than red.

'I *will* know,' he hissed.

'You cut yourself,' Dermott said.

Fainn shook his head. 'Something else did this.'

He sucked at the cut, a slice right across the serpent tattoo, drawing his own blood back, until the flow had stopped.

Without a pause, he bared his other arm, where a spiral of sleek weasels traced a helter-skelter from elbow to wrist.

With the tip of his knife, as he had done with the snake, he pierced the skin where the first weasel touched his wrist. A ripple ran through his stringy muscles and then the little animal pictures began to move of their own volition. Fainn

74

set the knife down, drew out a handful of leaves from a pouch, held them tight in the bloodied hand until they were crushed to dust and let them fall in a russet puff on the surface of the carved table.

'We shall see what is to be seen,' he said. 'We shall flush out who comes. Who dares touch Fainn.'

The trail of weasels scuttled off his skin and disappeared into the shower of crushed leaves, wriggled into the carved forest and were gone.

ELEVEN

The beast roared, loud as a lion. Huge teeth sank into Kerry's backpack and he was swung off his feet so fast he didn't even have time to cry out.

All Jack saw was a row of teeth that seemed a yard wide and a big, hoary head. Paws the size of dinner plates were planted on the path. The beast snarled, shook its head back and forth, jerking Kerry left and right. He looked like a rat in a terrier's mouth.

Jack's first instinct was to run. He bit back on instinct. Kerry yelled now as the dog, bigger than anything the Scree had unleashed on them, swung him about. Jack jumped back. His fingers found a solid branch and he grabbed as he forced himself forward.

The dog seemed to catch sight of him for the first time. It crouched low, dropping Kerry to the track, paws scraping ruts in the ground, its tongue as long as an arm.

Jack took three fast paces forward, pivoted on one foot, and smacked it as hard as he could, right on the end of its nose.

The beast howled in pain.

Jack snatched at Kerry who was still on the ground. He caught his backpack strap, and heaved his friend to his feet. Then, just as they had done in the dark forest, they were running for their lives.

The dog bayed. Trees shivered.

The boys went down that trail like roe deer in full flight. Jack felt as if his feet hardly touched the ground. They were running faster than they believed possible.

The dog raced after them.

It snarled and Jack cringed, expecting those teeth to snap like a bear-trap and end everything right here and now. Kerry was yelling. He pointed ahead and Jack saw a tall oak tree, wide branches stretching over the trail.

'Climb,' Kerry panted. They were only just a couple of steps ahead of the impossible hound.

Suddenly Kerry tripped on a rope strung across the trail. Jack saw him go down, bounce, roll and then the whole world tilted crazily and he was flying through the air as if he had been kicked by a giant horse. All the breath was punched out of his lungs. Kerry slammed into him with such force Jack saw little stars orbit in his vision. His chin struck his knee and his elbow caught Kerry a hard one on the cheek, and still the world spun.

Jack's stomach seemed to fall like a stone and he felt himself gag, then both of them were pitched downwards.

Something held Jack in a tight embrace, and then they were falling, even faster than they had risen.

They fell like dead weights then jerked to a sudden stop. Jack was upside down. Kerry was a tangle of legs and arms.

The dog growled. Jack looked down, and then wished he hadn't.

Twenty feet below them, the hound leapt up towards them. Its jaws opened, wider and wider, until they filled the whole world.

Then the pair of them were dragged skywards so violently that Jack felt as if his head was being torn from his shoulders.

Kerry squealed as they were crushed even tighter, swinging past the branches, out into the cloudy day.

A vast face loomed at them.

'Shouldn't have hit my puppy,' the monster said. Eyes glared at them. Brows as thick as porcupine quills were drawn down in a frown. A gale of breath that smelt of fish blew their hair backwards. 'He only wanted to play.'

Jack tried to say something, but he was mashed against Kerry in some sort of net that made it impossible to move and his throat didn't seem to want to open in any case.

'Poachers, are you? Here to steal my lunch and dinner? Well, this time I've caught you. Boiled or fried? Sliced or diced? Smoked or choked? Something tasty for me and the puppy.'

He swung them over his shoulder where they thudded against his massive back. It felt as if they had hit a rock face.

'Come on Tinker,' the giant rumbled, clicking his fingers. 'Home for dinner.'

The giant marched on and on, past grey crags shrouded in mist and then down the far side of a smoking mountain to where a stack of stone pillars formed a natural staircase down to the sea. A square wooden house stood near the shore.

'We have to get out of here,' Jack said.

Kerry wriggled until he could reach the hilt of his sword and with some effort he managed to draw it free. With all the jostling, he almost dropped it through the netting.

'You want me to stab him?'

'No. Just cut us out. We can run as soon as he puts us down.'

Kerry started working the blade across the net. In a few moments he had opened a space wide enough to get a head through. He was halfway free when the giant pulled up beside his house. Jack saw great slabs of meat drying on racks. And piles of bones picked clean and white.

'Hurry,' he urged.

The giant swung the bag off his shoulder, catching Kerry completely by surprise. The sudden motion sent his sword flying over their heads, whirring like a helicopter, then plummeting back down. The blade missed Jack's head by an inch, flashed past him and plunged into the giant's left foot.

The roar of pain was like a landslide. For a second, both of them went completely deaf.

Kerry managed to disentangle himself and pull Jack free. The dog was too busy to notice them.

'Come on,' Jack said.

'What about my sword?'

'Go and get it if you want.'

Kerry looked at the giant, who was holding his wounded foot, face screwed up in agony.

'That must have hurt,' he whispered. 'You think we should help him?'

What Jack thought was that they should run and not stop until they had put plenty of miles between themselves and the giant who now had two very good reasons to slice or dice them if he chose.

Then he looked at the giant's face, screwed up in obvious pain, and what he saw was not so much a giant as just a person who might need some help.

'Don't wiggle it,' he finally said. The giant's eyes opened. 'You'll make it worse.'

Jack risked a couple of steps forward. The dog opened its mouth and looked as if about to pounce but the giant reached out and pulled it close.

'It was an accident. We didn't mean it.' Beside him, Kerry nodded in vigorous agreement. 'But we can fix it for you, if you let us.'

The giant pondered this for a moment. He scratched his head. Finally he nodded.

'I can't get it out,' he boomed.

'Promise not to slice and dice us?'

'Wasn't going to anyway.'

'Okay. Take it easy. Just put your foot down nice and slow.'

Jack opened his pack and drew out the bag of stuff that

Rune the Cluricaun had used on Kerry's cuts and bruises. He sat astride the giant's foot. The skin felt as thick as a rhino's.

'This will hurt a bit,' he said, then, without further ado, he grasped the hilt, bent his legs and heaved with all his weight. The sword slid out with an odd sucking sound, and blood welled from the cut.

The giant groaned, but managed to keep still.

'Now the line,' Jack said. Kerry handed him the bobbin of fishing line, the strong nylon he'd used for hauling cod and halibut up from the estuary. It was tied to a steel hook.

Jack worked quickly to stitch the cut as best he could, then dabbed Rune's medication on it. The giant let out a huge sigh.

'How's that?'

'Much better.'

'We're really sorry,' Jack said, still wary. 'The sword just fell out. And I only hit your dog because he attacked Kerry.' He held his hand out. 'I'm Jack Flint, and this is my best friend, Kerry Malone.'

The giant looked at Jack's small hand, then engulfed it in his own.

'Finn McCuill. This headland is my piece of the shore.'

'Pleased to meet you, I think.'

'Tinker wasn't going to eat you,' Finn rumbled. 'Just scare you. Then you hit him. I've got a bit of a temper, see? When somebody hurts my dog. Runs away with me, so it does.'

'You set a trap for us,' Kerry piped up, indignant.

Finn shook his head. 'The net was for rievers. Thieves

and poachers. Don't see many of you little folk one year on another, but since the seasons went out of step and the clouds hid the stars, they've been coming here to steal my dinners. They'd starve me if I didn't watch out.'

'Your dinners?'

'Aye, the cattle and sheep. I prefer fish myself, but the fishing's gone off with all this funny business. I seen islands of ice go sailing past the front door. Anyway, thanks for fixing my toes, I'd have never thought of stitching it myself. It's a fine trick for a little 'un.'

He patted Jack on the back and sent him flying.

'And if I can do you a favour any time, just ask.'

TWELVE

Corriwen Redthorn had no idea where she was going, no sense of direction in the dark.

Connor held tight to the mane.

'I like this,' he cried. 'Never went so fast in the whole of my life. When I'm rich, I'm going to get one of these.'

Corriwen laughed, more out of relief than anything else.

'Just try to stay on. And try to stay alive.'

When the horses began to tire, they dismounted and unhitched the saddles. When the leathers slid to the ground, Connor bent quickly and came up with a short sword that had been hidden in a saddle-scabbard.

'Finders keepers,' he said. He drew a rag out of his little bag and wrapped the blade in it.

'Can't be seen with a sword. They're not allowed for the

likes of me. But I'll take it anyhow, because they'll hunt us for sure, high and low.'

'Well, I've got used to that.'

'But this time, if they catch us, they'll hang us.'

Together they found a coppice where they could shelter from the rising wind and the cold rain that was beginning to fall. Connor used a flint to start a fire and they huddled beside the heat, gnawing on the dried meat, deciding their next move. The wind picked up, sending little flurries of brown leaves circling about them, and making the fire flare.

'The whole land feels wrong,' Connor said. 'I haven't seen the moon and stars in I don't know how long, and the birds don't know when to nest.'

'I could have picked a better gate,' Corriwen muttered. She wished her friends were with her here and now. Connor, despite his bad leg, seemed a sturdy enough boy, but he wasn't the same as Jack and Kerry. Her heart ached for their company.

A hand on her shoulder startled her out of her memories.

'Did you hear something?' Connor scanned the trees around them.

'Only the wind.'

One of the horses whinnied and stamped its hooves.

Connor cocked his head, closed his eyes. 'Maybe a rabbit, if we've still got luck.'

Corriwen sincerely hoped they still had luck.

Something scampered through the leaves. From the far side of the fire, came more rustling and an odd high whistle.

'Don't sound like a rabbit,' Connor whispered. He picked up a stone.

A lithe brown shape emerged from the leaves. Two brilliant black eyes regarded Corriwen.

It whistled. Small and serpentine it squirmed out. It had a fierce, triangular head and at first she thought it was an adder.

'Weasel.' Connor sounded disappointed. Another whistle sang out and another creature burrowed up on the other side of the fire, then another and another.

Connor raised the stone, threw it hard and accurate, straight at the first weasel. Before the stone even hit the ground the animal whirled and was gone. The rest of them seemed to wink out of existence as they too spun for cover.

Corriwen shivered. The way the little beasts had glared at her was unnerving. Unnatural.

One of the horses neighed loudly and kicked at the ground, then both took off at a gallop.

In the crowded trees, something was moving, and fast. She got to her feet and Connor did the same, and they stood, almost back-to-back as around them the crunch and crumple of dead leaves grew even louder.

Corriwen saw it first. A hump of twigs and leaves seemed to be rippling in zig-zag lines as if something as big as a badger were racing underneath the fallen litter. As soon as she saw it, another line began, arrowing straight towards them across the clearing. A third snaked its way round the bole of a tree, keeping to the dense patches of leaves. It was like watching moles scutter through dry brown earth, but these things were moving faster than any moles, and they were bigger too. Connor bent and snatched up a heavier stone.

Corriwen tensed as the motion suddenly stopped. Around them, several heaps of leaves, each a yard high, had piled up. They trembled slightly as if whatever was underneath was breathing fast.

Then, without warning, the mounds of leaves exploded, scattering twigs and acorns and beech mast into the air.

'Evil magic,' Connor said. 'There must be a curse on this place.'

Leaves and branches, burrs and bark spun in vortices, solidifying as they whirled until, abruptly, they stopped.

Before them stood a semi-circle of man-shaped figures, thin as spindles, each made entirely of the detritus of the forest floor, shaggy with pine-needles and fir-cones. Twiggy fingers sprouted from dead-bark arms. Shiny chestnuts gleamed in pits where eyes might have been. Jagged lines of rose-thorns could have been mouths.

Corriwen felt a shudder ripple up and down her spine.

The first creature, taller than either of them, raised a knotted hand and pointed a stick finger. The others stepped forward. She could hear them breathing, dead and dry as worm-eaten wood.

Chestnut and acorn eyes glinted. Connor eased the sword from its rag, the first sword he had ever hefted in his life. It felt good in his hand. The figures rattled and rustled forwards.

'Do we run, or fight?'

'How do you fight dead wood?'

'I don't know,' Connor whispered back. 'But we'll find out.'

He steadied himself on his good leg. The nearest creature

was only feet away. It smelt of mould and toadstools, a hellish scarecrow bound together by some unnatural force.

It shot out an arm and gripped Corriwen's left wrist. Wooden fingers squeezed with shocking force, twisting her hand open. Her knife fell to the ground. She slashed at the arm with the other knife. It cut cleanly through. For a second she expected blood to spout, but the twiggy hand simply disintegrated in a brown explosion before whirling back to become a hand again.

The others closed in. Connor leapt forward at the second figure. The blade went straight through the chest with a tearing sound. Corriwen picked up her knife and slashed again, severing the tumbleweed head. The leaves spun in a lazy circle and reformed where they had been before. *Exactly* as they had been before.

'We can't beat them,' Connor said. She heard his bewildered horror.

'Yes, we can,' Corriwen said.

She stooped to the fire, dragged out a burning branch and thrust the flames right inside the leaf-creature. It caught alight in an instant, the dry twigs and damp chestnuts making a strange singing noise. In seconds, it was a pillar of fire. Staggering left and right, it barged into its neighbour and set it alight.

She thought she could hear a hiss of pain, but she didn't stop, Turning in a half circle, she lashed the branch through the rest of them. They scattered, spinning like fiery tops through the bracken and thorns, trailing flame, and setting fire to the undergrowth.

'We'd better move,' Connor said. A dog-rose went up in

a crackle of heat and shared its fire with a dead ivy coiled up a pine tree. Flames raced up the trunk to turn the waxy needles into an incandescent sheet and then, in the space of a dozen breaths, the whole coppice was an inferno.

'Come on!' he tugged her arm as flames licked about her feet. The leaf-creatures were nothing but spinning flickers of light now.

She let him pull her away and they ran from the scorching heat that chased them until they came to the edge of the trees and clear air.

In Wolfen Castle, Fainn gasped as rivers of fire seared through him. He pulled back his sleeve. The hairs on his arm were singed and an acrid smell rose from skin that was already beginning to blister.

He crossed the room and plunged his arm into a stone jug. The water hissed and bubbled as it drew the fire out from him. He grabbed his staff and in five long strides he was out of the room and making his way up the winding stairway.

Dermott the Wolf was in the banqueting hall, gnawing on a platter of pig ribs, washing them down with ale.

'What news, Spellbinder?'

Fainn said nothing. He showed Dermott the skin on his arm where the weasels had scampered. Now they were puckered and twisted.

'You should put a poultice on that,' Dermott advised.

'I have seen ... *her.*'

'What?'

'I have seen her! The warrior woman. I have looked in her eyes.'

Dermott stopped, a rib halfway to his open mouth.

'You saw her? Where?'

'In the east. Halfway to the Mourning Mountains.'

Dermot got to his feet. He drew a greasy forearm across his mouth.

'Have her brought to me. Find her. Take her!'

His face was thunderous. His wolf-cloak bristled as if charged with his anger.

'Captain!' He roared. 'Captain of the guard. Fifty men – a hundred! Fast horses. Spare mounts. Hurry. Hurry, damn you all!'

People scurried. Horses clattered. Armour clanked. The drawbridge went swinging down and a line of horsemen sped across it. Hungry people along the road watched them gallop past.

And silently they prayed for whoever Dermott was hunting.

Corriwen and Connor ran down the hill from the blazing coppice, with Corriwen urging him on. Behind them came angry shouts as people came running from the sparse fields with spades and hoes to try to beat out the flames.

'Fire-raisers! Stop them!'

They didn't look back. They scrambled through a hedge onto a road and straight into a troop of horsemen galloping towards the flames.

They skidded to a halt as the horses wheeled in unison.

'It's them,' a man shouted. 'Take them!'

The pair ran across the road into a field. Despite his bad leg, Connor could get up quite a speed, but neither of them could outrun horses. Corriwen held back a little to give him a chance and regretted it instantly when Connor slowed with her.

'Move your feet,' she cried. 'Get on with you.'

He lurched on, drawing his sword, but the lead horseman swung his mount to stamp him down. Connor went sprawling. Corriwen grabbed his arm, got him to his feet and they ran.

They veered left, towards some bushes, the only cover they could see. Hands reached to grab her hood and she shook them off, but it was to no avail. The horses ran them down, surrounded them and one man drew a sword to bar their way. Corriwen ducked under it, slashed his stirrup and managed to unseat him. She whirled, knives at the ready, when from behind she was hit such a blow she fell flat to the ground. For a second the whole world spun dizzily and all the strength went out of her legs. With a desperate effort she forced herself back up, dodged a swinging blade.

Connor screamed in rage and frustration. She saw him pivot on his good leg, land a clean blow across a man's throat and saw the man drop like a sack. Somebody kicked the legs from her and she was down again. Connor was growling and snarling like an animal, trying to fight his way towards her, but it was a hopeless effort. He had his stolen sword in his hand and whirled on one leg, slicing a circle around him, when a club came flying in and took him on the side of the head. It was all over.

On the ground Corriwen let out a cry of despair. A heavy boot came swinging in, caught her under the jaw, and it was all over for her, too.

THIRTEEN

They had dined like kings, even though Finn was surprised at how little they could actually eat. He had tied the canvas bandage tight round his foot and limped up towards the smoking peak of the mountain and when he came back down he carried a side of beef spiked on a sharpened log, cooked so well that the fat still sizzled on the seared surface and the smell of it made them groan in anticipation.

'Old Grumbles,' he said, carving off great chunks which they ate until they were stuffed. 'Best roasting oven in all of Eirinn.' Finn slapped half the side between two monstrous crusts of bread and went through it like a buzz-saw, bones and all.

'So what brings you to these parts?' Finn wanted to know.

'We came looking for a girl,' Kerry piped up.

'Maybe I should do the same.'

'No. She's a friend of ours,' Jack said. 'We've sort of lost her.'

He explained how they'd met Rune the Cluricaun, got lost in the darkwood and told him about the snakes in the forest.

'Aye, there's things woken right enough. From the old days before these hills were even raised. There's bad in the land. I keep my own company and my own counsel, as the McCuill always do, but I fear there's trouble brewing. Real trouble.'

The next day Jack and Kerry made their way to the crossroads. They had travelled for miles and miles, over hill and dale and across wide rivers and now they were far south of the farward gate.

Finn McCuill had carried them on a wicker basket strapped to his back. It was like riding a balloon through turbulence as the giant's strides tossed them about in the basket, but the countryside sped past in a blur while the huge dog scampered around, for all the world like an overgrown pup.

Eventually Finn set them down. Before them, low country spread out under dank clouds.

'This is as far as I go,' Finn said, barely out of breath after his long walk. Rune's potion and Jack's stitching had healed his wound overnight. 'Too many little people around here.'

'Like Cluricauns and Leprechauns?' Kerry asked.

'No. Little people like you. They squeak and scuttle. Too jittery for me.'

He crouched to their eye level.

'You did me a true favour, fixing my foot. You find trouble on your way, you just ask Finn. The McCuill always pays back.'

Jack smiled, sheepish. 'It was nothing.'

'Not to me it wasn't.' He drew a thin wooden tube from his pocket, about the size of a flute. 'Blow on this, and Tinker will hear it. I'll come apace.'

'Nice big guy,' Kerry said after the giant had strode back the way they had come.

'Turned out to be a big friendly giant after all.'

Now they were far from Finn's home and they paused on the brow of a hill. Jack opened the Book of Ways and they sat down to read the verses that scrolled on the page:

From rocky reach wends far the path
To peril, danger, hate and wrath
A friend in need, a friend now lost
New friends meet where roads have crossed
Comes here a ragged reiver band
A journey make through troubled land
The hunter rides; the die is cast
The sands of time are running fast
Journeyman, make haste, make speed
Or ever lose the friend in need.

'Even I get the picture,' Kerry said gloomily.

They reached a winding road and walked for five miles or more until they saw a crossroads ahead of them. The two roads intersected on a bare, flat straight with no real cover nearby. A single signpost pointed in four directions.

Jack eyed the scene warily. They would have to walk out into the open. They listened, but heard no sound but the thin drizzle.

'We'll have to risk it,' he said. Kerry shrugged.

'*New friends meet where roads have crossed,*' Jack said. 'Maybe this isn't the place. I don't see a soul.'

Side by side they strode to the crossing and stopped at the old wooden sign on which strange lettering had been etched. Kerry squinted, trying to make out the words when, in the distance, movement caught his attention.

'Horses,' he said.

Jack turned in alarm. Far to the south the sound of hooves came faintly on the breeze, and there was no mistaking the column of horsemen making speed towards them.

'And nowhere to hide!'

Another troop of riders appeared round the bend to the east, galloping just as fast. Kerry could make out bright pennants above the cavalcade. The pair of them spun in circles, desperately trying to find a place to hide before they were caught in the middle of the two groups.

'We're caught like rats,' Kerry snarled.

They stood, paralysed. The southern horsemen came on at full tilt, sending up mud and spray, and there was nothing the boys could do to escape over empty ground.

Something snorted just behind Jack's shoulder. He

half-turned and then something big nudged him on the back and he almost leapt a yard into the air. The cry of sheer fright that escaped him could have been heard a mile away.

A short, fat pony snorted again, shook its head and then barged past him, hauling on a low covered wagon. Jack's heart, which had leapt into his throat, slid back down again, but still hammered like a drum.

The pony and wagon trundled past, followed by another, and another, all heading south past the crossroads.

'Where the heck did they come from?' Jack muttered.

It was as if the line of gaudy wagons had simply winked into existence. Jack scratched his head, unable to comprehend how either of them could fail to have noticed the caravan of carts and chubby ponies.

The fourth wagon was rolling past where they stood when the tanned leather covering was suddenly pulled aside. Four brawny arms shot out, grabbed them by the shoulders and hoisted them inside. It all happened so fast the boys didn't even have time to yell.

But they did as soon as they saw what had hauled them aboard.

A muscular man with his hair in tight bunches stared at them. His skin had a strange bluish tinge, and his eyes were the colour of polished silver. But that wasn't what caused their jaws to gape.

He held them in a tight four-handed grip. Two pairs of thick arms reached out from each shoulder.

Now Jack and Kerry squawked in sheer fright.

The big fellow let go with two hands. He brought one to his lips in an unmistakeable request for silence, then clamped both free hands over the boys mouths to emphasise. He turned, carrying them as easily into the shadows within the wagon.

He snapped open the hinge on a thick hide bag that sat on a stool and drew the sides apart until they were more than a foot apart, and without ceremony, dumped Kerry head-first inside the bag. He disappeared completely.

Jack wriggled, trying to free himself, but the four-armed monstrosity simply flipped him up and stuffed him inside the bag. It was impossible. Jack saw the bag, and he knew it was only two feet deep at the most, but in a second he was inside it and the hinged lid was closing. He tried to jump up and out, but his feet felt as if they were sinking into warm wool and he could get no leverage. Complete and utter darkness enfolded him.

Jack groped with one hand until he found Kerry tumbled beside him.

'Are you okay?'

'You've got to be kidding,' Kerry shot back.

FOURTEEN

The darkness was warm, but uncomfortable. Jack didn't want to move in case it went further than he imagined. And he imagined a great deal of darkness around them.

'This is really weird,' he said. 'Did you see him? The four-armed thing?'

'See him? I couldn't take my eyes off him! Four *arms*. What kind of freaks do they grow in this place? And how did he get us in this bag? I saw it. It's the size of a ruck-sack. This place creeps me out.'

'They came from nowhere,' Jack said. 'I could have sworn there was nobody else on the road.'

'I don't know what's worse. Getting caught by the troopers or by that four-armed freak. What do you think he'll do?'

Before Jack could reply, they were suddenly thrown into

the air and landed in a fankle of arms and legs. Kerry's knee caught Jack on the nose and little lights spangled around him.

'Get off,' Kerry groaned from under him.

Outside the strange bag, there was still no sound. But they were tumbled over again and then everything stopped moving.

'You okay?'

'Apart from a sore dose,' Jack mumbled.

'We have to get out of this.'

Jack was about to ask how when daylight stabbed into the dark and they screwed their eyes shut against the glare. Two hands reached in and hauled them out. The big blue man's silver eyes looked them up and down.

'It's all right now,' he said, in a surprisingly soft voice. 'They're gone. And good riddance to them all.'

He set them on their feet and Jack looked about him. The little caravan was in disarray. Bags and trunks littered the road, all emptied, clothes and pots scattered around. The strange, bottomless bag they'd been stuffed in was lying at their feet. That explained the tumble and crash.

'Not very nice people at all,' a voice said and they both turned. Beside them stood a little man, no taller than Rune the Cluricaun, but wider, fatter and bald as an egg on top, but with the same curled whiskers on either side of his face.

'I knew we'd come across you,' he said. 'Rune said to keep a weather eye out and there you were, just about to be nipped by the Wolf-pack.'

Jack looked from one to the other. The blue man was solid and muscular. The little one almost round. He stuck out a podgy hand.

'Brand's the name. I lead this hapless band hither and yon.'

'What band?' Kerry asked.

Brand laughed. 'The *Vaga*band. Rogues and scoundrels all. Peddlers of mystery, magic and mayhem. This is Score Four-arm. You'll see he's well-named.'

The blue man held up four hands and waggled twenty fingers.

'Score,' Jack said. 'I get it.'

'Congratulations! The boy can count,' Brand beamed. 'We came here just in the nick of time. You'll be heading south, Rune tells me, so you're better travelling with us. We're good company.'

'That bag you put us in,' Kerry said. 'How did you do that?'

'Och, just a trick. The quickness of the hand deceives the eye.' Brand snapped it shut like a medic's case and slung it onto the wagon.

'It's a good place to hide what you don't want found. And it worked just fine when the Wolf-pack came searching.'

He reached high and clapped Jack on the shoulder.

'Come and meet the rest of the reivers. Changelings, foundlings and fairy-touched all of them. Rune says you'll fit in so you can't see the join. Tells me you're a pair of acrobats.'

Jack looked at Kerry and shrugged. A small crowd had gathered around them by now.

'Tigally and Tagelyn,' Brand said.

Two slender girls stepped forward together, so close they could have been glued to each other. They were identical in every way, from short spiky hair to eyes of lavender blue. They wore tight leggings, like gymnasts. 'Tig and Tag to the rest of us. Best tumblers in the business.'

The girls gave them twin dazzling smiles. Tag fell backwards. Tig tumbled over her and the pair spun together, on hands and feet, blinding fast, like one creature cartwheeling along the road.

'And Thin Doolan,' Brand said.

Kerry shrank back as Thin Doolan stuck a scrawny hand out. For a moment he thought it was one of the Rushen folk who had almost killed Corriwen in the Temair marshes. Jack took the proffered hand. He felt as if he was shaking hands with a skeleton.

'This here's Natterjack,' Brand said, 'We call him Toad for short.'

A squat fellow with a broad face and a mouth that seemed to span from ear to ear, blinked yellow eyes at them, and smiled a toothless grin. His skin was as warted as a Scree trooper, and greenish brown, just like a toad's.

'All right then,' Brand said. 'We should be on our way.'

'Where are you going?' Jack asked.

'South. Same as you. Hop aboard and take the weight off. We've a distance to travel between here and there and maybe there's a chance you'll find what you're searching for.'

'Did Rune tell you?'

'He did indeed. But you're not the only ones looking for

a red-haired girl.' Brand smoothed his moustaches. 'I heard she got taken some way north of here, and then she gave them the slip. If it's the same one you're looking for, she's a plucky one for sure. But now she's got a price on her pretty head.'

Neither of them knew how to respond to that. But it did sound as if Corriwen was making her mark in Eirinn, even if it wasn't for the better.

They climbed onto the buckboard beside Score Four-arm. He grinned, snapped the reins and the little fat pony took the strain.

In the distance they could see a pillar of dark smoke rising into the air and when they rounded the bend the source became clear. A wide coppice of trees up the hill from the road was well ablaze. Men were trying to beat out the flames with farming tools, but they were fighting a losing battle. Further along the road, the horse troop that had nearly caught them were milling about and somebody was yelling.

'Nothing but strife and trouble every which way,' Score muttered. 'The whole of Eirinn is going to ruin and rack.'

He hitched the reins around the buckboard brake and let the fat pony amble along with the rest. From a wide pocket, he took a bag of coloured wooden balls and threw them up ten, fifteen or more. The four hands wove in the air, smooth as oiled machinery until he had at least twenty balls whirling about his head in complicated patterns.

'You're a juggler, then.' Kerry stated the obvious.

'Juggler, fiddler, fuggler and more besides.'

'A fuggler?'

'Sure. That's when I juggle and fiddle at the same time. There's not many can do that.'

'I can play the mouth-organ,' Kerry said.

'Don't believe him,' Jack snorted. 'It sounds like a scalded cat.'

The band, the *Vagaband* as Brand liked to call his troupe, drew up their wagons close to the town square.

'We'll have some fun here,' Score assured them. 'And it seems to me they could do with it.'

The first thing Jack noticed was the armed men patrolling the streets. They kept their hoods up to make themselves as inconspicuous as possible. Brand had been right though. It was better for them to travel with this band, strange as they may be, than to be two boys alone on the road with so many patrols about.

'Friends and townsfolk,' Brand piped up. 'It's a dull life and the sun still hides, but here we are to bring a smile in fun and frolic. We promise mystery, magic and mischief. We will tumble and juggle and stir you with music to bring a tear to a blind eye.'

Thin Doolan gave a quick drum-roll. Natterjack played a riffle on a set of pipes.

'I give you Brand's Wandering Band. The Vagaband! Entertainment for your delight and delectation.'

With that, Tig and Tag came tumbling into view, joined

back to back, cartwheeling along the street, totally silent, eerily elegant.

'Beauty and grace in a double dose,' Brand announced. People stopped to look as the twins spun and whirled around each other, sinuous as snakes.

'Brilliant,' Kerry said. 'Never seen anything like that.'

Two of the guards had stopped to watch. Tig and Tag swirled round them, then up and over them without missing a step, somersaulting to the men's shoulders, flipping back to land together.

As they spun away, Jack saw something blur through the air towards Natterjack who caught it and dropped it into the bag they'd found themselves in. It happened so fast that he wasn't quite sure what had taken place.

Score Four-arm walked into the crowd, his hands moving in circles and spirals, twenty coloured balls in the air making intricate patterns that changed from second to second. He approached another pair of guards and stood in front of them, dazzling them with his juggling, while around him small children watched, fascinated.

Then Jack saw it happen. Three of Score's hands kept all the balls. His other sneaked out. Everybody watched the cascade of balls. Nobody saw the fourth hand snick the pouch from the guard's belt. The pouch came flying backwards towards Natterjack and nobody saw that either. It disappeared into the bag, as did the second guard's pouch, along with a gold-handled dagger from his sheath.

Jack giggled. Kerry looked at him. 'What's funny?'

'Didn't you see it? They're picking pockets. They're just a bunch of thieves!'

Thin Doolan wandered about with a wide, straw hat held upside down, encouraging people to make donations. It was clear this town had seen better days, for there were very few coins, but Thin Doolan didn't seem to mind at all. He wove among the people and the guards and every time he got close to a soldier, something went missing from the man's belt. A knife, a purse, a money-bag. He did it with such speed and skill that no one, except Jack and Kerry who were now watching closely, saw a thing.

'Now *that's* a talent,' Kerry applauded. Natterjack brought the bottomless bag up to Brand. Score pulled back from the crowd, still juggling so fast it was impossible to see how he did it. Tig and Tag came cartwheeling back to the wagons.

Brand pulled himself up to his full height.

'Friends and countryfolk. It has been a pleasure entertaining you all, though the pickings are slim today. It seems your need is perhaps greater than ours. So it's our pleasure to share our good fortune on such a grey day.'

With that, he opened the mysterious bag and began to flick big red apples to Score who spun them into the air, then tossed them unerringly to the children who snatched them fast. Brand brought out crusty pies by the dozen and Thin Doolan passed them around the eager crowd. Even the soldiers began to look hungry.

Jack saw one of them reach for his purse, then he saw the look of surprise on the man's face when he realised it was gone. He was about to warn Brand when a loud clamour started up on the far side of the square. The crowd around them turned as one, as the sound of men's voices and the thud of soldiers' boots grew louder.

Beyond the mass of people Jack saw a horse-drawn wagon, built like a cage. Between the press of people he saw two figures slumped inside, and inwardly he wished them well. It could so easily have been he and Kerry in the cage.

A troop of soldiers kept the people back as they trundled it away.

Jack saw a flash of red hair, and before he knew it he was off the wagon.

'It's Corriwen!'

Kerry was beside him in a flash, sword already in his hand. They raced across the square to where the cage had been.

Before they got ten yards Score snatched them both off the ground and hustled them back.

'Put me down!' Kerry yelled. 'You big four-handed freak!'

Score clapped a hand over his mouth and stuffed him in the back of the wagon. Brand shook his head slowly.

'That's the best way to lose her, and yourselves.'

FIFTEEN

'Score did the right thing,' Brand said. 'That would have been you on that jail-cart. You can't help anyone when you can't help yourself, am I right?'

Jack had to agree. It had happened to them before, and Kerry had accused him of cowardice before he saw sense. It was hard to see sense, though, when the one person they had come to find was caught and felled.

'You have to pick your moment,' Brand went on. 'And the moment always comes.'

'We have to find her,' Kerry blurted. His stomach still churned at the thought of Corriwen being carted away like an animal.

'That's the easy part,' Brand said. Score nodded. Natterjack stuffed half a smoked ham into his wide mouth, closed his bugging eyes and swallowed with a look of sheer pleasure. 'They'll race her to Wolfen Castle and spare no horse on the way. Bold Dermott and his spellbinder have been combing all Eirinn for your friend.'

'Then we have to get to her before that happens,' Jack said.

'More haste, less speed,' Brand assured them. 'We're on our way there for his Lordship's entertainment.'

'How far away is it?'

'As the crow flies? Two days. As the road twists, maybe four.'

'So we should get a move on!' Kerry insisted.

'Aye, we will. Once we're fed and watered and rested.'

Kerry hauled to his feet, drew his sword, spun around in clear frustration.

'Come on, Jack. Let's go.'

Jack looked at Brand who returned the look without his usual smile.

'Only if you never want to see her again.'

Jack grasped Kerry's wrist and sat him back down again.

'Hear him out,' he said. Kerry shot him a look, but Jack stared him down.

'We know the short-cuts,' Brand said. 'The *by-ways*. We'll get there ahead of them. And we can help you on your mission ...'

He paused and glanced at Score.

'... if you help us on ours.'

'What does that mean?' Kerry demanded.

'There's something in Wolfen Castle that shouldn't be there. We plan to liberate it.'

'More thievery?' Kerry demanded. 'We've got better things to do.'

'It's the Harp,' Jack said, in sudden comprehension. 'You're going to steal the golden harp?'

'It's the only way to get Eirinn out of these troubles,' Brand said. 'Dermott has turned its harmony to discord. And as you've seen, thievery is our stock-in-trade. And you two could be the very fellows to help us.'

'I knew this wasn't a coincidence,' Jack said. 'We've been set up all along.'

'The book was right,' Kerry snarled. 'It said time was running out.'

Brand waited for a reply.

'I think we have to go along with it,' Jack finally said.

Corriwen wondered if she had dreamed it. Her eyes had opened briefly as the prison-cart rolled through the town gate and onto the road, past a line of little caravans. For an instant, before the darkness rolled in again, she thought she saw Jack Flint.

She tried to swim up out of the miasma, ignoring the pain in every joint and the blood that clogged her nose, but the effort was too great. She slumped down again and the darkness took her away.

Jack opened his pack and drew out the roll of leather that protected the Book of Ways. Kerry shone the light onto the page and they waited until the words appeared for them.

In Mists of Time a low road take
Through skeins a stranger journey make
Careful though upon this travel
See the winding road unravel
Straight and swift as any ley
Never tarry, never stray
Peril waits at journey's end
New friends aid to find a friend
For Eirinn's harmony, beware!
Onward lies the serpent lair.

'I wish it would just say 'Go north' or 'Watch out for dragons'.'

Jack agreed. 'Brand says he'll help us get Corriwen. There might be safety in numbers.'

'But they're going to steal this harp. That's got to be risky.'

'I believe my father had something to do with the harp,' Jack said. 'That means it's really important. He would *want* me to help.'

'How do you know that?'

'Rune told me a traveller had come through the gates before. And he was the Journeyman,' Jack said simply. 'Remember, he fought the Morrigan long before we did.'

Kerry was still in an agony of frustration and urgency as the ponies ambled along. A few miles further, the road entered a forest where branches curved over their heads. Brand turned left at a fork and as they travelled, a damp mist thickened around them until they could barely see the road ahead.

'It gets a bit tricky along this way,' Score said, 'so even if we stop, don't stray from the path. You go into that mist and you'll never get out again. Not in this life.'

'It's only a bit of fog,' Kerry said. 'I've seen worse blowing onshore back home.'

Jack wasn't quite sure. There was something odd about the mist, so white and thick, rolling in from either side so that even the dank forest was completely hidden from view. As he stared at it, he could imagine he saw pale shapes writhing within its depths, and he remembered the words from their Book of Ways: In Mists of Time a low road take.

For a while there was silence. Even the rattling of the wheels was muffled by the fog, as if wrapped in gossamer. Ahead of them, the next caravan was a vague shape.

'Where is this place?' Jack asked. His voice sounded thin and smothered.

'A road few know of,' Score said. 'And fewer take. With good reason, too. Brand knows all the low roads. We call 'em *by-ways*. Takes us by and beyond.'

He turned to the boys, all hands juggling on automatic. 'The mist hides a whole shebang of things you don't want to look at. And don't you pay heed to anything you might hear, either. Short-cuts are fine and handy, but to travel them, you've got to go *between* places.'

Jack thought he got the meaning. He and Kerry had gone *between* places and ended up here in Eirinn. There were some things you just had to accept, he decided, or you could go crazy.

Kerry muttered under his breath and Jack saw he had quietly drawn his sword.

'This gives me the heeby-jeebies,' he said.

The words were barely out when a deep bass rumble shivered the wagon. Jack jumped.

'What was that?'

'Who knows, or wants ever to know? There's things lost in that mist. And worse things walking it.'

The rumble came again, so powerful and slow it made the hairs on the back of Jack's neck rise. Then they heard a squelching sound, once, twice, as if something very big was moving in thick swamp.

'Can this horse go faster?' Kerry asked. 'Like a whole lot faster?'

They moved on and the noise faded, bringing another silence for some time before that too was broken. Jack turned to listen.

It came again. A child crying beyond the side of the road. The cry of a child left all alone.

Jack instinctively moved towards the sound. Score touched his arm.

'Maybe it fell off a wagon,' Jack said. 'We have to help.'

'No baby with us. And it's not what you hear.'

Jack strained, trying to see through the blank gauze. A motion, barely perceptible, rippled in the mist.

'I see her,' Kerry said.

It was a girl, small, thin, ragged. She held skinny arms out.

'Help me,' Jack heard her whisper. 'Oh please help me. I'm lost and all alone.'

'Just you look straight on,' Score warned.

'She's just a kid,' Kerry said. He bent to put his sword down, but the hairs on Jack's neck were still walking and he clamped a hand over Kerry's wrist.

'Oh sirs. Won't you help a waif?' The piteous voice tugged at Jack's soul. 'Take me with you. Please?'

'Look,' Jack said.

The girl was closer now, almost close enough to touch, but filmy and translucent. Jack thought he could see other shapes beyond her, milling in the mist.

'She's floating,' he said, aghast. 'She's not on the ground.'

The girl stretched towards them. Through her, Jack could definitely see other shapes. Shapes that hurt his eyes.

Slowly the pitiful face writhed back into churning mist. Jack heard a giggle that sounded more than a little mad.

He closed his eyes and held tight to Kerry's wrist, wishing he had never heard a thing, never seen a thing.

The journey seemed to take a long, long time in that eerie place. Jack and Kerry clambered into the wagon and found a place to sleep, while Score juggled and watched the pony, never letting his eyes stray left or right. He had travelled the by-way before.

When the boys awoke, some hours later, the mist was thinning and the feeling of oppression was also beginning to lift.

Eventually they could see the trees on either side of the road as they rounded the bend and emerged on the brow of a hill.

And far in the distance, a dark castle hunched like a beast on the crags beside a storm-tossed sea.

SIXTEEN

Dermott the Wolf crouched beside the cage-wagon. He was as big a man as Corriwen had ever seen. As wide across the shoulders as she could span with both hands, and head and shoulders taller than the rest of the men except the strange thin creature who stood beside him.

The thin man was the dangerous one, Corriwen sensed. Dermott could crush her with his hands, but the one in the hood, face covered in tattoos, cloak fluttering, he looked as if he would pick at your soul like a buzzard on a carcass.

'So this is her then?' Dermott turned to Fainn, twirling his bullwhip in one hand. 'She doesn't look like much to me. She's more a girl than a woman.'

'She's a fighter, my Lord.' The leader of the troops stepped forward. 'It took ten to bring her down. And before that she unhorsed two lancers and then found a way to escape from a secure lock. She's got wierden-shee ways for sure.'

'That's still to be found out,' Dermott said, measuring Corriwen with his eyes. 'What's your name, girl?'

Her throat was still sore and dry. Her voice came out ragged.

'I am Corriwen of the Redthorn of Temair,' she said, knowing he wouldn't have any idea where Temair was.

'Never heard of you, nor your kin. So, you're a scrapper are you?'

'Only when I have to be. I'd rather walk in peace.'

'That's not what the runes say, is it Spellbinder?'

'That's true, my Lord. And the runes never lie. A red-haired fighting woman from a far place. Can there be two?'

He bent towards her. 'This is the one ... the one who dared *touch* me.'

Two guards opened the cage and dragged Corriwen out. Dermott examined her knives, running a thumb along the edge.

'Beat two of my horsemen, and yourself on foot. I'll give you credit for that, girl. But it would take ten of you to best me, maybe even more.'

'Why should I want to fight you?'

'Ah, why indeed?' Fainn hissed in Dermott's ear. 'So it is *written*.'

Dermott glowered. 'Where did you learn to fight, girl?'

'At my father's knee.'

'Aye, and you'll wish you were still sitting on it by the time we're done. We'll have fine sport with you, come the morrow.'

He glanced at Connor, slumped in the corner.

'And who's this wretch?'

'A poacher, my Lord,' a soldier said. 'Taken with the girl.'

'A cripple? Hardly worth the effort. We'll send lame dogs after him and watch him hobble.' He loomed over Connor. 'You poach my deer, boy, and you pay the price.'

Connor said nothing. He looked Dermott straight in the eye. He had nothing to lose.

They had seen the castle from the breast of the hill.

'Wolfen Castle,' Corriwen said. 'An evil place, I think.'

'At least this cart will be stopping. Looking on the bright side, they could have made me walk all the way, but now my teeth are rattling like nuts in a jar. And I'm hungry.'

'Aren't you afraid?'

Connor grinned. 'Sure I'm scared. Who wouldn't be? But I'll give him a fine run for his money. Maybe I'll get a chance to die like a hero and win a place in TirNanOg. You think they have good horses there?'

This time Corriwen had to smile. Trussed up like a duck all those long rattling miles, three days and nights, and Connor still had his optimism. Or bravery. Whatever it was, it gave her some heart.

And there was something else. The glimpse of Jack Flint's face in the crowd came back to her time and again until she was convinced she had seen him as they trundled her out of the village.

It had to be Jack. *Had to be.* And that meant he and Kerry had come through the gate to find her. They had not abandoned her. In her heart, all this time, she had known that neither he nor Kerry ever would.

Score Four-arm flexed his shoulders and threw a battle-axe straight at Jack's head.

Jack almost jumped out of his skin.

But something else happened.

Brand had ringed the wagons and they lit their campfires. After the unearthly mist, even the thin rain from low dark clouds was bearable. Natterjack got busy with a big pot that soon bubbled on the coals while Brand strode around urging the rest of the troupe to get practising.

'Big day tomorrow,' he told them. 'We have to put on a fine show, and they'll expect the best.'

Jack and Kerry stood by a big oak tree while Tig and Tag went through their somersaults and cartwheels, intricate movements that told Jack their minds were completely in tune. Score practised his juggling, this time with long knives and double-bladed battle-axes that twirled in the air, hissing as they went and it was a miracle he didn't slice himself with all that flying sharp metal.

Brand strolled over to him and Score bent down to listen, never pausing in his manoeuvre and then he turned smoothly and without any warning, threw one axe at Jack and another at Kerry.

'Jeez!' Kerry blurted.

And in the blink of an eye, before either of them had time to react, they were twenty feet up in the tree.

Below them, at head height, both axes were dug deep into the trunk, quivering like tuning forks.

'What was that about?'

Before Jack could respond, Score turned and flicked two knives at them, one after the other. Kerry yelped again and then Jack found himself fifteen feet further up the tree. And the amazing thing was that Kerry was even higher, white-faced and gripping a spindly branch with even whiter knuckles.

'What do you think you're playing at?' he demanded in a shaky voice. 'You could have killed us!'

Way below, Score grinned up at them, never missing a beat with the spinning weapons. Brand was rolling about on the grass, convulsed with laughter.

'All right squirrels, you can come down now.'

'Not with that loony chucking hatchets at us,' Kerry yelled back.

'Oh, that was just a wee experiment. Get yourselves down here. You've passed the entrance test to Brand's Vagaband.'

It took a lot longer to descend than it did to climb, if climbing was what had actually happened. They made it to solid ground and Score clapped them both on the shoulder, chuckling all the while.

'I knew it,' Brand told him. 'Didn't I recognise Rune's cobblery?'

He pointed at Jack's new boots.

'None like Rune for the shoemaking,' he said. 'Turned

you both into a pair of mountain goats, and that's just what we need. When Rune makes shoes, he puts all his skill into it. And he's made you both the best, as far as I can see. He told us you'd be at the crossroads.'

'But we've never done any circus stuff,' Kerry said.

'Well, you'll have to learn quick, if you want to save that girlfriend of yours.'

Kerry's face went red. 'She's not my girlfriend.'

'No matter,' Brand said. 'Once we get in the Wolf's den, you'd best be slick as spit. The place will be bristling with armoury. Not to mention that snake of a spellbinder who does the Wolf's bidding.'

Jack looked down at the castle. 'It's not going to be easy.'

'Nothing worthwhile ever is,' Brand agreed. 'But that doesn't mean we can't have fun. Like I said, mystery, magic and a little mayhem is what it's all about.'

It amazed them both how quickly they melded into the routine with Tig, Tag and the others. Rune's special shoes made all the difference.

By evening they were tired and bruised and sore all over. But Brand seemed quite happy with their progress.

SEVENTEEN

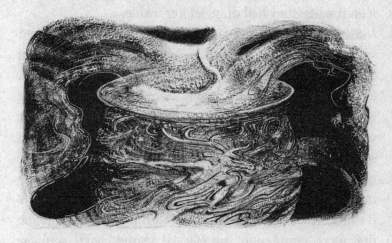

Corriwen was still in a cage, but no longer on the cart. She was high up, very close to the raftered ceiling in a great hall, the cage suspended from beams by a sturdy chain. It swung when she moved. Connor was in another suspended cage, still bruised and sore.

It was hot and the air was thick with smoke from a glowing fireplace. The walls were grey stone, here and there relieved by tapestries of hunting scenes. Wide wooden pillars cut from single trunks supported the arched ceiling.

There were other cages up here. It was clear from the desiccated remains crumpled inside them that some prisoners had not been taken out to be hunted. They had died here and dried to parchment in the heat and smoke.

Below, a long table, wider than a man was tall, stretched almost the length of the hall, with benches on either side. Dermott sat at its head, massive in his wolfskin cloak.

Behind Dermott stood a huge silver cauldron. Corrie had seen it when they had dragged her inside.

She had caught her own reflection in the burnished silver, pale and thin, as if she was hardly there at all. It had somehow drawn her into its carved surface, where a creature, half man and half stag, dominated a festive scene of dancing forest nymphs and strange creatures. The cauldron had seemed very old and mysterious and somehow ominous, though she couldn't say why.

From her vantage point, she could see beyond its rim into its depths where dark colours swirled, fast and oily, as if she was peering into the eye of a storm. It was like looking into the deepest night, so black it seemed solid, and the dark eye tugged on her with such power it gave her a dizzying sense of vertigo.

She pulled her gaze away. The tall, thin man in the fluttering cape sat hunched like a hawk, oblivious to the raucous feasting down the long table. Servants scurried back and forth and every now and again he would touch the cauldron with a long staff carved into intertwining snakes. A heavy vapour oozed up to the rim and the servant would reach in to draw out a ham, or a plucked goose, or a fat salmon to be taken to the hot coals and cooked.

The supply was never-ending. And Fainn seemed to be able to get the cauldron to produce whatever he wanted every time Dermott demanded more.

She had been right about Fainn, Corriwen told herself. Dermott was loud, brash and arrogant, the king of all he surveyed, and from what she had learned, very keen to be king of everything else worth surveying.

But Fainn, he was different. She had felt his poisonous touch the first time those hooded eyes had fixed on her.

Before they had hoisted the cage up to the rafters, Fainn had approached, as quiet as a spider and every bit as alien. The spiral tattoos on his face twisted and danced. Hands like bony claws raised the carved snake-staff towards her and her heart almost stopped dead when a forked tongue flicked out from one wooden snake mouth and tasted the air.

Unblinking snake eyes had fixed on her and she felt as if they sucked the life out of her. A voice whispered in her head, like the hiss of steam from a spout, like the rustle of dead leaves.

Who are you, girl? You are not what you say. Tell me everything.

His eyes bored into her. Her vision began to waver and a giddy sensation rolled in the pit of her belly.

I had you and you escaped. None escape Fainn's reach. But you, you are different. And there are others. I smell them. I taste *them on the air.*

In that instant, Corriwen knew he was looking for her thoughts. She felt the scrape of his mind against hers, the way she had felt the vile touch of the Morrigan in the dark of the Black Barrow.

Almost unbidden, a picture of Jack and Kerry together, racing for the homeward gate, began to form in her mind and with an enormous effort she turned the thought away and instead pictured her brother as she had found him on the slaughterfield.

The memory hit her with a solid blow of anguish.

She saw herself cradle her brother's bloodied head in her arms as she had moaned and rocked back and forth, devastated by her loss. The power of the memory was so great that she felt the connection between her and Fainn snap like string.

His black eyes widened in surprise as he stumbled back. Corriwen staggered against the bars of the cage. Fainn's carved stave dropped to the flagstone floor and for a brief, blurry instant, it coiled and looped on itself before becoming rigid once more.

Fainn picked it up while Corriwen stood, breathless and gasping as if she had run a great distance.

He glared at her.

You defy me, girl. You will regret it as long as you live. And you will regret it as you die.

Then the men hoisted her up towards the vaulted ceiling where the smoke gathered like the clouds over Eirinn.

The guards searched them all very thoroughly before the drawbridge swung down over the crevasse. As soon as the heavy door hit the blocks, the heartstone on Jack's chest gave a slow pulse.

They entered the outer ring of the castle, with Kerry close to Jack, who stayed beside Score Four-arm. The big juggler pretended to be at ease, but Jack saw his eyes flick right and left, taking in the sprocket wheel that raised the drawbridge, then scan the walls and turrets like a well-trained spy.

Brand walked ahead of them, in a green jacket, jaunty red hat and with a swagger in his step.

'Brand's wandering troupe,' he announced to the gatemen. 'And the Lord of the Keep is expecting us prompt. So be about your business and let us get about ours.'

Despite his diminutive stature, his voice carried authority and confidence and in only a minute they were through the second ring and into the main part of the castle where the walls were so high that little light reached the ground and they were surrounded by grey fortifications and thick, heavy stone.

The heartstone pulsed harder.

The guards on the battlements were armed to the teeth with pikes and swords, too many to fight. Jack looked about, wondering where in this maze of stone and turrets they had put Corriwen. When the second door closed behind him, he quailed at the thought of finding her and trying to get her out.

But nothing seemed to affect Brand's confidence.

They were marched round a narrow way until they reached a double door studded with bronze dead-nails. Four fierce men eyed them steadily before they were allowed entry and then Jack and Kerry and the rest of them found themselves in the midst of mayhem.

From up above Corriwen had heard Dermott's voice, demanding silence.

'Time to eat and drink,' he roared. He drew his sword and slammed the hilt down on the table. Plates and goblets jumped in unison.

'Half a moon to the midsummer and I will have all the kings gathered here. They will all bow their heads to me and be grateful for the privilege.'

The men cheered. They raised goblets and horns and clashed them together.

To Dermott, the Wolf of CorNamara!

'And this wolf has been on the hunt,' he boomed. 'There's a hunger in Eirinn that none can feed; none but Dermott of Wolfen Castle. And they know it. The kings don't remember what it is to fight. They grew fat and lazy on the easy times. Peace and harmony for generations and where has it got them? Wasted lands and empty fields, and now they all turn to the Wolf for help.'

He got up and strode to the cauldron and hit it with his hand. It rang like a gong.

'None had the strength or the will to win the Cerunnos Cauldron, so by default they lose their place. What's a king who cannot feed his people? No king at all, I say. So they come to me, the only one who could find and win the cauldron and reap its plenty. They come begging, trading their lands to fill their bellies.'

He threw his shoulders back. 'Let them come, I say. On the midsummer, they will see me crowned high king, and they will sell their lands and their souls. And those of you who marched with me, you will reap ten times over. Lands a-plenty.'

'And *then* they can have peace and harmony,' he said, chuckling. '*My* peace and harmony. Your lands will be ripe for the reaping.

'So today we feast from my cauldron. And tomorrow we hunt.'

He looked up to where the high cages were almost hidden in the smoky haze. 'Tomorrow we *kill*!'

They roared and clashed their tankards and fell upon the feast like beasts.

The smell of food drifted up.

Connor roused himself from the cage.

'I'm drooling like a starving dog,' he muttered. 'I don't mind so much them hunting me down. But do they have to torture me first? I'd sell my granny for a bite of that ham.'

'I thought you were an orphan.'

'But I must have had a granny somewhere,' he said. 'Hasn't everybody?'

Brand played it like a true ringmaster. He stood on an upturned tub and doffed his hat.

'My Lord Dermott, good sirs,' he began. 'It is a fine honour to be in such exalted company. At your request, we bring music and mystery for your delight.'

'Better be good,' Dermott growled.

Thin Doolan had a drum strapped to his thigh and played a roll. Natterjack squatted on his haunches with a big lambeg skin drum that he beat steadily with a long bone.

Score Four-arm opened his bag and juggled his coloured balls, using only two hands, but managing to get ten flying at the same time, then he picked up an old fiddle and bow and with his spare arms he began to play a jig, still keeping those balls flying.

'He said he was a *fuggler*,' Kerry said. 'Now, that's a neat trick.'

Jack cast his eyes around. The table was groaning with more food than he had seen in their journey across Eirinn and he felt a wave of disgust at seeing such plenty when there was so much hunger across the land. His stomach tried to argue with him when he smelt the roasting goose and he forced himself to ignore it.

Dermott was every bit as fierce as he had been told to expect, big and bearded and broad as an ox.

But it was the thin hooded man who sat close to the great cauldron who held his attention.

Fainn sat alone, aloof, eyes taking in everything. Jack felt those eyes light on him and he looked away, though he sensed a pause, and closer scrutiny. The heartstone felt it too, for it started beating again, slow squeezes against his skin and for an anxious moment, Jack believed it was beating loud enough to hear, and he willed it to stop.

Fainn's gaze felt like a physical touch, cold and foul. Jack's belly clenched tight as he felt it probe, lingering long, too long.

Then Fainn's soulless eyes passed on.

His stare reminded Jack of the snake that had lunged at him in the forest.

EIGHTEEN

As shows went, it was probably the best Jack and Kerry had ever seen. The fact that they were part of it made it more exciting.

And the fact that they just couldn't tell where pure sleight-of-hand ended and magic kicked in, helped take their minds off matters at hand and the likely outcome.

Brand produced thin reed pipes which he put to his mouth and warbled a tune in time with Score's fiddling – *fuggling* – for he never dropped a ball the whole time – and Thin Doolan's drumming.

Score threw a red ball into the air, and when Jack followed its progress, he saw the cages high above them. His heart skipped a beat.

Corriwen Redthorn stared down at him, her face pale in the smoke, both hands gripping the bars of the cage. He darted his eyes towards Fainn, then checked himself before he gave himself away and looked back at Score who played and juggled, but let his eyes wander all round, like a soldier working out tactics.

'Don't look,' Jack whispered to Kerry. 'She's here.'

He clasped Kerry's arm tight, making sure he didn't gawp. 'They're watching us.'

He turned away. The red ball reached the apex of its flight and fell slowly towards the flagstones. Just before it hit, Brand let out a piercing note on his pipes and the ball exploded in a fountain of glittering sparks, and Tig and Tag suddenly appeared before them, tumbling out of the smoking sparks, dressed one in red and the other in purple, joined back-to-back as if glued together.

They catapulted out from the sparking fountain in a blur of arms and legs, now up, now down, now on hand, now on foot, rippling around the great hall in rolling cartwheels and somersaults. They spun at the end of the hall and came whirling back, reached the far end of the table and then they were on its surface, tumbling past the astonished revellers, moving like a single nimble creature, never disturbing a plate or a goblet as they reached the centre and then spun around each other in faster and faster circles, sometimes joined, sometimes apart.

Jack thought that apart from the sight of Corrie Redthorn flying through the spume of the great waterfall on Temair, it was the most elegant thing he had ever seen.

Tig and Tag came rolling back down the table. Now they held each other's shoulders and formed one long single creature who arced to land feet first, feet first again until they flew from the end of the table, spinning together in the air.

Score threw another ball towards where they were about to land. Brand aimed his pipes and produced another shriek of sound.

Purple sparks cascaded and in the blink of an eye, Tig and Tag vanished in a puff of pink smoke.

Even the big fierce men around the table were impressed. Dermott slammed his goblet on the table in applause. But Fainn hunched even lower, mouth turned down.

Natterjack approached the table, squat and ungainly. He lifted an apple from a bowl, held it up for all to see, turned his hand and the apple vanished. He did the same with a leg of mutton, inches away from the reveller who was just about to carve a slice from it, faster than most eyes could follow. But Jack, watching from behind Score Four-arm saw him perform a truly amazing feat. While distracting attention with his free hand, his wide mouth opened in an impossible gape and a long tongue flicked out, grabbed the mutton and whipped it into the big mouth. Natterjack's bulging eyes blinked hard, seemed to disappear deep into their sockets, and the meat vanished in a blur.

Score put his fiddle down and drew out a dozen sharp knives. Thin Doolan picked up a bowl of apples and threw them all into the air at once. Score's arms snaked out and the knives were all in the air, spinning among the falling apples and the astonished audience saw each piece of fruit sliced in half before it hit the ground.

Then Thin Doolan picked up a long knife one of the trencherman had used to carve his meat, and before anyone could stop him, he threw it straight for Score's head.

The juggler didn't miss a beat. The knife came whirling in at him and he plucked it from the air to join the others in the deadly dance around his head.

Brand clambered on his tub.

'My Lords,' he crowed. 'Many have tried and many have failed to deter Master Score from his performance. However, I am sure that one of you fine warriors is more skilful. Master Score welcomes you to do your best ... or your worst.'

Dermott laughed and slapped his hands on the table.

'Now there's a challenge, if I ever heard one.' He pointed at a brawny man near the end. 'You, Coglan. I've seen you beat the best. Let's show them!'

The man turned in his seat, drew out his blade and without seeming to move, shot it at the juggler.

Jack saw Score's eyes acknowledge the incoming blade. He changed his stance just a fraction and caught the knife by the handle, inches from his eye, and it joined the others in the air.

'Well caught, strangeling,' Coglan growled, nudging the man next to him in encouragement. He stood, hefted a short sword, swung his whole body into the throw.

Score turned aside, snatched the sword, spun on his heel and without pause threw it at the nearest wooden pillar where it hit point-first and dug itself deep into the timber.

Somebody roared approval and then the whole table of revellers were on their feet, each one determined to show his mettle. The blades came thick and fast and deadly, but each one Score caught effortlessly and with astonishing speed and accuracy, threw it to thud into the pillar.

In mere seconds, the timber was spiked with quivering blades thrumming like bass strings.

And in the meantime, Jack and Kerry, who were as impressed as anyone in the great hall, watched Thin Doolan and Natterjack weave their way around the guests while their attention was diverted. Thin Doolan seemed to suck in his breath and when he turned side on, he was barely visible, as if he'd been ironed flat. He divested the roisterers of purses, jewels and anything else and passed them to Natterjack who made them disappear in his own special way.

Tig and Tag came cartwheeling past Score and towards the pillar. For the first time they separated with an audible snap, tumbling around the post and then they spun upwards, using the spiked knives and swords as a ladder, weaving an intricate dance as they spiralled higher and higher together in perfect synchrony.

Brand nodded to Jack and Kerry. They had practised all day, with the help of Rune's boots, but still they were both nervous. There was too much at stake. Score winked encouragement.

'Come on, Jack,' Kerry said. 'No business like showbusiness.'

He skipped forward, crouched, then leapt up, higher than Score himself. The juggler caught him with two hands, spun him with the other two and Kerry landed lightly on the left pair of shoulders. Jack followed, letting the boots do the business, to land on the opposite side.

Jack risked a glance overhead. Corriwen's pale face was

pressed against the bars of the cage, barely seen in the smoke up there, watching them in amazement.

'Now for real magic!' Brand leapt from his tub, dug into the bottomless bag and produced a long coil of rope. He tossed it into the air and when it was still rising, he produced his pipes again and began to play a fast tune.

The rope uncoiled as it rose, wavering in the air, snaking up and up until its top end disappeared into the pall of smoke up at the rafters.

Then it stopped. And it stayed. Brand's fingers danced on the pipes and the rope swayed like a snake, but remained upright.

'Sorcery!' a voice shouted from the table.

Brand kept playing and the rope kept swaying, its knotted end lost in the smoke.

'Now,' Score said. He held his arms out on either side. Jack and Kerry stepped out, and Score took their weight on his hands. His muscles bunched, and then they were flying. Jack felt his stomach flip as if he had stepped into a fast elevator. Up and up he sailed, and the faces below seemed to shrink.

He caught the rope with both hands, feeling it twang as Kerry grabbed just below him, then began to climb, hand over hand, putting all his strength into it. He reached the top knot, maybe forty feet high, where the light was dim.

'Wait for it,' he told Kerry.

Down below, Score collected his multi-coloured juggling balls, tossed them around his head, then launched them up to where Jack and Kerry clung to the rope. Instantly Brand changed the tune on the pipes. The balls popped, loud as fireworks, scattering sparks all around and sending out a billow of blue smoke, completely concealing Jack and Kerry.

'Go for it!' Jack swung on the rope, letting his momentum carry him back first, then forward. When he got to within a yard of the top of the great pillar, he gritted his teeth and let go, trusting to the day's practice. It was a long, long way to fall. His fingers found the cross-beam and he clambered onto it. In a second, Kerry was behind him. Across the hall, they saw Tig and Tag reach the same height on the opposite pillar, clambering like squirrels up the ladder of blades. Both acrobats gave them a cheery wave and disappeared into the shadows.

Below them, Brand played three shrill notes on the pipes. Jack saw the knotted end of the rope vanish as the line simply fell in a heap to the floor far below.

The men at the table applauded. Even Dermott was impressed.

'Clever. Clever indeed.' He turned to Fainn who glowered thoughtfully beside the great cauldron.

'Almost as good as your Pictish magic, would you say?'

'Tricks and sleight of hand,' Fainn growled. 'Fairground games for farmers.'

He rose to his feet and strode to the centre of the hall. He picked up the limp rope, testing it in his hand, then looked askance at Brand, who smiled innocently at him.

'Smoke and mirrors,' he hissed. 'Nothing more.'

'As you say, my Lord,' Brand replied, politely. 'We are just a travelling band of entertainers and jugglers. Our japes are no magic.'

Fainn seemed to shrink back into the shade of his hood. He raised his carved staff.

'But there is something here. I smell it.'

'Enjoy the show, Spellbinder,' Dermott bawled. 'It's a day for feasting.'

Fainn pretended not to hear. He sniffed at the air, eyes scanning left and right. Thin Doolan and Natterjack edged out from the crowd.

'I smell treachery,' Fainn hissed. 'It reeks like carrion.'

He brought his staff down, pointed the carved snake-heads into Brand's face. 'Mischief. Mischief and ill-will.'

He gestured with one thin hand and the staff came to sudden life. Brand took a step back as two snakes uncoiled from each other, tongues flickering, eyes gleaming with toxic ferocity.

From the crowded long-table, a collective gasp shuddered round the hall.

High above, hidden by the coloured smoke, they could see Corriwen clearly. Jack put a finger to his lips, then he edged across the beam with Kerry close behind.

'Have you got it?'

'Sure I have.'

'Then blow it up.'

Jack continued, step by step, until he was within two yards of the suspended cage. Behind him he could hear Kerry huffing and puffing. He closed his eyes, took a slow breath as he counted to three, and then made the leap across space and caught the bars.

'Hey Corriwen,' he managed to say, more out of relief than anything else. 'Fancy meeting you here!'

'I waited for you,' she snapped back. 'And you never came.'

For a second Jack was completely taken aback. Then her face broke into the widest, happiest smile he had ever seen and she grabbed him through the bars and held him so tightly his eyes watered. It wasn't just the embrace that brought the tears.

'But I always knew you would, Jack Flint.'

'Shhhh! We have to get you out of here.' Still clinging to the bars with one hand, he drew out a metal hook Brand had given him, slipped it into the latch and opened the gate.

'Now we have to swing this a bit. Get us closer to the beam.'

Kerry gestured urgently at them. 'Come on!' In one hand he held a life-sized dummy, complete with a mop of red hair, that Natterjack had sewn together from sheep bladders. Kerry's face was still red from the effort of inflating it. He threw it across and Jack stashed it in the cage. From down below, no one would tell the difference.

Together he and Corriwen used their weight to swing the cage until they were close enough for her to leap out. Kerry caught her with both hands and held her tight.

'Missed you like crazy, so we did,' he said. 'We've been hunting all over.'

Jack landed beside them. 'Break it up, you two. We have to get moving.'

'What about Connor?'

'Who's Connor?'

Corriwen pointed at the next cage. A ragged boy was up at the bars watching everything. They could see his twisted leg.

'He's a friend of mine. We travelled together.'

'He'll slow us down,' Kerry said. 'We came for *you*.'

'I said, he's a friend.'

Kerry looked the boy up and down. 'Doesn't look like much to me.'

'We fought together,' Corriwen retorted. 'He tried to save me.'

Jack looked at Kerry. This hadn't been part of the plan, and speed was of the essence.

'We don't need extra baggage,' Kerry insisted.

'Don't be an ass,' Jack hissed. 'Let him come.'

'Dermott will hunt him and kill him,' Corriwen said very quietly. 'He goes or I stay. It is my honour. He is a friend.'

'Okay,' Kerry said. 'I take it all back. Let's get him out.'

Corriwen smiled and kissed him hard on the cheek. Kerry's ears went bright red.

Jack turned on the beam, leapt the gap and landed on the side of the cage. He pressed against the bars.

'You'll be Connor.'

'I'll be the late Connor by tomorrow.'

'So let's make today count.' He looked at the twisted leg. 'Can you jump?'

'Watch me,' Connor said. 'To get out of this, I'll fly like a bird.'

'First, we need another decoy.' Jack said. He tugged at

the boy's tattered cape. 'You don't need this.'

'Whatever you say,' he replied. 'It's only a few holes joined together.'

He unclipped a circular brooch-pin and let the cape fall in a heap. From down there it might just be convincing enough to give them time.

Together they swung the cage close enough. Jack held him by the arm and made the leap effortlessly. Connor's one good foot reached the beam, but his crippled leg caught the edge and he began to fall backwards, arms pinwheeling for balance.

Kerry leapt forward and snatched him by the front of his tattered tunic and held him firm. He drew him back upright until they stood together on the high beam.

'Beholden to you,' the boy said. He glanced down. 'I'd have been Connor stew for sure.'

'More like hamburger,' Kerry said. 'Raw.'

'Come on,' Jack said. 'Let's get out of here before the smoke clears.'

It took them twenty seconds, hand in hand, across the narrow beam, to reach the part where it dug into the wall. There was enough space to crawl through under the eaves and onto the slate roof.

'Fresh air,' Connor took a big breath. 'I feel like a smoked ham.'

'You smell like one too,' Kerry said.

They scrambled down the roof and made their way to a small tower with a narrow window. Inside, Jack closed his eyes, trying to remember the layout Brand had described to him, then led them together up a narrow winding staircase.

Two doors faced them, left and right.

'Which one?' Kerry whispered. Jack still clung to Corriwen's hand, as if he was scared to let her go again. Inside he was so relieved at finding her, yet he was also apprehensive in case they were caught before they made it out of this place.

Think! He told himself. But in the excitement of the past few minutes, he couldn't.

'Oh, just try one of them,' Kerry decided. He reached beyond Jack, snatched the handle and opened the door.

A table stretched in front of them, old and knotted, and intricately carved with mountains and roads and rivers in stark relief. Beyond it, a pit of fire belched oily smoke that completely obscured the ceiling the way Brand's diversion had hidden them in the great hall.

'That's Eirinn,' Connor said. 'It's the whole land, carved into wood.'

'I don't like this place,' Kerry said. He sniffed the air. 'It's like that place we were in. The Black Barrow. It smells really bad.'

The heartstone hammered against Jack's skin.

Jack pulled Corriwen's hand and they turned back. Kerry closed the door, glad to be out of there. The other door led upwards until they found themselves in a dark passageway. Jack closed his eyes, found his sense of direction, and urged them on.

They had just reached the end of the passageway when the ragged boy held up a hand.

'Someone's coming!'

Jack had heard nothing. But Connor's face was pale in

the gloom, and Jack could tell by his tone that they were in trouble. He quickly turned back and they followed him at a run, until they came to an opening they had passed, ducked inside, and found themselves in complete darkness.

They held their breath. The heartstone thudded hard and strong. Jack clamped a hand over it and felt it pulse in his grasp. Now he heard someone approaching.

Someone paused at the opening. They heard a snuffle, like a hound on the scent before then the footsteps resumed and slowly faded. Jack stepped out into the passage, drawing Corriwen after him.

Something lunged at him. He leapt so fast that Corriwen was dragged with him and they landed in a sprawl.

'Snake!'

Connor darted forward, snatched it by the tail and spun it around his neck, then suddenly slashed his hand down. There was a faint crack and the snake's head snapped clean off. It slammed against the wall in a splatter of venom.

'Got to be fast for snakes,' he muttered. Kerry was behind him, still in the dark. Something else slithered against his foot and he stumbled, barging against Connor. He felt a stab of faint pain in his ankle, and then his whole leg went numb. A sinuous shape slithered off into the shadows. Connor caught Kerry under the armpit as he lurched.

Together they hobbled after Jack and Corriwen, Connor on his good leg helping Kerry along.

'Did it get you?'

'Don't know. I might have just pulled a muscle,' Kerry said through clenched teeth.

Along the passage a door slammed and a man's voice roared a curse.

'Big trouble,' Connor gasped. 'Time to hurry.'

Jack and Corriwen reached the far end of the passage and now he had his bearings. It opened onto a balcony that led round a battlemented wall, and there was no guard here. High above them the wolf-head flag whipped in the wind. Ahead was the outer wall. All they had to do was cat-walk across a narrow buttress that joined the inner and outer walls, keeping close to the stone, and staying low.

A fast movement close on their left made Jack's heart leap and he shrank back until he saw Tig and Tag somersault over the battlements. Brand's bottomless bag was strapped to Tag's back. They landed silently beside the four fugitives.

'Ready?'

'I think so,' Jack said. He turned to Kerry. His face was ashen and screwed in a grimace of pain.

'Are you okay?'

'Hurts,' Kerry groaned. 'Burning . . .' His knee began to buckle. Sweat trickled down his forehead. Connor caught him before he fell.

'He's been bitten,' he said. 'I'm sure of it.'

'Help him to the wall,' Jack said, thinking quickly. 'I'll be back soon. If we're running, get him out fast.'

He beckoned to Corrie. 'I need your help. Kerry can't do this.'

Despite her puzzled look, she nodded and they followed the twins back through the window and up the spiral stairs to the top of the tower. The metal tool that Brand had made was just as efficient here and Jack opened the door in a minute.

The harp stood on a pedestal. Even though the shutters were bolted, its gold surface gleamed with a light of its own. It was beautiful, perfectly wrought in every way except one.

All its strings had been slashed.

Jack took its weight and for an instant the heartstone let out a clear, single note. Even with its strings cut, he could feel the latent power of the golden harp in his hands.

'Be swift, Jackflint,' Tig urged. Tag opened Brand's bag wide and he lowered it inside. She snapped it shut and handed it to him. It weighed next to nothing, as if it was as empty as before. They moved to the doorway and stopped. Below them, another cry echoed up. Someone was coming.

'The window!' Corriwen eased the bolt back and daylight flooded in.

'It's a long way down,' she began to say, but Tig was already over the sill, Tag close behind.

'Climb on us,' Tag said as she dropped. Corriwen clambered out and saw the twins had formed a human ladder. Jack lowered himself until he swung below them and Corriwen climbed down all three until her feet reached a ledge. Above them, a head loomed through the vent and a man cursed. Corriwen edged on the ledge to the next vent, pushed it open and climbed inside.

A bulky figure came clattering down the stairs. Instinctively Corriwen crouched as the man rushed round the corner. Not expecting to find anything in his way, he tripped over her, tumbled ten feet and hit the wall with a crunch and lay still.

They raced past him and onto the roof, while angry cries echoed from the walls. Connor was huddled out of sight, holding Kerry tight.

Jack leaned over the battlements. The chasm below was shadowed and sheer as it dropped to jagged rocks.

Tig produced a rope, tied one end to a pennant-post and hurled the other over the wall. Thin Doolan, on the far side of the chasm, caught the end and fixed it to a wagon-wheel.

Tig bowed. Tag did the same. Then in a sinuous display of acrobatics, they went swinging down the rope.

'It's a long way down,' Connor said. 'And I'm not half so nimble.'

Jack used the leather cuff Brand had given him, tied it firmly around Kerry's limp wrists and they sent him sliding down the rope. Corriwen followed, then Connor. Jack closed his eyes, banishing the image of fearsome rocks below as he zoomed earthwards over the chasm to land with a thump. Then they were running for the wagons.

On the battlements, men were shouting orders. Brand skipped across the drawbridge, hat in hand, but there was no sign of Score Four-arm. As soon as Brand's feet were on solid ground, the drawbridge creaked and the ropes strained as it lifted up and began to swing closed.

'Open the gate!' Dermott's voice ripped the air. 'Open the gate, damn your eyes.'

Then Score came scrambling over the battlement and clambered down the wall, head first, all arms and legs.

Close to the moat, Jack saw Natterjack draw deep breaths, and as he did, his squat body expanded so fast that in seconds he resembled a warty beach ball.

Score launched himself from half-way down the wall, right across the chasm, and hit Natterjack so hard the squat fellow bounced. All the air came out in a rush and he shrank back to his previous size.

Score helped him to his feet, as a volley of arrows came arcing over the top wall.

'Obliged for a soft landing, friend,' Score said. He heaved Natterjack along behind him, leapt on to the buckboard, and they were off and out of range in moments.

'I jammed the gate,' he told Jack. 'It'll hold them for a while, but not for long. Just now they'll be trying to pull their swords from the pillar, and that won't be an easy task, for I dug them deep. But they'll be after us soon enough.'

'These ponies don't have the speed,' Corriwen said.

'Aye, maybe. But we liberated a couple of Dermott's mounts.'

He jerked his thumb behind him and they all turned to see two huge black horses hitched to the back of the wagon.

'Just in case we need a bit of speed,' Score said. 'You can't get better than Dermott's stable.'

Behind them Wolfen Castle was in uproar.

Ahead of them lay the open road.

Corriwen put her arms around Kerry and helped him to his feet.

'Together again at last,' she said. 'I've waited so long for this.'

NINETEEN

'Get that damned-forever drawbridge *down*!'

Dermott's rage could be heard echoing two miles up the winding road from Wolfen Castle.

'The ropes have all been cut, my Lord,' a man called out. 'And the wheel's been broken.'

'Saddle the horses,' Dermott ordered. 'Muster every man.'

Another man came running round from the stables and stopped ten feet from Dermott. He didn't want to get within striking distance, not while bringing more bad news.

'It's the horses, lord,' he said, breathless. 'There's two of them stolen.'

'We'll get them back, don't worry. Those rievers will pay me with interest. I'll tear them to pieces. I'll gouge their eyes. I'll *crush* their bones.'

The man backed away.

'It's the other horses,' he said. 'They're all lying down in the stalls. Asleep. They must have been given a potion.'

'A potion? My horses? They poisoned *my* horses?'

Dermott let out a great snarling bellow. His sword was suddenly in his hand, a huge double-edged blade. He swung it about, needing to hurt somebody, cut something.

Dermott was blind with fury. The sword just missed the man and clove a wooden mounting block in two. The fellow turned to run, but Dermott's whip lashed him round the legs and he sprawled flat. Dermott gave an incoherent roar and sliced the unfortunate messenger's head from his neck in one ferocious blow.

Fainn had discovered the theft. And he had found the headless snake in the passageway.

His rage was as searing as the heat from the smoking pit.

'Thrice,' he cursed. 'Three times defied!'

He stood in his dungeon room, quivering with such intensity he looked as if he had a fever. The tattoos writhed on his skin.

He picked up the headless snake and laid it on the long table where he had cast his dark spells over Eirinn. The second snake coiled up his arm, its venom sharp on the air.

'Gone,' Fainn hissed. 'Stolen! Thieves and vagabonds.

Oh, such a curse I will weave on them. They will wish they had never drawn breath.'

He picked up the torn head and pressed it hard against the end of the cold coils, muttering in his strange language until the snake twitched. The bloody ends seemed to knit together as he spoke. Glassy eyes stared brightly and its tongue tasted the air. Its twin spiralled around it, head to head, and then both went suddenly rigid. Fainn had his staff back.

He held it out over the map of Eirinn.

'Thunder and hail, ice and rain,' he chanted. 'Strip every blade and leaf. Storm and gale, curse and bane, find for me the thief!'

His hands spread across the carved map. Far beyond the castle walls, the clouds suddenly darkened and lightning flickered.

Fainn swept from the room, a dark bearer of darker news.

He had to tell Dermott that the red-haired fighting woman was gone.

Then he had to tell him about the harp.

They were five miles from Wolfen Castle, on the edge of the forest that crowded the valley. Far behind them they could make out the brooding shape of the great keep, but still there was no sign of pursuit.

Brand drew up the wagons.

'A fine show,' he said blithely. 'Maybe they will invite us back for the coronation.'

Score chuckled. 'If we ever go back in there, we'll not come out again.'

'Perhaps. Dermott and his spellbinder won't sleep tonight, for all their drinking.'

Jack lowered Kerry to the ground. He was breathing fast and shallow and sweat dripped into his eyes.

'He's been bitten,' Jack told Brand.

The little man pushed his way in and rolled up Kerry's leggings. Two blotchy puncture marks stood out clearly.

'Oh dear,' he said. 'This needs fixing.'

He rummaged around in his wagon and came back with strips of cloth and some foul-smelling ointment which he slathered on Kerry's bites.

'He'll be better by morning,' Brand assured them. 'Snake bane works fast.'

Jack looked ahead of them to where the road disappeared into the trees.

'Shouldn't we get a move on?'

Brand shrugged. 'No hurry Jack. And the time's not right.'

'Once they get that bridge down, they'll be after us like an avalanche.'

'Well, whatever an avalanche is, that won't be happening tonight, to be sure. Didn't Thin Doolan feed the horses a bag of his special oats? They won't wake until dawn.'

'We were lucky to make it out of there.'

'Ah, now isn't the fun in the risk? And anyhow, you saved

the young lady and this poor young fellow from a death worse than fate.'

Corriwen's face was smudged and she seemed thinner than Jack remembered, but her smile was the same. It lit up the day.

'I knew they would come for me,' she said. 'I just didn't expect them to put on such a show.'

'I still think we should put some distance between us and Dermott,' Jack said. 'He's going to be awfully mad.'

'Mad before and mad now. Makes no difference. Anyhow, you remember the way we came, on the *by-way*. That's the way we go back, but not at night. The low road hides many secrets in the dark, and not any that I'd like to meet.'

Brand clapped Jack on the shoulder. 'Settle down and take some rest. Young Kerry needs it more. None of them will come on foot. I'd say in all it was a job well done.'

He climbed inside the wagon and came back again with his mysterious bag.

'Thin Doolan and Natterjack found some of your property amongst the baubles they lifted.' He reached in and drew out Corriwen's knife-belt where her two blades sat side by side in their matching sheaths, then hefted the sword that Connor had picked up.

'You'll be needing these, take my word for it. It's a wild road ahead.'

Corriwen looked at Jack but he shrugged. They both knew dangers awaited. She drew Jack close to her again, still hardly able to comprehend that she was free and that they had managed to get her out of the cage and out of the castle.

Thunder woke Jack well before dawn, woke him with such a start he was sitting up before he even knew it. The crash was so loud it crackled in his ears and the lightning sent purple after-images dancing behind his eyelids.

'Not a good sign,' Corriwen said. 'It reminds me of Mandrake's work.'

'That Fainn, I think he's every bit as bad as Mandrake.' Jack shivered, remembering the cold, poisonous stare. 'But much more powerful, I think. I felt it when he looked at me.'

They had spent the early night round the fire, swapping tales of the adventures they'd had since they'd stumbled through the stone gate and into this world. Brand's potion seemed to have had an effect, because Kerry fell into a deep sleep and Connor soon dozed off, leaving Jack and Corriwen together.

'I thought I'd lost you,' he told her. 'You could have been anywhere. Then Kerry found your tracks, where you'd fallen and we came after you.'

'It all seems like a bad dream,' she whispered.

'Hopefully the bad part's over,' he said. 'Though I'm not so sure.'

'I don't understand.'

'I've been thinking about all this. When we were in

Temair, all I wanted to do was get home. Then we met you and we got into all sorts of . . . trouble.

'But everything that happened led us on to the next, like it was *meant* to happen. The Major always told me there were no coincidences, and I think he was right. You were thrown through the gate and we followed. Then we met Rune, and that was no coincidence. Then Brand and his circus. And now we've stolen the Harp and we're part of it.'

'You *were* part of it,' Corriwen said. 'Whatever the Harp is for, it's not your fight. We should find our way home now.'

'I'm not so sure. In Temair we had to finish the quest before we got home. The Book told me we are part of a quest here. And I don't think we can get home until we see it through.'

'What quest?'

'It's to do with the Harp. I don't know why. But I've a feeling we're going to find out.'

She clasped his hand. 'I want to go home. To help rebuild Temair. That's my destiny.' She looked into his eyes. 'But whatever you have to do here, I'll be with you.'

'I know that,' he said. 'I really do.'

Before he knew it he was asleep and he didn't wake up until a great peal of thunder shook the earth.

'Time to move,' he said. The thunderhead was moving up the valley from Wolfen Castle, spitting lightning as it came. Nearby, a stand of trees bent under its power and over the roaring of the wind, they could hear trunks split and crack.

'That doesn't look natural to me.'

'Fainn sends a storm,' Corriwen said, gathering her meagre pack together. Jack slung his own bag over his shoulder and grabbed his amberhorn bow. The storm was coming fast.

Score and Brand were already busy with the troupe. Ahead of them the dawn mist was like a wall, thick and white. It swallowed the narrow road in the space of a couple of paces.

Downslope, where the road meandered towards the dark castle, the big drawbridge finally cranked down and as soon as it hit the blocks, a whole cavalcade charged out in an explosion of horses and harsh cries.

Jack gauged the distance. They could be here in fifteen minutes, not much more.

'Somebody's woken angry,' Brand said. Connor snapped awake in mid-snore and looked around, still dozy from sleep.

'Rise and sparkle,' Brand ordered, nudging him with a foot. 'The by-way won't wait for sleepyheads.'

Already the first of the wagons was rolling towards the mist.

'And where's young Kerry?' Brand wanted to know.

Jack turned. Kerry's sword was still dug into a dead log, close to where he'd slept. But of Kerry himself, there was no sign.

'Where's he gone?'

'You'd better find him quick, young friends. Once we're in the mist, there's no turning back, and the time to move is now.'

'He can't have gone far,' Corriwen said.

'He'd better not have,' Jack said, impatient to be as far away from Dermott's anger as they could get. He cupped his hands to his mouth and called Kerry's name. The wind snatched his words away.

'He was cold last night,' Connor said. 'Before he slept he said he couldn't get warm.'

'Let's spread out and find him.'

Brand stopped them with a gesture and pointed towards the castle where the horde was spilling out. 'We don't have time now. The misty way won't stay open, and we must be gone.'

He took his bag from the wagon and hooked it on the pommel of the nearest horse. Digging in a pocket, he brought out a small, intricately carved flute.

'They'll be here before we know it,' he said. 'And the Harp needs to be protected. You carry it for now.'

'What about you?' Jack asked.

'They'll follow us for sure. Into the misty way. I'll make certain of that.'

He handed Jack the flute. 'You guard the Harp and we'll find you. Just blow the flute when you need help the most.'

With that, he hopped on the wagon and was away without looking back.

Down the road, the horsemen were galloping full tilt.

Jack urged the others into the trees and in seconds they were hidden from the road. He called out again. On his left, Connor was beating down thick ferns. He heard Corriwen call for Kerry, but there was no response.

He pushed on, agitated now and getting more concerned. Kerry had gripped his sword like a talisman since he found it on the slaughterfield on the day they'd fallen into Temair. Jack couldn't think of anything that would make him leave it.

He made his way down a slope towards a deep tarn when he heard Corriwen.

'Jack! I found him. Over here.'

Her urgent tone told Jack something was badly wrong. He and Connor barged through the ferns until they reached her. Jack stopped dead.

Kerry was curled up on the ground, his eyes wide open and staring blindly. His whole body shivered as if he was freezing.

'He's sick,' Corriwen said.

Jack touched Kerry's brow, but his skin was cold and dry, not even clammy. Kerry let out a long hiss of breath and seemed to rouse, very slowly. He moved, as if he was walking in deep water, every action slowed down.

'Come on man,' Jack urged him. 'We have to hurry.'

Kerry looked at him blankly, as if it took a while for Jack's words to register, and rather than wait for a response, Jack put an arm round his shoulders, feeling the tremor run through his whole body, and led him back to the two horses Natterjack had stolen.

The last of Brand's wagons was trundling towards the wall of mist and in seconds it was enfolded in white skeins.

The cavalcade raced by in furious pursuit, looking neither right nor left.

Jack and Corriwen crouched together as the horsemen galloped up the road. As they watched, the mist seemed to recede, quite slowly, but gaining speed. One of the men

155

urged the riders and charged ahead towards where Brand's wagon had disappeared.

In a matter of seconds they reached the white bank of fog and plunged straight ahead, and immediately the clatter of their hooves began to fade.

The mist pulled back further, showing the road winding through the trees. Of the horsemen and Brand's troupe, there was no sign at all.

They waited for a while, just in case, then Jack and Corriwen helped Kerry onto a horse and Jack climbed up behind him. They were just about to move on when there was a clamour from inside the valley where the road disappeared. Three horsemen came bolting out of where the mist had been. The horses were steaming with sweat, eyes rolling. Foam and blood flecked their flanks.

And as the men drew closer and passed by, they could see their terrified expressions. One man held tight to the reins. His eye sockets were red holes. He screamed madly as he passed, a sound that sent shivers up Jack's spine.

'They must have gone off the road,' he said. 'I pity the rest of them.'

TWENTY

In Wolfen Castle, Fainn sat silently beside the pit in the floor where deep fires glowed. His eyes were closed, but he could see them, four of them on two stolen horses.

The vision was blurred, as if seen through a dark veil, but he laughed gleefully. It was the kind of laugh that would send shivers down a man's back, had they heard it, though there was no one to hear, not here in Fainn's low domain.

Now he could see them, they would never escape.

He crouched alone, feeling the baleful heat from the underground pit.

There was something else about these fugitives that he couldn't put his finger on, something very important and very powerful. He had felt it, sensed it.

He didn't know what it was. But that would change.

He would find out as sure as day follows night.

They stopped, exhausted. The horses stood, heads down, panting for breath.

They were in a different forest and for now there were no sounds of pursuit.

Brand had bought them time, but more men had picked up their trail and harried them for miles until Corriwen spotted a trackway that led off the road and had wheeled her mount, almost pitching Connor off. He'd jumped down, sword in hand and in two swipes, felled two bushy saplings and as soon as Jack's horse passed, he shoved the cut ends deep into the ground, effectively hiding the path from the road.

'Once a poacher ...' He grinned brightly as he climbed back on. Using deep cover, they travelled on until Corriwen stopped at a small dell and they waited in total silence, holding their breath as the patrol hurried past.

'They'll soon work it out,' Jack said.

'But it'll take them more time to work out *where* we turned off,' Connor said. 'They might be big hard men, but I know woods. They won't catch me again, I can tell you.'

When the sound of horses had disappeared completely, they followed the track deeper into the forest. Kerry still hadn't said a word. Finally Corriwen led them off the trail and they kept going through the trees for hours before risking a stop by a stream. Corriwen dug a hole in the bank and gathered enough wood for a fire, using the overhang to hide the smoke.

Jack led Kerry close to the heat. He walked as if he was half asleep, and allowed himself to be sat down on a log.

'He's cold,' Jack said.

Corriwen put both arms round Kerry, offering him her own body heat, feeling the faint tremor of his shivers, while Jack fretted. After ten minutes or so, Kerry blinked and seemed to come awake. He looked around, bewildered.

'Where are we?' His voice was faint, barely a breath.

Jack was beside him in an instant. He touched Kerry's cheek, where the fire had warmed it. The cold had dissipated a little.

'We had to run,' he said. 'You were sick.'

'I'm starving,' Kerry said. He yawned. 'Anything to eat?'

Jack almost laughed, and then he almost drew back a fist to knock Kerry's head from his shoulders. They'd have been safe and gone if he hadn't disappeared. His anger subsided as quickly as it flared. It wasn't Kerry's fault.

'We have to take a look at you,' he said. 'You were bitten and Brand fixed you up. I think it's working.'

Kerry still seemed sluggish. Jack rolled up his leggings, and saw that the two small holes on Kerry's pale skin were now edged in an angry purple.

'That don't look too good,' Connor said, crowding in close. All around the puncture wounds, Kerry's skin was turning blotched black, and the bites themselves were weeping. Jack touched the spot. Kerry didn't react. The whole area seemed nerveless.

'Maybe it's not working. What cures snake-bite?'

Corriwen didn't know. Neither did Connor. Jack had read something about serums, back home in the real world, but he also knew you had to be sure which kind of snake had done the biting, and he knew there would be no serum here.

'I could tie it off,' he said, 'but then he'll get gangrene or something.'

Corriwen drew a knife. 'I could heat the blade and burn it.'

Jack stayed her hand. 'Only if we have to. I don't want him to lose a leg. First we'll try a poultice. See if we can draw the poison.'

He pasted some of Rune's cure-all mixture and bound the wound with a wad of burdock leaves held with a scrap of leather. They eased Kerry to a nearby oak and sat him down to rest, hoping the poultice would have some effect.

Far away in Wolfen Castle, Fainn had not moved from his seat beside the fire-pit. He stared down into the red waiting for a picture to form.

He saw them faintly, by the light of a fire. They were beside a river, three of them around the embers. Two horses were hobbled some way off.

Dermott had scoured the road up and down for twenty miles, and it was clear they had cut off the track and into the forest.

Silently Fainn rose from the edge of the pit and crossed to the great table and the map of Eirinn.

He could still see them, again as if through a veil, but that was enough.

He bent over the map, following the road where it meandered into the valley and through the dark forest that stretched to the edge of Dermott's landhold to the mountains in the north.

He traced the road, moved off to the left, to the north until he found the river.

A twisted smile spread on his face.

He stalked off to find a fast messenger.

Jack unhitched Brand's bag and brought it to where they rested. He reached inside and drew out the golden harp.

Connor's eyes opened so wide they could have popped out.

In the firelight he could see the pure rich gold gleam on its intricately carved arch. It was maybe a yard high and wrought with such wonderful craftsmanship that it glowed as if lit from within.

'It's so beautiful,' Corriwen said.

'But it's broken,' Jack said. 'All the strings have been cut.'

The strings, woven from threads of pure gold, flopped in tangles.

'Tell me I'm seeing things,' Connor said. 'If that's what I think it is, then we're done for.'

Jack held the Harp close to his chest. Under his tunic,

the heartstone did not beat, but he felt it vibrate, like a tight plucked string.

'Dermott's going to hunt us to the ends of Eirinn. He'll never stop.'

'I know,' Jack said.

Corriwen touched the harp. 'What is it?'

'That's the Harp of Tara,' Connor said. 'People say Fainn used dark magic to help Dermott find the golden harp. And the Cerunnos Cauldron. I never really believed it until I was up in that cage and saw the spellbinder sit beside the cauldron. It's got the Horned God carved on it and they say you can get anything you want from it. It *never* runs empty. That's how Dermott was able to keep famine at bay. He had all he needed while the rest of Eirinn went hungry.

'My Da, that's my foster Da, he was a woodcutter. He was old when he and Mam found me, half drowned and just a baby. My real Mam, she was dying already, but she had borne me up to save me, so they thought. They were old, but they gave me a home and raised me as theirs and I did my very best for them till the end.'

They listened quietly. Connor closed his eyes for a moment then continued.

'Da loved the old tales. Just a woodcutter, but he remembered every one of them, and that's how I know about the Harp. The Harp of the Seasons.'

'Brand was on a quest to steal it,' Jack said.

Connor continued. 'A long time ago in Eirinn the sea people, the *Fir Bolg*, were at war with real folk. And they were winning that war. They took hundreds captive and slit their throats or strangled them and put them in the bog-tarns of CorNamara, which is what they did, for they worshipped dark gods and that was their sacrifice.

'Anyhow, the king of the West, the Dagda, he said enough of this, and he gathered all the chiefs together and they raised a high stone on Tara Hill, which was the sacred place to the Sky Queen and the Dagda said if she came to Eirinn's aid he would give her his son, whose name was Conovar the Fair. All the chiefs said this was a mighty thing to do, and they made him chief of chiefs over them.

'Then, on the midsummer, at sunrise, the time for the sacrifice, with Conovar lying on the rock, a sunbeam shone through the stones and blinded the Dagda. When his knife came down it hit the rock and shattered into a million pieces that swirled around his head, and among them, the Sky Queen herself appeared.

'*You have shown your heart and your courage for the good of Eirinn. I pledge my aid to you and your people down the ages.*'

'And then she tells him she will send a champion to lead them against the Fir Bolg and drive them back into the sea. This champion, she said, would find three sacred things. The Cauldron of Cerunnos, which would never empty and would ensure the land was never hungry. The Harp of the Seasons, which would ensure the spring would always come and summer after that to make the land green. And also there was the Invincible Club, which would defeat any foe.

'Then, from the west, comes a travelling man, who says he has been called to pledge to the Dagda.'

Jack felt the same twinge of excitement as he had when Rune had told him the story.

The travelling man. The *journeyman*.

'Strange in his ways,' Connor went on, 'and his talk, they say, but he did all that she promised. Then he led the armies out to the badlands where they took the revenge on the Fir Bolg for all their atrocities and killed them by the thousand. The rest were driven back to the sea where they still live in the kelp and the deep channels. Except for a few who escaped to the bare mountains far away and became Fell Runners.

'And then, when there was peace, the Dagda went back to Tara Hill alone to thank the Sky Queen, and that's when she showed her real self to him and they fell in love and had a daughter. They said she was the most beautiful ever born.'

He nudged Corriwen. 'Not as pretty as yourself, of course.'

She snorted and cuffed him on the ear. Connor chuckled and went on.

'The Sky Queen said that peace would last a long time, but people would covet the three great talismans, so they must be hidden in secret places that only the Traveller and the Dagda's son know. The Harp would sing its harmony and the Cauldron would see Eirinn was never hungry. The Club was sent far away to keep it from ambitious men.'

Connor looked up. 'And that's the story as my Da used to tell it. But these past years, the seasons have turned up all wrong. Snow in summer. Frost in spring. Ice and hail and storms. The crops fail and the cattle die while Dermott the Wolf gorges like a pig and holds the other chiefs to ransom.'

'And you think this is *that* harp?' Corriwen asked.

'It's *that* harp,' Jack answered. 'I helped Brand steal it. I did a deal with him so we could rescue you.'

'And put yourself in so much danger, Jack Flint.' Her eyes were filled with gratitude and admiration.

Now Connor touched the gleaming surface, very gently and with great reverence.

'It's been silenced.' His tone made it sound like a foul crime. 'Fainn must have cut its strings and stopped its song. And for that, folk have gone hungry and sick.'

He took his sword in his hands. A single tear ran down his cheek.

'When I get the chance, I'll cut Dermott down for what he's done.'

Corriwen patted Connor on the shoulder, then wrapped him in her arms and hugged him tight. Jack made himself busy, carefully stashing the Harp back in the bottomless bag which he tied to the saddle-horn.

'Now it starts,' he said. 'Like I said.'

'What?' they both turned to him.

'There are *no* coincidences, just as I said last night. Brand left the Harp with us for a reason, maybe so he could lure Dermott into the mist, or for some other reason. But now it's our responsibility.'

'What's he talking about?' Connor wanted to know. Corriwen hushed him.

'On Temair, we had a job to do before we got home. I think this is our job *here*. It's what the heartstone and the Book of Ways are all about. What being a Journeyman is all about. I'm sure of it.'

He touched the heartstone, now still, but warm on his skin.

'We were brought to Temair, and now we've been brought to Eirinn. There must be a purpose in all of this.'

'To right a wrong?' Corriwen suggested.

'Maybe. Yes. That's what the Book of Ways told us. But I think there is something bigger going on. I can't say why I think that, but it's how I feel. We have to protect this harp.'

'I'm with you,' Connor said.

'Dermott really will keep hunting us, so we have to get away, as far as we can. We should move at first light,' Jack said.

Corriwen agreed. Connor shrugged. His smile returned.

'Whatever you think. I'm happy just to be out in fresh air again.'

'You told us Dermott hunts with dogs?'

'And kills with them.'

'So we have to put distance between them and us.'

'Which way?' Corriwen asked.

Jack opened his backpack for the first time in days, and drew out the Book of Ways.

In the light of the fire, the words resolved, line by line. Connor looked on, fascinated, as Jack read:

North from chase, but find no hide
Journeyman has far to ride
Evil eye counts every stride
Peril lurks on every side

Climb bare hill but ware the mire
Far from rage of thunder dire

Find the shore and walk the strand
Yet ware the tide and ware the sand.

In the night the lost await
Hunger stalks on runners gait.
Where the ocean finds lands end
Seek a haven, seek a friend.

'Now that's really clever,' Connor said. 'More witchery.'

'It doesn't sound promising.'

'We have to go north,' Jack said. 'But there's warnings all over it.'

'We have to find the Homeward Gate,' Corriwen said. 'And get back to Temair.'

'I'll guide you,' Connor said. 'I know every trail, and if I don't, I can find one.'

'Have you ever been north?' Jack asked.

'Never been anywhere but here,' Connor said. 'Though I truly think I've outstayed my welcome. In the north, there's sour badlands. Bogrim and Fell Runners and the like, so they say, but maybe up there is better than down here, with Dermott in full cry. And if you could use another sword-arm, I'm your man till the end.'

Connor stuck his hand out and Jack shook it firmly.

'The more, the merrier,' he said, though he didn't feel merry at all. 'We'd best get some sleep, because we have to be up and away before they know it.'

TWENTY ONE

A thud in the dark. It sounded like a body falling on soft ground.

Jack's eyes opened instantly, his hand on his amberhorn bow. There was cold rain on the air, and a breeze shook icy droplets from the branches overhead. In the gloom he could barely make out Corriwen and Connor, close to the dying embers.

The heartstone pulsed with its own mysterious energy.

Something moved, so slowly at first he thought he'd imagined it. He waited, breath held tight.

Then he saw it. Kerry was on the ground where he had slumped from his position against the tree. Jack let out a breath of relief. His eyes began to close again when Kerry moved.

Kerry *slithered* away from the tree.

The sight froze Jack. He could hear damp leaves scrape under Kerry as he inched forward, eyes wide and staring.

The heartstone quivered.

Wake up. *Wake up!* The voice in his head yammered at him to get out of this nightmare.

Kerry's tongue flickered out. Too long to be a human tongue, too fast and reptilian.

And Jack couldn't wake himself.

Kerry hissed and came right up close, swivelling from side to side, as if taking bearings. Jack was motionless, lying on his side. His tunic was half open and the heartstone just visible against his skin.

Jack felt the tickle of Kerry's tongue against his skin, and goose pimples crawled where he had been touched.

Kerry's hands came forward, strangely sinuous and fluid and reached for the heartstone, and still Jack was paralysed.

Wake up *now*!

His brain shrieked the command to himself but his body still couldn't move an inch.

Kerry's hands drew the heartstone out, still attached to the silver chain, and he brought his face close. Black eyes scanned it avidly.

'Not black,' Jack's mind whimpered. 'His eyes are *blue*!'

The stone was in front of him, between his eyes and Kerry's. And when Jack looked through the translucent talisman, his heart almost gave out completely.

Kerry's face was a mask of scaly plates. His pupils were no longer round, but vertical, like slits in glass. The tongue that flicked out was thin and black and forked at the end. Suddenly he dropped the stone and slid away.

Jack let out a long, silent breath that seemed to have been backed up in his lungs for hours. He turned slightly and a thorn stabbed him in the knee. The sharp pain made his eyes water.

And in that instant he knew he was not dreaming. He was awake with his hand on the amberhorn bow, a thorn in his knee, and his friend coiled like a snake under a dead oak.

Jack Flint suddenly felt more afraid than he had ever been in his life.

Jack lay awake in the dark for a long time as the damp overtook the fire and finally snuffed it out. He waited until the only sound was the steady drip of rain on leaves. Then, very carefully, he crept away from the campsite, inching his way on the ground so as to make no sound and no obvious motion.

In the hollow, Kerry stayed dead still, hissing softly as Jack crept silently over the fallen oak. The very sound made Jack shudder.

He waited until he was sure that he couldn't be seen. Water had gathered on the ridges on the dead bark. As quickly and quietly as he could, Jack prised away some of the loose wood until he formed a little runnel, and the rainwater began to trickle down to splash on the ground just beside where Kerry lay. Jack watched the drips gradually build into a puddle of cold water, and while he hated to make Kerry suffer, he knew what had to be done.

In his lair below Wolfen Castle, Fainn saw none of this.

But he *had* seen the beating heartstone.

Somewhere in distant memory, he recalled hearing of such a talisman. In the far days of the Dagda, there had been a man ...

There had been a heartstone. A charm of great power.

This, he told himself, *was something he had to have*.

This was something that could change *everything*.

They were up before dawn, though Jack had not slept at all.

Kerry did not move. Jack forced himself to his feet and went across to the hollow. Kerry was completely motionless. When Jack nudged him, he didn't blink. His breathing was so shallow it was just the faintest reptilian hiss. His limbs were stiff and cold.

Jack wasted no time in binding Kerry's hands and feet with some line from the fishing reel, hating himself for treating his best friend this way, but knowing there was no alternative.

The horror he had seen in the night had not been Kerry. Not the friend he'd known since childhood.

He slid Kerry's sword into a scabbard on the horse's saddle and relit the fire to get some heat into his own stiff muscles.

When Corriwen awoke and saw Kerry tightly bound at the base of the tree, she was horrified. She whipped out a knife and bent to cut him free. Jack pulled her back and made her listen. His voice woke Connor and he told them what had happened.

'I made sure he got cold in the night,' Jack said. 'The rainwater. Cold slows snakes down and it worked. Something's got into him. That snake bite has done something horrible.'

'You can't beat Fainn's magic,' Connor said. 'He turned weasels on us in the woods and they changed into monsters made of leaves and twigs, but they were *alive*.'

'But we burned them,' Corriwen said. 'We beat them.'

'We can't beat this,' Jack said miserably. 'I don't know what to do, but we have to. Whatever Fainn has done, surely it can be undone.'

'There's no cure for Fainn's curse,' Connor said. 'I don't think there's any for snake magic. He'll be suffering inside all the time, more than anybody should suffer.'

He was about to say more when a clamour of noise reached them through the trees.

'Dermott!' Connor hissed. 'He's come for us.'

Jack immediately scooped Kerry up, grunting with the weight. Kerry was rigid, as if all his muscles had seized.

Jack ignored the involuntary shudder of revulsion that ran through him as he heaved his friend over the saddle, lashed his wrists to the pommel and hauled himself up. Connor sat behind Corriwen on the other horse and they were gone with a wild hue and cry behind them as horsemen crashed through the undergrowth.

They had a slight advantage, because Dermott's men were weighed down with weapons and armour, and Thin Doolan had picked out two of the best horses in the castle stables.

Grey drizzle soaked through their clothes and Kerry bounced like a dead weight. They reached a rocky pass and went down it, Jack leading the way, heading north-west. At least, he told himself, the compass in his head was still working. Ahead the land rose through trailing clouds and they could sometimes see the rugged peaks of black mountains in the far distance. They looked forbidding, but with Dermott's hunters behind them, they had no choice but to head in that direction.

It was mid-morning before they had to stop and let the sweating horses rest a while.

Corriwen examined Kerry closely, concern making her face grim.

'We've only just found each other,' she said, distraught. 'And now we could lose him.'

'We'll find a way,' Jack said, with more conviction than he felt.

Then they were off again through the rills and passes of the foothills, crossing fast streams amber with peat. Every once in a while, they found a ridge they could use as an observation post, and each time, they saw the dogged pursuit through the swirling clouds.

Connor shook his head.

'We're leaving no trail. We've come through water and kept to stony ground, but they follow us at every turn. I don't understand it.'

'Maybe they're good trackers,' Jack suggested.

'No. They're not that good. Not as good as me and I've been watching to see we don't leave tracks. Something's giving us away.'

Jack drew him and Corriwen away from the horses for a moment. He glanced across at Kerry, silent and still where they had put him.

'He reached for the heartstone last night,' Jack said. 'Kerry would never have done that. Something was making him do it. Using him. Whatever it was might have seen the stone.'

'Fainn!'

'What if ...' Jack paused. 'What if he's using Kerry's eyes?'

'Blind him!' Connor said.

'Don't you dare!' Corriwen shot back.

'No. I mean, blindfold him. Cover his eyes so he can't see. We'll soon know if they lose the trail.'

'It's worth a try,' Jack agreed.

Kerry fought. As soon as Jack touched him, he swung his head round with reptilian speed and tried to bite. Jack snatched his hand back and heard Kerry's teeth close with a snap, and then Kerry squirmed, body flexing and heaving, trying to sink his teeth into Jack's legs. Connor darted behind him and flung his whole weight down, using both hands to pin Kerry's shoulders and force his face into the ground. Kerry bucked and heaved. Jack managed to tear a strip of leather and bind it round his eyes. As soon as the light was cut off, Kerry went completely limp.

Jack turned to Corriwen. Her face was a mask of anguish. He felt her horror and despair.

An hour later, it was clear they had shaken off the pursuit. Connor the poacher made sure they left no trace as they travelled up towards old pine forests that clung to the steep hillsides and then down the far side into rugged country that stretched towards the dark mountains.

'I wish we could find a Bard,' Corriwen said as they pushed through the pines. 'He would know what to do.'

Her words jolted Jack. Perhaps because somewhere inside him, he had known what to do.

'You could try it,' Corriwen said gently.

'Try what?'

'You know what. Use the heartstone.'

'It might crack in the flames.'

'Maybe it will.'

Something cold twisted inside Jack. 'I can't lose it.'

She turned on him, eyes blazing. 'Can you lose a friend?'

Sudden shame burned in his heart. He reined the horse to a stop. 'Fire,' he told Connor. 'We need heat.'

He and Corriwen pulled Kerry down from the saddle. He hissed and struggled but to no avail. Jack remembered Finbar's words on Temair when he too had needed a drastic cure from the dark touch which had invaded him.

Be a friend to him now . . .

They had to be Kerry's friend, no matter what the cost.

Connor had a good blaze going in no time and rolled some logs for them to sit on. They dragged Kerry close to the flames and laid him down.

Connor looked expectantly from one to the other, waiting for an explanation. Jack said nothing. He reached inside his tunic and drew out the heartstone on its silver mount. It glowed almost black, but still translucent. It felt alive in his hand.

'What's that?' Connor asked.

'It was my father's,' Jack said.

TWENTY TWO

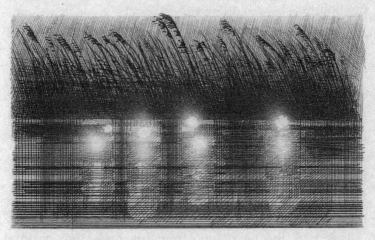

Fainn roared in pain and rage.

He clapped his bony fingers against his face and when he lowered them again his eyes streamed with blood. He lurched to his feet, using the hem of his cloak to wipe away the bloody smears and his vision gradually cleared.

Shaking with pain and fury, he bent over the table-map of Eirinn.

'I'll find you!' he snarled. 'I *will* find you. And then ... you ... will ... suffer!'

He held the end of the cloak over where the bogs of CorNamara showed in clefts and tarns beyond the pine forest and squeezed hard. Droplets of blackening blood splashed the carved surface, and where they landed, acrid fumes rose up.

Jack doubled over and was violently sick.

Kerry, or what had once been Kerry, hissed and fought. They kept the blindfold on, because Jack didn't want to look into those dead black eyes, and he didn't want whatever had control of his friend to see into his own.

'Be a friend to him,' Corriwen said. 'That's what the Bard told us when we held you down.'

'I remember,' Jack said tightly. 'It's something I'd like to forget.'

They used their combined weight on his arms and legs to hold Kerry down and keep him still.

Jack took the heartstone from his neck, then used a branch to lower the stone on its chain into the heat of the fire. He watched as the stone changed from black, to purple, to hot red, then searing white. And it still didn't shatter.

'Tight now,' he told them. 'Keep him still.'

And he placed the stone on the centre of Kerry's bare chest.

The scream that erupted sent a flock of birds clattering into the air half a mile away and echoed all round the hillsides.

Kerry twisted as if hit by lightning. He hissed and spat and then, without warning, his mouth gaped as if he was gasping for air.

A long, black tongue emerged from wide open jaws. His mouth opened wider still. *Impossibly* wide, Jack thought. His jaw joints made a horrible creaking sound. The black forked tongue lashed the air.

Behind it, the bloated pale head of a snake appeared.

Jack stepped back in horror. Corriwen let out an anguished wail. Connor just held tight to Kerry's shoulders as the snake oozed out, pulse by grotesque pulse and began to roll into a coil on ribs. It opened its mouth and Jack saw fangs swing forward as its eyes locked onto his.

'Kill it,' he gasped.

Kerry bucked again and Corriwen was thrown to the side, but she rolled back, a knife in each hand and stabbed the snake in each eye. They popped with a sickening wet sound. Its blind head hit the ground. Jack snatched Kerry's sword and sliced it in half. Blood sprayed and both halves twisted and coiled, but Jack skewered the head end on the point and shoved it into the fire. It sizzled like crackling.

Overhead, lightning blasted down in savage forks and the ground shook.

Connor kicked the other half into the flames while Kerry, still blindfolded, rolled, got to his knees and was violently sick. He groaned, retched again. Jack matched him, stomach heaving with the horror of what he had seen.

Then Kerry reached up and pulled the blindfold down.

'Jeez man,' he said, still doubled over. 'I must have eaten something awful.'

He knuckled his eyes and looked at Jack.

'Whatever it was, I'm not eating it again.'

'I don't remember a thing,' Kerry said. 'What happened in the castle? And who's this new guy?'

He blinked as if seeing the world through fresh eyes, then saw Corriwen. His puzzled expression turned to one of pure delight. He grabbed her in a huge bear-hug and spun her around until she was dizzy.

'Where have you been? We've been looking all over for you.'

Corriwen introduced him again to Connor then they sat round the fire while Kerry ate ravenously and Jack filled him in on all that had happened since they'd come through the misty by-way and gone to Wolfen Castle.

'Sounds like a real bundle of laughs,' Kerry said, through a mouthful of food. 'You sure you're not making all this up? I don't remember swallowing any snake.'

Jack laughed and felt the awful fear and tension drain away. The relief at having Kerry back to normal again had changed everything, even if Dermott and his men were scouring the land for them and they were still in awful danger.

'We're not out of the woods yet,' he said. 'And we've a long way to go. The book says we have to cross bogs and get over the mountains to the sea. So now we should rest and get our strength back.'

Despite his own suggestion, Jack couldn't sleep. His mind was churning, turning over everything that had happened since they had arrived on Eirinn. He stared into the flames for a long time, trying to puzzle out all the questions that crowded in on him.

Finally he blinked and turned. Kerry was staring fixedly at him. Jack's heart lurched.

'What's up?' Kerry cocked his head, a half smile on his face and relief flooded through Jack. 'Can't sleep?'

'Too much going on in my head.'

Kerry shuffled closer and took his hand. 'You saved me again. You're making a habit of it.'

What are friends for? Jack almost replied, but the words stuck in his throat.

'It was Corriwen,' he confessed. 'I was scared I'd break the heartstone.'

'I don't blame you,' Kerry said. 'You know how important it is. And it was your dad's.'

Jack shook his head. 'Corrie was right. She made me think about what I would hate to lose most. I was just being selfish.'

He drew out the heartstone, let the firelight catch it. 'It's still only a stone. But you're ... you're the best friend a guy ever had.'

Kerry dunted him on the shoulder. His eyes were bright. 'Quit that, man. You'll have me blubbin' next.'

Then, before Jack could respond, Kerry grabbed him and held him in a tight hug. Jack just let his own tears flow.

The other two were sound asleep.

'So,' Kerry asked. 'What's the plan?'

'That's what I've been thinking about. Everything since

we came here has led to this, and remember what the Major said about coincidences?'

'There aren't any.'

'Right. Brand deliberately left the Harp with us. There must be a reason for that, but whatever the reason, we've got it now. And I'm not going to let Fainn or anybody else get their hands on it. Fainn's worse than Mandrake. I think he's more powerful, and I know he's seen the heartstone. He's not getting that, either. I'd rather destroy it.'

'And then how would we get home?'

'We'll figure something out,' Jack said. 'But we've been given responsibility to keep the Harp safe. That's our job now. I might never find my father, but I know that's what he would have done. Corriwen was right. We have to do the right thing.'

He turned to Kerry. 'We've seen how the people here are starving. Somebody must know how to fix it and bring the seasons back.'

'And how do we find that person?'

'We trust the book, and we trust the heartstone,' Jack said. 'And we stick together and trust ourselves.'

Before dawn the band of four were on their way.

The Bogs of CorNamara were as bleak as Jack had ever seen. They spread out around them on every side, mile after mile of moorland pocked by black tarns of slimy water and studded with old weathered rocks that stood like dead sentinels.

For a full day, they trudged through it, finding their way, sometimes *feeling* their way, until night began to fall.

Far behind them glittering lights began to appear on the slopes that led down to the bog, first a few, then dozens, all widely spaced on the far hills. It was clear that Dermott's men were combing the land. The fires they had lit meant that they wouldn't venture here by night.

'Can't blame them,' Kerry said miserably. 'I don't like this place in the daytime.'

'It's bad lands,' Connor said. 'Men don't come here. Nor in the mountains. Bad things hunt there.'

'There's always stories about lonely places,' Jack said. The bog was indeed lonely and somehow threatening in its desolation, but he didn't want them all to get spooked. It would be a dreary night and they needed some sleep, Jack more than anyone. But if Dermott's troops wouldn't venture into the bog, he knew they could gain some distance if they travelled by night.

They led the horses by the reins, listening to the odd, sucking noises in the dark. Things lived in the slick waters. Jack hoped it was frogs and newts, or even moorhens. Occasionally the tarns would burp some rotting gas that smelt like the slaughterfield of Temair, but at least, Jack told himself, there were none of the great *roaks*, the carrion birds that had stalked them in Temair.

As it grew darker still, the whoop of the wind and the soughing of reeds sounded like whispering voices.

Connor touched Jack's shoulder.

'I hear things,' he said. His short-sword was tight in his grip.

'What sort of things?'

'Don't know. Like people calling me. Whispering in my head.'

'It's just the wind.'

'No, it's not the wind. They tell me they're cold. And lonely and lost.'

Something plopped in the tarn and bubbles burst in gulps. The smell of marsh-gas spread around them. They held their breath, listening.

... So cold ... so very cold ...

A voice moaned in Jack's head, a voice that sounded like oozing mud.

'Bogrim,' Connor said, shuddering. He made a sign in the air with his fingers, warding off bad luck.

They skirted a tarn. Jack fumbled in his pack and drew out the little Maglite torch, flicked it on, and swept the beam in an arc. A greenish vapour floated knee high above the pools and beneath it, dark water.

Shapes moved in there. Forms drifted under the stagnant scum, rising to the surface.

... so cold ... so lonely ...

Another bubble burst like soft tar, belched green gas that swirled up, condensing in the night air. It writhed in the torchlight, elongating as it rose. It spun in an eddy of air and in its centre, Jack thought he saw a face.

Kerry gripped Jack's arm.

'You see that?'

The face wavered towards them, pale as a dead fish.

... join us in the dark ... sink with us ...

The beam caught another shape rising from the quagmire.

A young girl's hollow eyes fixed on them, her mouth open in a silent scream. Her translucent arms reached towards them.

'Bogrim,' Connor said again. 'The drowned dead.'

... Come sleep in the dark cold ...

Corriwen had both hands clamped to her ears.

'Make them stop,' she cried. 'I feel their despair.'

The wraith floated towards Jack and he saw the twist of rotting rope tight around her neck. Her wispy arms enfolded him and immediately, a feeling of dismal cold rippled through him.

And with it came a sense of deep sadness and lonely despair.

He pushed forward, through the apparition, felt it suck the heat from him, and then he was beyond it, leaving him with an emptiness in his heart as if he had been drained.

'Come on,' he said. 'They can't hurt us. Not physically.'

'They hurt my soul,' Corriwen said miserably. 'They are so, so lost.'

The plaintive voices pleaded and the wraiths crowded in on them, begging for warmth and an end to loneliness.

'Sacrifices,' Connor said. 'Strangled and sunk. They can't ever escape.'

'Come on,' Kerry said. 'This place is creeping me out.'

At that moment the light failed and they were in darkness.

'Oh, screw this for a game of soldiers,' Kerry said.

He fumbled in the dark before he found a clump of bulrush, broke off a hank and twisted the reeds together. There was a flash in the dark as he flicked his lighter and got the rush-heads to ignite. Yellow light spread around them as he held it high to show the way. The wraiths shrank back.

'I don't think we've far to go,' Jack said. 'The ground's getting more solid.'

Together they pushed on, battling against the oppressive misery of this place, while the wind rippled the reeds in moaning gusts until they reached higher ground.

'It's so depressing,' Kerry said, wading through the lingering mist. 'All that misery. I just want to cry.'

He lowered the guttering torch.

And the night *exploded*.

Jack and Corrie were thrown backwards. Kerry vanished in a blinding blaze of light. Connor was blown flat onto the heather. The horses reared, eyes wide with fear.

The floating mist caught in a series of stuttering flares that leapt from one tarn to another, turning the night into a weird pink day.

'Marsh gas,' Jack said, helping Corriwen to her feet.

The nearest tarns were now pools of flickering light, as the trails of fire spread out all around.

The wraithlike shapes writhed and twisted in the heat, and in an instant, the miasma of misery lifted from Jack's heart. It felt as if a physical weight had fallen away.

The apparitions in the marsh were drawn into the rising columns of flame, a silent, drifting multitude, spinning in a gauzy procession, faster and faster, gradually losing shape and form.

They watched, spellbound, as more and more of the wraiths were sucked into the heat, merging and melting into a pale cloud that rose ever higher into the night air.

In his head, Jack heard a whispering sigh that faded as the cloud began to dissipate high above them, and the flames guttered and died.

'They're gone,' Corriwen said. 'I think the fire set them free.'

'They'll be warmer now, I bet,' Kerry finally said. Jack suddenly convulsed with laughter that was very close to hysterics, until he doubled up, unable to get his breath.

'What?' Kerry asked. 'Did I say something funny?'

TWENTY THREE

They had reached solid ground but the flares of exploding marsh gas had surely pinpointed their presence to the hunters. In the morning, men would zero in on them for sure.

They were hungry, wet and tired, but there was no rest for them here at the base of the black mountains. They climbed a series of rocky tracks that were just wide enough to let the horses pass and when they got high enough they turned to look back.

Across the expanse, lines of men and horses had started down towards the bogland. Dermott was taking no chances. He'd comb the entire barrens if he had to.

In Wolfen Castle, Fainn's bloodshot eyes stared madly. The thieves had found their way into the bogland, herded there by the frigid wind he'd sent to drive them on.

From there, with hordes of hunters behind them, there was only one way to go: into the black mountains.

And if they made it across those dark peaks, he knew where they'd reach. If not, they'd die there and Dermott would have the Harp again, and he, Fainn, would find that dark heartstone. And sooner or later he'd learn its secrets.

He turned from the smoking pit and stalked out of the chamber into the great hall.

Dermott was brooding. He sat in a scatter of bloodied feathers that drifted around his feet. In among them were the torn bodies of the messenger pigeons that had brought news of the thieves' escape from the trees and into the bogs, then the further news that they had fled into the night. Dermott just could not control his anger, and could never be relied upon to refrain from killing the messenger, even if it was a pigeon.

'You lost them!' He turned accusing eyes on Fainn.

'A temporary misplacement, my Lord,' Fainn muttered.

'My harp! That damned harp. I want it back.'

'As ebb follows flow Lord, you shall have it. It is time to end their game.'

'You have them?'

'We will have them soon. They head west, towards the ocean. I have ordered the black ships to raise sail. And summoned a sea-wind to speed us.'

Dermott's face visibly brightened.

'To oars then!' he boomed. 'Every hand to the rigging.'

They had picked their way up, through gullies and ravines where fast water cascaded from high melt snow until the air sharpened and squalls of hard hail stung their cheeks and blinded the horses. They climbed on and up, sheltering behind the beasts when they could, and taking the brunt of the hail when they couldn't. Every now and again, a motion would catch Kerry's eye and he would spin in alarm to see a boulder tumble down a scree slope. Jack thought he could feel eyes on him, but couldn't be sure. The stone here was dark, almost black, as if pushed up from hot depths. No tree grew. Behind them, the bogland was a wet moonscape, pocked and cratered. The long sweep of trailing horsemen were just dots in its vastness.

The final ridge took them by surprise. It had taken them all day to reach the heights where razor-sharp edges and towering stacks made the going almost impossible for the horses until Corriwen blindfolded them when they stalled on a narrow track, and led them slowly uphill.

Wind whistled in cols and ridges, wails of lost souls. It was cold and barren. Jack was in two minds as to whether he preferred the bleak hills to the black bogs. Both were dangerous and miserable.

When they breasted the ridge, Jack sank to his haunches and called a halt. His legs were aching and shaky. Connor stood beside him, breathing quite easily and Jack felt a pang of shame at feeling so weak when this boy with one good leg had matched him step for step the whole climb and seemed none the worse for it.

'Glad you said it,' Connor said. 'I'm about dead on my toes.'

'You've done pretty well so far,' Kerry said.

'Only because of those things in the bogs. I don't like dead people. Especially ones that move. And moan inside your head.' He let out a breath. 'It's pure cowardice that keeps me going.'

They rested an hour, no more, and then Jack said they had to continue. The far side was a nightmare, muscles accustomed to climbing that now had to be used for descent. The slopes were steep and slippery from rain. Avalanches of rock-chips trickled down from above, threatening to cover them, and from below their feet, threatening to tumble them down.

The fell runners swooped on them when they were barely halfway down the far side.

They moved with frightening speed.

The fugitives were working their way through a narrow pass when Jack caught something out of the corner of his eye and turned round, expecting to see Dermott's hunters closing in.

'You see something?' Kerry stood beside him.

'I thought I did.' Jack scanned the rocky valley sides.

'Every time I look round,' Connor said, 'they disappear.

Maybe it's mountain sprites. They hide in the rocks.'

'As long as they stay hidden,' Jack said.

When the going got easier, they climbed into the saddles again and let the horses find the track down.

At the end of the valley, the avalanche came swooping down the slope towards them. It came so silently that at first Jack thought he was seeing things. In the first instant it looked like rolling grey boulders, bouncing and tumbling over the splintered rock, then it suddenly leapt into focus.

'Fell runners!' Connor barked a warning and their horses reared in alarm.

They were tall and thin as skeletons, leaping from rock to rock like spiders. Eyes bulged in gaunt faces where every dark vein showed through and as they ran, their mouths gaped, showing sharp feral teeth.

'What in the name . . .' Kerry almost fell off the horse.

Corriwen heeled her horse and it took off. Jack and Kerry were right behind as the grey horde, fifty or more, came charging down the hillside faster than any man could run, tattered rags flapping in the wind. Kerry risked a glance over his shoulder and saw them gaining, every stride ten feet or more, and on every face a dreadful, implacable hunger.

'Come on, Jack!' Kerry yelled in his ear, holding onto his belt. 'They're catching up.'

Jack urged the horse on, up and over a lip and down a gradual slope, but the horse was tiring fast. Beyond them the slope dropped towards a flat plain where the mountains ended.

'We'll never make it,' Jack said, holding tight to the reins. 'They're too fast.'

Behind them the fell runners snickered and howled, sounding too much like a pack of hungry hyenas for Jack's liking.

Ahead, Corriwen's horse faltered.

'We have to do something.' Jack raised a foot from the stirrups and pointed at his leather boots, then at Connor and Corriwen just ahead of them. 'They'd be faster on a horse each.'

Kerry looked at him, not comprehending. Then it dawned.

'You think we can take them?'

'We have to give it a try.'

Jack spurred the horse, got it alongside Corrie and Connor. He grabbed Connor by the neck of his threadbare tunic and hauled him off. The boy yelled in fright and surprise and for a second, the horse almost juddered to a halt under the triple weight, but as soon as Connor was on its neck, Jack swung one leg off. Kerry rolled and hit the ground on his feet, moving fast.

With only one rider, the horse gathered itself. Corriwen turned in her saddle and saw Jack and Kerry on the track with the horde of fell runners arrowing straight for them. She began to rein her horse.

'Go!' Jack cried. 'Don't stop.'

Then the boys *moved*. One second they were on the track. The next they were up and running over the hard rocks, leaping like mountain goats, almost faster than the eye could follow.

Kerry bent to snatch a handful of stones and his sling was already swinging when the nearest hungry runner got to within twenty feet of him. He wheeled, splitting from Jack, leapt from one rock to another, spun as he landed and let fly.

It took the lead runner between the eyes with a sound like a hammer blow. Blood spattered and it went down in a clatter of bones.

Jack had his bow ready for the next one who came bounding in a ragged grey streak, laughing like a thing demented. His arrow went clean through its neck and lodged in the eye of another runner ten feet behind. Both fell dead.

Jack and Kerry hared after the horses but sufficiently off the trail to lead the hunters after them.

'These boots are pure magic,' Kerry said. 'I thought those things were fast, but we're . . . we're just *super-freakin'*-sonic.'

'Come on!' he yelled. 'Come and get me, you bunch of bony freaks.'

Forty yards on, Jack had found a high vantage and was on one knee, sending a volley of arrows into the main pack and finding a target for each one. Kerry's sling was just as deadly. They kept up the fusillade until the attack petered out.

'That stopped them,' he crowed. 'What a team!'

The fell runners milled together, out of range. Two of them tore apart one of their fallen and without a pause, began to feast noisily.

'Gross!' Kerry groaned. 'That would turn your stomach.'

They scampered off the rock and found the trail, running

easily while the land zoomed past them until they reached the long downslope towards the plain below.

When they got there, they discovered it wasn't a plain, but a vast beach.

And there was no sign of Corriwen and Connor.

The Book of Ways had told them they must cross the strand. Jack and Kerry walked down through the tide-line where sea-bleached tree-trunks jutted like tumbled bones, and real bones, great white curves, angled up from deep sand, ribs and skulls filled with huge teeth, as if this was a place where all the monsters of the deep came to die.

Far, far in the north, a faint smudge told them where the beach ended. It could have been twenty miles away, or fifty. They couldn't tell.

Kerry searched until he found what might have been horse-tracks that were slowly filling in with fine damp sand. They were barely visible, but he convinced himself and Jack that they were real.

He pointed north. 'That way.'

Jack scanned the extent of the long shore. The faint sound of waves whispered across the sand and he thought he could make out their motion in the distance.

'The tide's far out,' he said. 'And we're a long way from the hills.'

'Takes ages for the tide to come in,' Kerry said, but there was something in this empty expanse that made Jack feel nervous and exposed. Here and there, as they walked, they stumbled into a patch of softer sand that gave under their feet and sucked them up to their ankles.

'What if they hit quicksand?' Kerry asked.

Jack didn't want to think about that. They plodded on, leaving two pairs of fading footprints behind them and the sand grew wetter and wetter until every step was a sheer slog.

They reached a narrow inlet and stood for a moment, considering whether to go seawards or landwards to attempt a crossing when Jack spotted something out in the west.

A black sail was just visible on the far horizon.

A thin cry carried to them on the wind.

Kerry grabbed Jack, pulling his gaze away from the black shape in the distance.

'Did you hear something?'

'A bird,' Jack said.

'No, I don't think so.' Kerry ran along the edge of the inlet. 'I see them. Come on!'

Jack ran up beside him. More than a mile away, Corrie was jumping up and down, waving her arms. Connor was astride one horse.

Jack looked back out to sea. Another black sail had appeared. Before he could say anything, Kerry was hauling him by the arm, slipping in damp sand until they found a place shallow enough to cross. The inlet was only a hundred yards wide, but the sand underneath was soft and cloying.

Fainn stood with Dermott on the foredeck of the black ship. The Lord of Wolfen Castle paced, clenching and unclenching his fists.

'You're sure they're here?'

'They are here, my Lord. And we have a tide wind.'

He gestured with one hand and the steersman made an adjustment so they tacked close to shore at the wide mouth of an inlet. Fainn pointed across the sands.

'I see them now. Hunted from the hills, and they have no escape. The tide will work for us, and I have turned the wind shoreward. You shall have them.'

The boat entered the inlet. Behind it, a fleet of low, sleek craft, each bearing a wolf's head on its prow, turned in unison.

Fainn walked to the stern and raised his snake-staff aloft, facing the sea, chanting words which none of the crew understood.

And the ebbing tide turned and began to flow.

The water came in fast as they ran. One minute they were running on sand, then they were splashing through waves.

'The tide, Jack,' Kerry cried. 'It's coming . . .'

'Run,' Jack said. 'We can beat it.'

If they didn't they'd be swamped. They scrambled towards the distant shore.

It was then that Jack remembered the words of the Book of Ways.

Climb bare hill but ware the mire
North from sound of thunder fire

197

Find the shore and walk the strand
Yet ware the tide and ware the sand.

In the night the lost await
Hunger stalks on runners gait.
Where the ocean finds lands end
Seek a haven, seek a friend.

They had climbed bare hill and braved the mire. And now they were in the tide and sand.

'Seek a haven. Seek a friend.' Jack repeated the words to himself and as he did, he thought of Brand and what he had said as he hurried towards the misty road.

'The flute!' he cried. 'It has something to . . .'

He jabbed a hand into his backpack and drew out the little flute. It could summon Brand, or other Cluricauns. *Maybe.* Jack kept moving as he put it to his lips and blew hard.

No sound came out. He tried again, and still got nothing at all. He looked at the flute in his fingers. It was made of bone, not the polished wood he recalled Brand handing to him, then remembered. *It was the wrong flute.* Finn the Giant had given them the bone one. And he was far, far away.

Jack snatched for the wooden flute and blew on it. This time he got a cacophonous shriek, like the whistle of an old train on a dark night. He blew again and felt as if his eardrums would burst.

Far from the foreshore, beyond where Corriwen and Connor raced from the rising water, something stirred.

Jack splashed on, Kerry beside him. Way on the far high tide mark, the loose sand seemed to shift and roll. Pieces of straw and dry seaweed tumbled up into the air.

And down from the mountains came a blast of wind that swept out onto the long strand like a storm.

It almost stopped them in their tracks.

But it did stop the black ships. Their sails caught the full blast and they veered out of control.

The wind was so strong it was pushing the tide back. Jack put a hand over his eyes and turned into it, peering through the slit between his fingers, and saw the water that had threatened to cut them off was being forced out, leaving the spine of sand free.

'Come on. Just a bit more and we're there.'

Behind them the black ships swung and ploughed into the inlet's bank. On the deck, Fainn and Dermott the Wolf cursed like demons.

Jack gasped for breath, legs aching from the effort of pushing against the headwind.

Corriwen and Connor were up on dry sand now, picking through the strand-line towards the cover of the trees.

And a huge beast with a wide gaping mouth and huge teeth came charging out at them.

TWENTY FOUR

The horse reared and almost threw Connor off. Corriwen moved like lightning. She pulled his sword out, rolled from the saddle and braced herself.

The beast came charging straight at her and she angled the sword to take it in the throat. The mouth of teeth gaped even wider.

'No!' Jack cried. 'It won't . . .'

But then it was on her and she was down on the sand, kicking and struggling.

Jack and Kerry crossed the distance in five seconds and grabbed two handfuls of hair, trying to drag it off.

And Finn's big dog was licking Corriwen Redthorn's face with its great wet tongue.

'Come on, Tinker,' Kerry pleaded. 'Let her up before she drowns.'

'I wondered why he took off so quickly,' Finn boomed. 'That whistle's so high, I can't hear it myself, but Tinker always heeds the call.'

They had managed to drag the dog off until Corriwen, dripping with saliva, got to her feet and then it bounded excitedly around them as they climbed up the beach slope and into the trees.

Behind them the black ships were stuck on the sandbank and Jack knew the sailors would have to wait for a full tide before they got moving again. They were safe for the moment.

Finn strode towards them through the forest, shuddering the trees with his footfalls. Corriwen looked up at him in awe.

'Well met, little people,' he rumbled. 'And twice as many as before.'

He hunkered low and looked Corriwen up and down. 'Two old friends and two new. Welcome to Finn's headland.'

They reached Finn's home before nightfall. The giant carried the four of them in his creel mile after mile round the rocky north shore.

For the first time in ages Jack Flint felt out of danger.

They ate slices of a huge fish as wide as a horse while Jack put a splint on Connor's badly bruised thigh. They discovered his horse had bolted for miles across the sands and thrown him off.

'I don't think it's broken, but you should keep it still for a while.'

'How can I do that and keep running?' Connor gritted his teeth as Jack worked.

'We'll think of something.'

'They'll come around the point on the high tide,' Finn said. 'And south of here, the little people are scouring the country for folk who sound just like the four of you. They say you stole something.'

'Well,' Kerry said. 'We did ... sort of.'

Jack told Finn everything that had happened to them, then drew out the golden harp. The cut strings drooped like precious threads. Finn held it daintily in one hand.

'Isn't this beautiful,' he said. 'I never saw the like in my life. And it's a crime to see its voice cut.'

'Brand says it's the Harp of Seasons.'

Finn nodded. 'That figures with what's been happening, I suppose. I always imagined it was much bigger than this little thing.'

'We can't let Dermott get his hands on it again. And we can't go home until we get it to Tara Hill, wherever that is.'

'Nobody knows where Tara Hill stands. It's a fairy hill. It comes out of the mist when the Sky Lady decides and not before. You're as well searching for gold at the end of the rainbow.'

'Doesn't sound like mission impossible in a place like this,' Kerry said, 'with leprechauns and giants and creepy dead people that float about the bogs.'

'Well, all I know is that no mortal can find Tara Hill. It's got to call you, I believe.'

'So we'll just sit here and eat your fish,' Kerry said, 'And wait for the call.'

Finn laughed. 'You can stay as long as you like, but Dermott and that spellbinder of his, they won't give up easily, and they won't give up any time soon.'

He stroked his big square jaw. 'Those boats need a wind to get round the point. Wind and tide together, so they won't get here for a day or two, three at the most. That should give you some time to think, and your little brains are a lot quicker than mine I hope, for I can't think of a way. This is as far north as you can get, and the whole south land is hunting your runaway hides. Beyond here's only a few misty islands and cold ocean.'

'We could check the book,' Kerry volunteered.

Jack already had it in his hand and the pages were riffling back to front in their papery whisper. Finn rubbed his jaw, fascinated.

Harried close, o'er sea and hill
Beset on every side by ill
Journeyman must ever flee
Bearing Eirinn's harmony

Yet standing on the furthest reach
Where ocean beats on stone
No escape, east south or west
But surely travel on.

No rest, no rest, till end of quest
The time is now at hand

To trust a friend, to steel the heart
And stride from land to land.

'It's like I told you,' Finn said. 'Hunters all over the south, and nowhere left to run.'

'Maybe we could get a boat?' Kerry looked hopeful. Finn shook his head.

'Nothing those sail-ships can't catch.'

'Then we're stuck here at the end of the earth,' Connor said.

'We must make a stand,' said Corriwen.

'Yes,' Jack said, with more sarcasm than he intended. 'Four against the world.'

'Five,' Finn said. 'And Tinker. He's good for a bite or two.'

'Yeah, he can lick them to death,' Kerry snorted.

'It's not your fight,' Jack said. 'It's our quest. We have to see it through or we'll never find the homeward gate. It's some kind of rule.'

'I'd be no good anyway,' Finn said. 'I might be big, but I'd rather fish than fight.'

'Me too,' Kerry said wistfully.

Finn had estimated three days at least before the black ships rounded the point, but whatever wind Fainn managed to conjure up hauled them off the sandbank and into deep tide water and then carried them past the long strand and round the cape. They made it in only two days.

And by then, a horde of hunters had hemmed the fugitives in on the rocky headland that was Finn's lonely home.

The sound of horns and drums came faint on the wind. Beyond, to the north, grey waves swelled as far as the eye could see.

Jack was desperately thinking of how to get out of this when the heartstone gave a slow beat against his skin.

Danger. But he already knew that.

They hadn't had enough time to think or plan. And Dermott and Fainn were coming fast. They'd be trapped between the ships and the hunters.

Jack pointed to where the sea disappeared in thick mist.

'What's in that direction?'

'Some bare islands. I've never been there.'

Below them, waves crashed against the rocky headland. From this height Jack could see the great hexagonal stones packed together like giant pencils. There was something familiar about the shapes. He was sure he must have seen a picture of them somewhere in one of the Major's travel books. The pillars marched out for half a mile, gradually descending until they disappeared under the surf.

'What's that?' he asked Finn.

'That's the sea wall.'

'The what?' Kerry asked.

'Oh, it's an old story,' Finn said. 'My great-great-seventeen-times-great-grandfather. He's supposed to have raised the dyke to keep the kelpie out of the reach. It's a kind of stone fence.'

'Where did it go to?' Corriwen wondered.

'It was supposed to stretch over to some island.' Finn scratched his head and frowned in concentration. 'See if I can remember.'

His face eventually brightened. 'Blind Fingal's Island. That was the name. Never seen it. Never been.'

'If it's a dyke, then it's been worn down by the tide,' Connor said.

'Like I said, it's an old story. My Ma used to tell me about it. About Finnan Flannan and the Kelpies.'

'I don't think we've got time ...' Jack began.

But Finn seemed not to have heard him.

'She told me it was true. I was only knee high, but I remember the rhyme. The Kelpies were hunting in the reach eating all Finnan's fish. And they swam too fast for him to catch, with spear or net.'

Finn squatted down beside them, closed his eyes, and began to recite from distant memory.

> And climbing high, he looked and saw
> The furnace of Gerumbel's maw
> A hillock High, the stone he smote
> Then stuck it down Gerumbel's throat
> In fire and flame and steam and smoke
> Gerumbel then began to choke
> And quaking all from ridge to ridge
> His struggles raised the stony bridge.

'Nice story,' Kerry said.

'That's how he raised it high enough to keep the Kelpies

out.' He scratched his head slowly, thinking again. 'Finnan broke off the top of a hill and jammed it in the hole up there on Gerumbel. Old Rumbles, I call it. He sat on the rock and the mountain bucked and heaved, but it couldn't throw him off. And all that force pushed up the rocks and formed the dyke. And it went right out to Staffa. I remember now. That's Blind Fingal's Island.'

Finn looked up at the smoking peak.

'We should be getting out of here,' Jack said. 'There's logs down on the shore. Maybe we could lash them together. See where the tide takes us.'

'You go,' Kerry retorted. 'I've had enough water to last a lifetime. Rafts! Remember what happened on the last one? And there's things in there, Finn. Kelpies, you say?'

He turned, but Finn had gone, surprisingly silently for one so big, with Tinker at his heels. In great strides, he was climbing the slope of the rumbling mountain to a rocky shoulder where smoky steeples poked up. He heaved at one, swaying it back and forth with all his weight until it cracked free. Finn bent low. Even from here they heard his grunt as he straightened up with the huge rock cone across his shoulder, then he began to climb, shoulders bent, until he was standing in plumes of white steam.

The mountain trembled.

'It doesn't like it,' Corriwen said. 'Can mountains think?'

'I surely hope not,' Connor said.

At the top, Finn rolled the rock over the lip and the column of steam was suddenly cut off.

The ground shuddered violently and the four of them

were bounced into the air to land in a tangled heap. Then the sides of the mountain began to swell.

Below them the water frothed and lashed where it met the line of pillar-stones.

Then, as they watched, great hexagonal stacks began to rise, one pillar at a time, grinding up from below the water.

'The Giant's Causeway,' Jack said. 'It was true!'

The mountain shuddered again. From its top Finn bellowed down to them.

'Finnan's Dyke! There's your bridge.'

And the pillars kept rising, one beside the other, fitting together like puzzle-blocks, row on row as the causeway began to appear, further and further out to sea in a curving line.

'It's like the Book told us,' Corriwen said in wonder. 'Stride from land to land.'

'Come on,' Jack said. He slung Brand's bag round his neck, then he and Kerry helped Connor down the slope until they reached the giant pillars which marched like a stairway down to the causeway.

Then they were on the new bridge, its rocks covered in limpets and barnacles.

And together they walked out over the sea, not knowing what they would find.

TWENTY FIVE

The land was far behind them now, but the ships were closer. Jack knew they would try to cut them off.

'We must be prepared to fight,' Corriwen said. 'They have the wind in their sails.'

Jack knew he and Kerry, with Brand's special boots, could have raced on ahead, but that was not an option, with Corriwen and Connor.

'Leave me,' Connor said. 'I'm slowing you down.'

'No chance,' Kerry said. 'It's one for all and each for everybody else. That's our rule.'

Behind the hunters, the Grumbling Mountain – *Gerumbel* – Jack corrected himself shivered again, quite visibly across the distance. Finn was still astride the plug-stone. But the mountain seemed bigger now, its sides less conical.

'It's swelling,' Jack said.

'Finn had better move,' Kerry said. 'If that thing blows ...'

The mountain heaved. A smoking spire blew off like a rocket.

'Come on, Finn!' Jack yelled into the wind, although he knew the giant would never hear him.

Then the top blew. One second Finn was standing on the plug-stone, keeping in the heat and pressure. Then he was gone in an enormous blast of smoke and steam.

A vast wave rushed from the mountain base, higher than a house, churning up rocks and boulders.

'Oh Finn!' Jack wailed.

'Jack. I think we should get the hell out of here.' Kerry's eyes were fixed on the seismic wave that sped towards them.

But Jack was still gazing at the blasted top of the mountain. There was no sign of Finn.

'He sacrificed himself for us,' Connor said. 'He must have known.'

'Jack,' Kerry said in a shaky voice. 'That big wave ... it's heading this way.'

It was, and so were the black ships. They had veered with the wind and were now so close that figures could be made out in the rigging.

'Come on,' Jack said bleakly, but as he turned, something else caught his attention.

Close to the shore, the great stack of pillars was beginning to subside. Jack stopped, still holding Connor's shoulder. His mouth fell open.

'What's wrong?' Corriwen asked. Jack could only point.

The pillars that formed the causeway were sinking back into the sea.

Kerry swore without repeating himself for almost a minute.

'The bridge,' Jack finally found his voice. 'It's going down.'

And the four of them were stuck on the middle of it, with the black ships closing in.

'Pray for a miracle,' Jack said, and something smashed on the stone at his feet. Splinters of glassy rock bulleted out, stinging his legs. Beside Corriwen, another rock fell from the sky.

'Fall-out!' Kerry dodged a boulder that slammed into the dyke. In a matter of seconds, the sea around them was churning with falling ash and stones.

'Run!' Jack yelled, turning Connor around.

'I can hop,' he said. 'Best I can do.'

'Then hop it, man,' Kerry told him. 'Hop for your freakin' life.'

Now a black shape tumbled down, trailing smoke and steam. Jack saw it expand in his vision, bigger and bigger until it seemed to fill the entire sky.

'Oh no! It's the top of the mountain!'

Instinctively he cringed as the rock passed over them, screeching like a hellish express train and slammed into the outermost ship. One second the ship was heeling against the wind, and then it was gone. Completely gone.

A fountain of water reached for the sky and a colossal wave surged out, catching the other ships and driving them shoreward at phenomenal speed.

But the causeway was still collapsing as the pillars disappeared in a continuous wave, like a row of dominoes.

They had a mile or so to go before the bridge vanished into the sea mist while behind them it was vanishing underwater.

Jack and Kerry took Connor's weight and they started moving as fast as they could on the causeway.

All the time Jack could see the final vision of Finn the gentle giant in the blast of heat and light. Tears coursed down his cheeks, thinking they had come so far only to lose a friend.

And it seemed it was all for nothing.

The ships surfed the enormous roller, helpless against its implacable force. Dermott held a rigging rope. Fainn stood, arms folded, wind whipping his batwing cloak around him, watching the shore rush towards them.

'Lost them again!' Dermott roared. 'They thwart me at every turn!'

But Fainn was also watching the land-bridge that had appeared so suddenly. It was now disappearing just as quickly, and their quarry was stuck out there.

All he cared about was finding the bodies afterwards, and that black stone the boy carried.

Dermott could have the stolen harp back, and he had the cauldron that could feed the whole of Eirinn as he chose until such time as they decided to re-string the Harp and let the seasons turn once more.

But that black stone heart ... he hungered for it.

Another man was blasted over the side. Fainn watched, curious, as he struggled desperately then disappeared in white water.

The keel hit rock. Fainn braced himself for the impact, closing his eyes and using all his powers to turn his weight to nothing. He smiled as he watched the great stone pillars sink faster and faster.

The sea-fog swallowed them and for a few mad moments, Jack imagined them falling off the end of the bridge into nothingness. He could barely see more than a couple of yards ahead of them.

Jack estimated they had fifty seconds, no more, before Finn's causeway disappeared under their feet.

'Jack,' Kerry cried. 'I don't think we're going to reach anywhere.'

'Try!' Jack gasped. But for Rune's special boots, he'd have flagged and dropped a mile back.

'Let me fall,' Connor urged him. 'Save yourselves.'

'Keep moving,' Jack ordered. 'We all go together.'

The heartstone was pulsing fast. Mere yards behind, the thud, *thud*, thud of the pillar-rocks sliding back to the seabed was like a constant drumbeat, and over that, the roar of the rushing wave grew louder and louder.

The rocks beneath their feet began to sink. Jack felt himself stagger to one side, found his balance. On the next step the stone he was on dropped two feet and Jack's stomach lurched.

Then he was running through water. A puzzling darkness closed around him.

The wave hit.

It came with such awesome force that they were catapulted forward. Kerry screamed. Corriwen held him tight. Connor slipped from Jack's grasp and then his fingers suddenly found him again.

Everything went black.

A vast echoing sound sang in his ears. Bubbles frothed around him. Connor struggled, kicked, then seemed to go limp. They were tossed head over heels, unable to breathe. The weight of water on them felt huge. It crushed their lungs, tried to suck the air out of them.

Then he felt shingle under him. The weight of the water ground his face down into it, scraped him along, then threw him up.

Jack opened his eyes and saw nothing, nothing at all. Something crashed into him and knocked him flat on the smooth stones. Jack shook his head, groped for Connor and heaved him onto what felt like a shore. Corriwen tumbled beside him and coughed out a lungful of water and then Kerry was gasping and floundering like a landed fish.

Jack rubbed his eyes. A dim light came from somewhere high, a mere pin-point in all the darkness. He rubbed again, and very slowly his eyes began to make out shapes.

He saw black stone walls.

Fronds of seaweed draped all around them. A crab scuttled away. They were in a cave.

Jack got to his knees, staggered to his feet, clambered up the shingle. He turned to his sprawled companions.

A hand came out of the gloom and fingers clamped over his face.

TWENTY SIX

A face with staring white eyes bent over him, while cold fingers explored his features: eyes, nose, ears and mouth.

'Have I mapped this face before?' an old voice asked. 'Welcome, traveller, to Fingal's island. A fortunate swell swept you here.'

Jack turned his face up, towards a shard of light beaming through a pinhole high above. He saw that the old man's eyes were as white as marble. This old man was blind.

He took Jack's hand in his own, a surprisingly strong grip, and helped him to his feet.

'After a long forgotten time, it seems our paths have crossed.'

'Not me,' Jack stammered. The hairs on his neck were on walkabout again. 'I've never been here before.'

'And the voice is familiar. But younger. *There's* a mystery.'

'I'm Jack Flint. You must be Fingal, the one Finn told us about.'

'Fingal I am. I am the Bard of Staffa Cove. The last Bard on Eirinn.'

'A Bard!' Kerry sounded enormously encouraged by this. The only Bards he had met so far had been the good guys.

The old man turned to him and his hands searched Kerry's face.

'A good face, this. But runs with the heart and not the head, eh?' The blind eyes crinkled and Fingal chuckled, much the way Finbar had done.

'And a young lady,' he said. 'On an adventure too. There's good blood in your veins girl.'

Connor eased to his feet, trying not to slip on the wet sea wrack, his tousled tawny hair now hanging straight and wet down his back. Fingal embraced him, then, as his fingers found his contours, he paused, a thoughtful look on his face.

'The water carries you again, foundling. The Selkie women smile on you.' He turned and walked deeper into the cave, leading them to a pool of shining water.

'This is Fingal's Cove,' he said. 'It is hidden from the eyes of men. You are safe here, you and the burden you bear. The Selkie guard us well.'

He told them to sit. Here, the stones were water-smooth and dry. Very suddenly Jack felt the strength drain out of his legs and he gratefully lowered himself beside a peat fire and let its heat soak into him.

The old man fed them well. Kerry couldn't remember

ever tasting better seafood. Connor looked suspiciously at a big lobster and counted its legs, but after one taste he was converted and tore into it.

'Where does the light come from?' Kerry asked, pointing to the pool.

'At low tide, the water leads out to the sea shallows. Daylight shines through.'

'Neat,' Kerry said, with his mouth full.

'And you have tales to tell,' Fingal said. 'The sea-maids carry word of Dermott's anger and his fast ships. They say the ships foundered under Gerumbel Mountain.'

'They did, sir,' Connor said. 'Finn plugged it with a stone, and then it blew its top.' He paused, looked down. 'He did it for us and it cost him.'

'All good deeds come at a price,' Fingal said. 'Gentle Finn would know that.'

He turned to Jack and his fingers unerringly found the heartstone. He weighed it, feeling its warmth. The stone pulsed almost imperceptibly.

'So far from home, and think you lost, Jack Flint. But these friends are family to you, and dearer than any kin. What you carry, Fainn wants, though he doesn't know its power. Two burdens you bear. One is the heart of Eirinn, the other the Heart of Worlds. Neither Dermott nor Fainn must get either.'

'That's what we're trying to avoid,' Jack said. 'It's not been easy.'

'Then there are things you must hear from me. All roads come together, and there is more than one quest here.

Some truths you must find for yourself, when the time comes.'

He closed his blind eyes. 'And that time, I fear, is coming fast.'

Huddled in a plaid cloak, drawing its edges around his ancient frame, he began to speak.

'You know about the Harp of Seasons, and the Great Cauldron. The Dagda bequeathed them to Eirinn before he went to join the Sky Queen. But there was a third talisman, the Oaken Club, which makes the bearer invincible. To be sure that no man would ever wield it wrongly, he sent it to a safe place, where it has been protected since.

'Now Fainn's witchery uncovered the secret places of the Harp and the Cauldron, and the brute Dermott cut the strings. With no spring to seed crops, and no summer to ripen them, the hunger has been terrible. Those prudent kings who had stored against hard times, Fainn sent plagues of rats and mice to eat them empty. And the seaward fishers, he sent ice to lock their ships in harbour. Dermott could then set any price on what he would dole out. That price has always been utter submission.

'But Dermott is a false king. No king at all, but a usurper and a traitor.'

They all leant in closer. 'You have been to Wolfen Castle. It was once Seahold Castle where King Conovar and his wife Eleon ruled the west lands. Dermott was the Reeve of the Marches, but when he met with Fainn his ambition turned to dark ways. There had been no war for so long none could remember, but Dermott warned of predictions that the sea people would return to Eirinn. Children had been stolen from shore villages. Ships had vanished. Conovar allowed Dermott to train an army to defend the people.

'But then Conovar became ill and wasted away. None could find a cause of it, but Fainn, he's the one responsible. A heart as black as sin, that one. Queen Eleon had just given birth to their first son, only a baby. Dermott now had great power, because he led the army, and he coveted the throne. Conovar was barely cold when Dermott decided to marry the queen. But when he made his proposal she refused him utterly. Dermott was so enraged that he snatched up the baby prince by the leg and hurled him from a tower into the sea far below, saying none of Conovar's blood would take the throne. And Queen Eleon was so stricken with grief that she threw herself from the window after her baby.'

Fingal nodded. 'So nothing stood in Dermott's way and he set his flag on the castle wall and called it Wolfen Castle from then to this.'

'What a rotten sod,' Kerry said. 'Somebody should give him his come-uppance.'

'That too is written in the runes,' Fingal said. 'At the hands of a red-haired woman.'

'He believes I'm that woman,' Corriwen said.

'Old prophesy says that the usurper of Seahold Castle will meet a red-haired fighting woman in battle, and that when his fate is decided, the true heir of Eirinn's Seahold will return to claim his crown.'

'No wonder he's worried,' Jack said.

'But he needs the harp. And of course, he wants the

oaken club and would have it if he could take it, but it's well guarded.' Fingal patted Jack on the shoulder. 'So he's a very angry man.'

'Tough,' Kerry retorted. 'He's chased us all over the place and we've still got it.'

'But we've gone as far as we can,' Jack said. 'There's nowhere left to go.'

'Why not consult your Book of Ways?'

Jack started back.

'How did you know?'

Fingal laughed gently.

'I have no eyes, but I hear the whisper of the waves and the chatter of the Selkie. And I read the runes better than Fainn himself. After all, I am the Bard.'

Jack opened the book. After a few minutes he began to read aloud.

Brave the turning ocean race
Trust in fortune's tight embrace
Take to flight by cockleshell
Face the rip-tide's parlous swell.

The time is close to end of flight
Then journeyman, prepare to fight
For Eirinn and for Eirinn's plight
And turn to battle evil's might

Heroes will return and bring
The harmony that summons spring
To Tara Hill, its song re-born
And with them will a king return

'As usual,' Kerry said. 'Riddles and rhymes.'

Fingal chuckled.

'Heart, not head, Kerry Malone.'

'No. I'm just kidding. It takes a while to work it out, but it's always right.'

'So what does it mean?' Connor asked. 'We're stuck here on this island and once Dermott gets those ships off the beach, he'll hunt us down. We're stuck!'

'Don't give up,' Fingal said. 'Not when you've come this far.'

'Where can we go from here?' Corriwen asked.

'There is one place I know of. A hidden place, but not far.'

'What is this place?' Jack asked.

'The Black Island. Few go there. Fewer return.'

'What's on it?' Jack queried, focussing on what lay ahead.

'A force of great power. And a trial. Maybe an end to the quest. You must be the masters of your own destiny now.'

'Well, we came to find Corriwen,' Jack said, 'and found ourselves in the middle of all this. We stole the Harp, but the odds have been against us all the way. I'd like to change that.'

'Then I will ask the Selkie folk to help,' he said. 'Rest now. Dermott will sail with the tide, and he will not give up until you are dead, or he is. I will beseech the Sky Queen that it is the latter, of course.'

Kerry and Connor dropped to their mats and dozed off. Jack and Corriwen sat together, watching the dwindling flames. Jack couldn't sleep. Too much was going through his mind.

Fingal sat on his stone, still as a statue.

'Maybe you should stay here,' Jack said. 'It's stupid for us all to risk it.'

Corriwen laughed softly.

'Jack Flint! You should be ashamed of yourself, treating me like a helpless girl. Didn't your book speak of heroes? If you're going to be a hero, I want to be one too. And anyway, somebody has to watch your back.'

Fingal nodded. 'Heroes all, and so young. But it's not the perils of tomorrow that keep Jack Flint awake, hm? So now you must ask the question that you have been wanting to ask since I touched your face.'

For a second Jack was tongue-tied at being so easily read. But he was also scared to ask in case he was wrong.

'It's my father,' he finally said. 'That's my other quest. My real one. To find him. And you said you thought you recognised me. I just wondered if he might have come here.'

'That's the question,' Fingal said gently. 'And I will answer.'

He held his hands to the heat of the fire.

'A long time ago, so long I cannot count the years, a traveller came seeking help. He crossed Finnan Flannan's causeway and paused here to rest. It was the days when the sea people, the *Fir-Bolg* were massing in the fight for Temair, and they had already consigned the slaughtered to the bogland.'

'We met some of them.'

'Aye, their cursed souls lay long in the cold, unable to leave the tarns ... until some young heroes set them free.'

Fingal went on with his story. 'The stranger rested here, then travelled on across the water. When he returned from the Black Isle, he bore with him a great sword with a fireglass hilt and a cairngorm stone set in it.'

'The Redthorn Sword,' Corriwen said. 'Cullian's sword.'

'Was that his name? Maybe. It was so long ago, the mists of time shroud my memory. But this travelling man came back stronger and ready for battle and he crossed to Flannan's point to take his skills to the Dagda King and win the battle. And after that came peace in Eirinn from then until now.'

'And you thought I was him?' Jack said.

'My hands remember what my old mind forgets. But he was older, and taller, though he spoke in the same voice.'

'My father,' Jack said. 'It *must* be him. I'm trying to find him. Can you help me?'

'All I can do is help you on your way. And it is the same way he took. The only one who can help you in that endeavour is the Sky Queen. Maybe, at the end of your quest, you might ask her a favour. She listens to those who would do her will.'

'I'm not doing anybody's will,' Jack said. 'This whole thing has been dumped on us. We just have to get the Harp to a safe place so we can get home.'

'Ah, Jack, I think you know better than that,' Fingal said softly. 'Many do the Sky Queen's work, and she chooses well. This is not your choice, but hers. All is destiny, and destiny must be fulfilled.'

'Easier said than done.'

'A wise man would tell you that nobody said it would be easy.'

'A wise man already did. He was a bard, too.'

Fingal woke them while it was still dark.

'Up with the tide,' he said. While they slept, he had made up a pack of food and stuffed it in Kerry's backpack. 'It's near the low ebb.'

Jack looked at the pool in the centre of the cave. The water had dropped ten feet or more and it gurgled and whirled as the tide sucked it down and then let it rise again. On the far side, a little round basket bobbed on its surface.

'What's that?' Kerry asked suspiciously.

'It's a coracle,' Fingal said, laughing. 'You might call it a cockleshell.'

'Are you kidding me?' Kerry spluttered. 'Look at it. I'm not getting into that thing. No way. Not in a million years.'

'It's the only way,' Fingal said. 'Unless you want to try going back the way you came.'

'Come on,' Jack urged him. 'It'll float.'

'It'll sink,' Kerry snorted. 'I'll drown.'

'I promised you a long time ago, in another time and place that I'd never let you drown,' Jack said, though even he looked askance at the little craft.

When they'd finally persuaded Kerry to get aboard, they were crammed together like nestlings. Kerry was pale and getting paler by the minute as the water rose and fell.

'The seventh wave at tide's low ebb,' Fingal said. 'There's magic to my back door.'

They were raised and dropped and Jack started counting. The water frothed and swirled. Four waves, five. The sixth took them very low and Jack's stomach did a nauseous flip. It rose, higher and higher until they were almost at the pool's edge and then, very suddenly they were dropping.

There was a huge sucking sound and the coracle plunged down and down and down. All Jack saw was rock and seaweed and a couple of big green crabs that held tight to the walls. His stomach lurched. Kerry yelled in alarm. Jack's ears popped.

Then they were out of darkness and in open water beside a jagged rocky face.

TWENTY SEVEN

A strong wind and stronger current carried them away from Fingal's cove. The island seemed to drift past them like a great ship as they bobbed along, surprisingly quickly. The little coracle sat high in the water, just a basket of reeds and sealskin. Kerry's knuckles were tight on the rim.

'This is pure suicide,' he muttered. 'Why can't we pick a better world? Where people are nice.'

'Like back home with mad Billy Robbins?'

'Like somewhere warm, with good fishing. And burgers and beans.'

Jack managed a laugh.

'What's burgers?' Connor asked, and this time Kerry forgot his terror and burst into a fit of the giggles until he started to make the coracle spin and his knuckles went white again.

Jack closed his eyes and he thought of what Fingal had told him about the travelling man and the sword. It *must* have been his father, here on some quest long, long ago.

Journeyman, Jack thought. *He can travel between worlds.* Which one he had finally gone to, Jack was determined to find out, even if he had to die trying, once this was all over. *If* it was over.

Corriwen's cry jerked him out of his thoughts.

They were well out at sea now, Fingal's island a smudge on the horizon. Corriwen was pointing astern.

Four black ships were tacking towards them, sails billowing tight.

'Fingal was right,' Connor said. 'Not all their ships were wrecked.'

Jack turned to look ahead. There was no sign of anything at all except a distant bank of sea-fog, and they had no sail to speed them along. His fingers found the heartstone and he felt its smooth contours as it beat softly with its own life. He opened Brand's bag and looked again at the golden harp. Such a small thing to be such a powerful talisman. The strings hung uselessly.

Jack glanced back to see the four ships had gained on them, and he wondered whether to throw the bag overboard. That way neither Dermott nor Fainn could get their hands on it.

But then again, he thought, that was not a choice. His only choice was to find a way through this and get home to begin his own quest.

'We could really use an outboard,' Kerry said. 'A big forty horsepower beast. That would give them a surprise.

'Is that some kind of spell?' Connor asked. 'You'd be as well asking the Kelpies for a tow.'

'I wish the Undines were here to help,' Corriwen said.

'What's that?' Kerry asked, looking dead ahead.

Jack held his shoulders to risk standing up, waiting until they had reached the crest of the next big wave to try to get a glimpse of what lay ahead.

'Just brace yourself. It's going to get a bit rough.'

'Jack,' Kerry cried. 'Don't you let me . . .' His jaw dropped as the little cockleshell spun as it rose up a foaming wave and he saw what lay ahead. 'Oh *freak*!'

That was all he managed before a great maw opened up to swallow them.

A whirlpool had sucked them in. A vast hole in the middle of the sea, whirling like a black summer storm on Temair.

Beneath them was a corkscrew hole that seemed to drill right down into the bed of the sea.

Connor let out a wail of fright as he began to slip over the side. Corriwen grasped him by his shirt and hauled him back, but the motion turned the coracle round in a complete circle, throwing them against its lip with centripetal force. It slammed down against the vertical wall, bounced hard and Kerry was thrown right over.

There was a brief cry and then Kerry was gone. He went straight into the side of the maelstrom. Jack saw him alongside them for a second and then the boat was spun away. Kerry's pale face sank into the deep green.

'No . . .' Jack's yell was smothered under the roar.

'Where is he?' Corriwen gasped, face ashen.

'Gone.' Jack moaned. 'He's . . . *gone.*'

Don't you let me drown! Oh, he had heard that before. Too often. It was as if Kerry had somehow had a premonition of what was to come.

The boat bobbed, tilted again, throwing them from side to side.

Then a shape appeared in the deep green. Something moved so fast it was barely discernible. It came speeding in from the side, angling up and through the whirling water-wall above them.

For an instant Jack thought it was a big fish, something that hunted in the maelstrom. Instinctively he ducked.

But it sailed right over him. All he saw was a lithe body sparkling in its own spray of droplets, and silken tresses of green hair that trailed behind it like a veil. A crecent tail thrashed powerfully, sending it soaring in an arc right across the whirlpool, from one side to the other. Its head turned and Jack saw big, lustrous eyes fix on his.

Undine, he thought.

The creature had a half smile on her face. A slender arm dragged something behind it, hauling it through the glassy wall. She continued on over the void and disappeared back into the water again.

And the bundle she had dragged with her tumbled to land, coughing, spluttering and cursing incoherently in their midst.

Kerry belched a gout of salt water. He opened his eyes

and saw Jack and Corriwen staring down at him in utter amazement.

'I told you not to let me drown!' he bawled. 'Didn't I tell you?'

'It was a Selkie,' Connor said, astonished. 'Fingal said they'd help us. I never saw anything as beautiful in all my life.

'Look,' he cried. 'There's more of them.'

They swam together in a swirling race, graceful as dolphins, beautiful and lithe. Luminous eyes gazed inquisitively at the four in the boat. Jack could see kindness in them.

'That was a miracle,' Kerry gasped. 'I really thought I'd had it.'

'So did we,' Corriwen said. She grabbed him in both arms and hugged tight. Then she raised her hand and rapped her knuckles hard on Kerry's skull.

'Don't you ever do that to me again,' she said.

'I'll do my best,' Kerry said. 'Honest. Cross my heart and hope to die.' He let out a huge breath. 'Or not.'

The current whipped them along, but behind them the four ships had tacked again in the cross current and came closer still.

'They'll catch us for sure,' Connor said.

'Oh, don't be such a pessimist,' Kerry said, pretending to scold. But his eyes too were fixed on the dark sails.

At that moment the tail-wind dropped. Immediately the sails went slack and the ships faltered on the edge of the maelstrom. Moments later, three boats were sucked under and disappeared in a crash of timbers. The fourth veered away at the last second and disappeared from view as the current carried the coracle into the white bank of sea-fog.

They drifted in a silken silence through a damp twilight, huddled together for warmth. Some time later, Corriwen shook Jack from a troubled sleep.

'I hear a ship,' she whispered. She was shivering from the cold and Jack pulled her close.

Out there, he heard a loud creak, more like a groan than a creak, and recognised it as straining timber, then dim lights of tallow torches glowed through the fog.

They crouched low as the lights came nearer. A man's voice called out and somebody replied. Connor awoke with a start and Jack whispered him to hush. Kerry snored, head back and Corriwen pinched his nose until he jerked awake, hand already reaching for his sword.

'Damn this fog,' Dermott's voice bellowed. 'Can't you do something about it?'

'I have tried, my Lord,' Fainn replied. 'But some power keeps it in place. But they are here. I can smell them.'

'Well, keep on sniffing, Spellbinder. We'll quarter the sea until we find them. Come on swabs, get grappling. We'll get them by hook and crook.'

The ship approached and the lights brightened, haloed in mist, and a shape loomed next to them. Something flew over their heads and splashed in the water some yards away.

'Grappling iron,' Kerry whispered.

The rope tightened and cut through the water towards them. The coracle spun as the ship's bow wave pushed them aside and then the three-pronged hook came surging up out of the water and disappeared from view.

The hulk slid past them. Dermott bellowed again as the ship vanished into the mist. The creaking of timbers grew fainter with every minute, until they were alone again, and the long night passed, slow and cold, until finally the dawn came, turning the sky from black to grey.

Somewhere in the distance, Jack heard a murmur and as they drifted closer, it became a deep regular pounding.

'Surf,' he said. 'We're getting close to something.'

'I hope it's a nice sandy beach,' Kerry said. They heard rollers swell somewhere in the fog as they were swept towards it. Big waves were rising and breaking, just out of sight.

Jack knelt up on what had become the prow, just because it was facing the way they travelled, peering out into the fuzzy gloom.

'I don't think it sounds like a beach,' he said.

'Oh don't you start the pessimism stuff,' Kerry said. 'Try to look on the bright side.'

'Okay,' Jack said. Perhaps their luck had changed.

He turned back to see what they were heading for.

And a vast black cliff suddenly loomed out of the fog as the waves drove them straight for the broken rocks at its base.

TWENTY EIGHT

'Looks a bit rough,' Kerry said. 'In fact, it looks awfully rough.'

'See if you can find somewhere to beach this thing,' Connor said.

'Beach? It's a freakin' great cliff, man.'

Jack counted the waves. Every seventh would be much higher than the rest.

'It's forcing us in and there's no way to steer. We have to get ready to jump.'

Jack flipped open his pack and drew out their two coils of rope. He handed one to Kerry and fixed the end round Corriwen's waist. The second he fixed to Connor and cinched it around his own chest.

'When we get close,' he told Kerry, 'we go first. We can make it.'

'Oh, don't be such an optimist,' Kerry said, ashen-faced, eyes unable to look away from the pounding water. Jack secured their weapons and Brand's bag so they wouldn't slip.

The seventh wave was immense. It picked them up and surfed them right in towards the cliff. The coracle smashed against a knife-edged rock which ripped a gash in the thin hull. Water flooded in.

Jack steadied himself. He clapped Kerry on the shoulder. 'It's up to you,' he cried. 'Don't you let her fall.'

Kerry turned away from the water and looked Jack in the eye. The challenge was enough to make himself forget his own fear. Jack saw it.

'I won't,' he said. His jaw set and he gritted his teeth.

'Now!'

They leapt. Jack hit the rock with hands and feet. His fingers found a minute crevice and his toes, in Rune's boots, found some friction. Kerry thudded beside him.

'Onwards and upwards,' Jack urged, and together they began to climb until the ropes tightened behind them. Jack risked a look up. Despite the mist, he could make out a narrow ledge.

'If we get there, we'll be okay,' he said, with more optimism than he felt.

It took them five minutes, but finally they hauled up and got their feet on flat rock. A few yards along, the ledge widened, enough to give them space to brace themselves and then they started dragging the ropes, hand over hand, until the sweat of exertion began to drip from their chins. It seemed to take forever, but finally they had Connor and

Corriwen up beside them and they sagged on to the ledge, breathing hard.

'How high does this go?' Connor asked. The sheer face vanished in mist. It could tower for miles, Jack thought. Below them, now out of sight, the waves hammered against the rocks and over that, a deep hollow sound boomed like a great heart.

'There's a cave below us somewhere.'

'You think we should try for it?' Kerry asked.

'Too risky. We'd have to clamber down and it could turn out to be a dead end, then we'd have to risk the waves again.'

'I'd rather not,' Kerry said. 'We'll have to climb.' He got to his feet and faced the cliff wall. To his right, the ledge widened out even further and he eased himself along it. Then he vanished from view round a jutting point. Two seconds later, he came back.

'There's some sort of crack here. Like a gully. It looks a bit easier.'

Still roped together, they shuffled along the ledge and found the crevice sloping, steep but not as sheer as the cliff itself. They began to climb, and after a hundred feet or more, they found a set of steps cut into the bare rock, steps so worn by time and weather that they were almost eroded flat. Jack was in the lead, with Connor roped behind when he stopped abruptly and Connor bumped into him.

A hollow boom shuddered the rock under their feet, low and loud, like a distant drum. A blast of cold damp air thickened the mist and then seemed to suck it away from them.

The boom echoed from the walls. The mist sucked away

again and they saw a huge round hole in the ground. Jack had almost walked into it.

'It goes down to the sea,' Jack said when he got his breath back. 'That's what's making the sound. The waves push the air up, then draw it back down again.'

They gingerly skirted the gaping hole, and pushed on into the mist when Kerry let out a sudden yelp as a great beast loomed out of the fog, eyes glaring, its gaping mouth studded with curved teeth. Kerry's sword was suddenly in his hand as he shoved Jack further back.

The thing glared at them. But it didn't move.

Kerry backed away, sword ready. Then he stopped, took a couple of wary steps forward.

'I don't believe it,' he said. 'It's a Viking boat.'

'How on earth did it get here,' Jack asked, when his heart slowed a little.

'High tide?'

'If it gets this high, we're really in trouble.'

They gathered around the ferocious prow. The head was as big as Kerry was tall, and the mouth a full yard wide, silently snarling at them. Horns like scythes curved forward, expertly carved in hard black wood. It looked like some kind of guardian.

They edged past its sleek sides and clambered over ropes which held it fast against the rock. Round shields hung along the gunwales, and a long mast lay prone along its deck, wrapped in a heavy canvas sail.

'It didn't float here,' Corriwen said. 'People must have dragged it this far.'

'Would have taken hundreds of them.'

'So we should be very quiet. They could be anywhere.'

In total silence they edged along the narrow path until they suddenly came out of the mist. It lay below them, like a flat white sea. Above them, a line of peaks soared into the sky. The track flattened out and they found themselves approaching two tall stone pillars, one on either side. Lines and characters, so worn they were hard to make out, covered their facing sides.

'Wonder what that says,' Connor said.

'*Trespass no further, stranger,*' Kerry said. 'On the left, that's what it says.'

Kerry's ability to understand the Book of Ways had astonished Jack in Temair, because all through school his dyslexia made reading so difficult.

'And on the right it says: *Proceed and Prepare for Battle.*

'I'm too tired to fight,' Connor said. 'I could sleep for a month and then have forty winks.'

They warily passed the pillars, walking slowly until they came to a wide fissure which cut across the path. It looked as if a whole section of rock had just slipped and dropped away. The gap was twenty feet across or more. They looked down into darkness.

'We can't go back,' Corriwen said. 'We'll have to cross.'

'Sure,' Connor said. 'I'll just hop over.'

'We could climb round the edge,' Jack suggested.

'No handholds,' Kerry replied. He turned to Jack. 'You think you could make it?'

Jack estimated the distance, then nodded.

'I wouldn't have had a hope before, but with these boots, it'll be a doddle.'

Jack unhitched the rope from Connor. Kerry did the same with Corriwen and explained the plan to them. Jack went first, taking a short run, timing his steps and then leapt. For a second his heart lurched as he looked into the chasm below, and then his feet were on solid ground again. Kerry landed beside him.

Corriwen cinched the rope on the far side, tied herself on and then, hand over hand, came swinging across, while Kerry held tight to the safety rope, just in case. When she got to their side, Jack found that he'd been holding his breath the whole time.

Connor came next, slower than Corriwen, and when he neared the edge, Kerry waited to haul him up.

Relieved, Jack turned to pick up his pack.

The heartstone kicked hard.

And a gargoyle of a creature leapt at them, so fast all they saw was a flicker of motion and a flash of red. Something whickered in the air. Jack caught a gleam of metal, inches from his neck and next thing he knew he was twenty feet away on a high slab of rock.

Corriwen's knives seemed to leap into her hands as she ducked under a blade as long as a man.

Kerry somersaulted over the blade as it swung round to cut him off at the knees.

The creature leapt aside and disappeared as fast as it had attacked.

Jack jumped down and the three of them stood, scanning the clefts and walls above them.

'What was it?' Kerry asked, 'It looked like a monster.'

Jack shook his head, searching all round.

Then it was back again, appearing as if from nowhere.

Connor was just getting to his feet. He loosened the rope at his waist and let it drop.

The demonic creature was on him in an instant. Jack saw his arms windmill as he fought for balance and then he toppled off the edge. The rope caught around his ankle and hissed as it was dragged over the rim.

The thing swung at Jack. He was up and over the singing blade before he knew it and then he was on the ground again. The rope was snaking away from him as Connor fell and he frantically grabbed at it.

Over the edge, Connor's wail of fright echoed from the sheer walls.

The rope skidded through Jack's hands, burning like hot metal. He braced his feet hard against a rock.

Then his arms nearly popped out of their sockets when Connor reached the end of the rope and jerked to a sudden stop. A high screech tore the air as the rope tightened on Connor's injured ankle and his weight hit the end of the drop. The sudden strain almost pulled Jack over the edge. He grunted in pain and effort, using every ounce of strength and will to stop that from happening.

The gargoyle went for Kerry. It's blade came swinging for him and Kerry's sword shattered into a dozen pieces. It slammed him into the air and he hit the rock face with a sickening thud and slid down in a heap.

Corriwen shrieked like a banshee and darted in, both knives flashing. Metal clanged on metal. Corriwen's knives flicked out of her hands and clattered to the ground. The gargoyle leapt and she rolled as its sword sliced and almost took her head off.

It whirled and came for Jack.

He was still heaving on the rope, gasping for breath. Every time Connor swung out, the strain and the pain in his arms was enormous. One of Corriwen's knives had landed at his feet and he eyed it, gauging the distance and the possibility of snatching it with one hand.

But with Connor's life depending on his two-handed grip on the rope, he couldn't risk it.

The gargoyle flashed towards him, sword whirring like a propeller. Jack was helpless. If he defended himself, Connor would fall to his death.

It glared at him, eyes shadowed by scaly skin, jutting teeth like needles, and scything horns ready to slice flesh.

Jack stared it in the eye.

'Fight me.' A harsh command.

Jack shook his head.

'Fight me, or die where you stand.'

It slashed. Jack swung back, slipped and felt Connor drop a couple of feet. The blade hit the rock an inch from his head and bright sparks burned the skin around his eyes. He held tight to the rope, managed to get to one knee then both feet. He hauled on the rope and managed to raise Connor a little higher.

'Kill me if you like,' he gasped. 'But he's my friend and I'm not letting him drop.'

'Fight me,' the thing roared. 'You trespass! All must fight!'

'If you kill me, then you kill him as well. And he's

crippled. Let me bring him up and then I'll fight you. But not before.'

It stalked towards him, hideous face glaring, sword gleaming and deadly.

Jack kept staring back and slowly began to haul Connor up. He didn't flinch, didn't blink.

It paused. 'You would die for him?'

Jack nodded. His throat was suddenly so dry he couldn't have spoken a word.

'If I have to. But I won't let him fall.'

Very slowly, the sword lowered until its point touched the ground.

Corriwen had regained her feet and was moving towards her knife. The creature held up a hand to her without turning round, even though Corriwen hadn't made a sound.

'Stay,' it said.

Jack grunted again and raised Connor a bit more.

'Fool,' the thing said.

'Maybe. But he's a friend of mine.'

It stood stock still. Jack risked squatting to get more leverage on the rope. As he bent, the heartstone slipped out of his tunic and dangled in the air.

The creature drew a sharp breath.

'You wear his . . . the talisman.'

It backed off two paces and stood still as a statue, still glaring. Then, puzzlingly, it sheathed its sword, raised both hands to its ogre face and lifted it. Jack saw now it was a mask hinged at the top. It swung open and red hair spilled out in long snaking braids. A pair of startling blue eyes stared at him as it dropped the demon-mask.

A tall, striking woman gazed at him.

'So much time gone by,' she said. 'And now this.'

Jack thought he saw her eyes glaze slightly.

'And you bear his courage in you.'

This time Jack's heart kicked against his ribs.

She changed her stance, bent towards him and the blue eyes speared his, catching the light and twinkling like stars.

To Jack she looked like some kind of fierce goddess.

He kept his eyes on her as he braced Connor's weight.

'I'm Jack,' he ventured. 'Jack Flint.'

'I know you, Jack Flint. It gladdens my heart to see you here. And it rends my heart in two.'

She held his eyes with hers as she bent to take the trail of rope.

'But you and I, we shall never fight again.'

TWENTY NINE

The warrior woman raised one arm with such power that Connor came swinging right over the edge of the abyss and landed with a groan. He rolled, untangled his leg from the rope, and gingerly got to his feet, face creased in pain.

He saw the red-haired woman for the first time.

'Thanks,' he mumbled.

'Thank your friend,' she said. 'He saved your life, more than once.'

'I got lucky,' Jack said. 'I was nearest to the rope.'

'Well, but for you I'd still be falling,' Connor said. ' That hole goes down a long way.'

He took a tentative step, more a limp than a step, and his joints creaked alarmingly. Then looked again at Jack.

'Have you shrunk?'

Jack stared back in amazement. 'You've grown!'

They both looked down at Connor's bad leg. It was completely straight, and it was the same length as the other one.

'It's a miracle,' Connor said. He raised his leg a few times, checking to see if it was real.

He turned to Corriwen, who was helping Kerry to his feet.

'I thought I was dead for sure, and when I reached the end of the rope, I thought it would pull my leg off. But it's gone and straightened me out. Look at me!'

He took another step, a painful one, but as he did, a smile lit his face. His tangled mat of hair had been smoothed by the seawater and he looked completely different from the crippled ragamuffin Corriwen had rescued in the forest. The gold torc on his neck gave him an oddly noble look.

'Your friend's gallantry saved you all,' the woman said. 'Him you thank for your welcome on my island.'

She bent towards Jack and clasped him on the shoulders with both hands, leaned forward and fixed him with those startling eyes. For the first time he noticed she was bristling with weapons of all kinds, in sheaths and quivers all over a scaled tunic.

'Your heart is straight and true. I am Hedda. They call me The Scatha, which means warrior-woman. You and yours are welcome ever to my home.'

She led them along a winding path so narrow they had to walk in single file.

Wherever they were going, Jack thought, the place was impregnable. The only way to get here was by leaping over the crevasse, and only Rune's boots had enabled Jack and Kerry to risk it with any confidence. The twists and turns in the path cut in the rock would have made this place impossible to attack. One person could hold off an army, and he had no doubt that this fierce, handsome woman would have no difficulty in doing just that.

They followed behind her until the path stopped abruptly at a cliff wall that soared above them towards the clouds. Whorls and patterns, very similar to the tattoos that adorned Hedda, were carved in the face. She touched one of the carvings and a stone door opened inwards. She ushered them into a cavernous room lit by torches and heated by a roaring fire. Somewhere in the distance, a low, regular booming shivered up through the stone floor.

They stood, all four of them gawping at the array of weapons studding every inch of the walls; daggers, spears, bows, harpoons, swords of all shapes and some weapons Jack had never seen before, even in books.

All except one great sword which caught his complete attention. None of his friends saw him go still as stone.

Their eyes were fixed above the row of shields which formed a continuous frieze.

Hundreds of skulls were pinned to the walls, crowding right up to the ceiling, strange white skulls with dagger-like teeth and weird bony crests.

'The Fir Bolg,' Hedda said. 'The sea people of old who made war on men in Eirinn. They sacrificed a thousand good men to their demons and put their bodies in the bogs where their souls lie cold and restless. In one day, I took two heads for every one they slaughtered. And then we went to war on them and drove them back into the sea. A few escaped to the mountains and became the fell runners.'

'We came across them in the hills,' Connor said. 'Ugly things. All ribs and teeth.'

The woman looked at him then cocked her head as she scanned his face, inspecting him closely. He'd tied his hair into two braids to keep it out of his eyes. Jack thought he looked like a young Viking chief.

Without warning, her hand shot out and Connor flinched, but not quickly enough. Her fingers snatched the tattered tunic and pulled him towards her, hauling him up on tip-toe. Her free hand raised the brass pin-brooch that held the rag in place.

'Where did you find this?' she asked.

'Always had it,' he replied. 'Since I was little. It was my mam's. It's mine now since she's dead.'

'Your mother.' She held him close. 'What was her name?'

'Don't know. Nobody knew. She died of cold and drowning. But my Ma and Da, my foster parents, say she pinned me on her shoulder with this so I wouldn't drown. All they got out of her was my name, before she breathed her last.'

Hedda slowly unclasped her fingers and let Connor sag back.

'Omens,' she said, almost a whisper. 'We are at a crossing of the ways. Strange things indeed come to pass.'

'You're not kidding,' Kerry muttered. 'And all I wanted was a quiet life.'

Jack elbowed his ribs. The great sword on the wall had sent a tremor through him. He sensed something important was happening. He too felt as if he was at some sort of crossroads now, about to take a step that would change his life. It seemed she had plucked the thought right out of his mind.

'Runes don't lie,' she said softly. She beckoned them across the room to a massive table beside the fire.

'Sit. We will eat, tell each other tales of the past and consider what is to come.'

She tugged a cord on the wall and sat down on a carved chair, then poured out five goblets of amber liquid and passed them round. The first sip was heady and sweet, and Jack felt its warmth creep inside him, heating him to the core.

He closed his eyes, letting the exhaustion of their climb drain away when a huge hand clapped him on the shoulder. He opened his eyes and saw a big face smiling down at him. For an instant he thought it was Finn McCuill, until he realised it was another woman, and one almost as tall as the giant who had forced up the causeway and sacrificed himself so they could escape.

'Eat first,' she boomed. She ruffled his hair with a meaty hand and Jack thought his head was going to spin off. 'You can sleep later.'

He glanced at the table and realised he must have dozed off for several minutes, for it was laden with platters of food in such quantity that it looked like a king's banquet. Kerry and Connor were stuffing themselves. As soon as the smell of hot food hit him, Jack realised he was absolutely famished.

The giantess sat herself down on a bench at the far end of the table and helped herself to a side of crisp bacon which she ate heartily with her huge fingers, and quaffed from a bucket as if it was a delicate tumbler.

'This is Fennel,' Hedda said. 'My armourer.'

The giantess chuckled. The walls seemed to shiver. 'Armourer, cook. Housekeeper. Sweeper-up-afterwards. A woman's work is never done.'

'But the best armourer in all of Eirinn. I suspect we will need all of her skill.'

'How do you mean?' Jack asked.

'Because if you are here, as the runes foretold, a battle looms.'

'Not again,' Kerry mumbled through a mouthful of food. 'Can't a guy get a break?'

'Men rarely challenge me,' Hedda said. 'Most quail at the crevasse leap. Some brave it. Most die. That is the way of the Scatha. Who fights and lives for one hour, whose hearts are good, I welcome and teach, as I will teach you.

She clapped Kerry on the shoulder. 'As they say in Eirinn, our songs may be sad, but all our fights are happy. There has been little song in Eirinn these past years, and now it is time to fight.

'Fingal's runes told me that four would come. Two travellers and a lord and a lady, come to me to aid Eirinn.'

'Well,' Kerry said. 'They got it half right. This is Lady Corriwen Redthorn, of Temair.'

Connor turned to Jack. 'I never knew you were a lord.'

'I'm not,' Jack said.

Hedda rapped her knuckles softly on the table, enough to command silence.

'Listen to my story,' she said. She closed her eyes for a moment, as if gathering her thoughts, then she spoke again.

'Men come here to challenge the Scatha, to gain honour or knowledge. Always the kings of the Westlands met me across the crevasse and were strong and brave enough to live the hour, and I taught them the ways of battle, for they were ever good and fair.

'So I taught Conovar, though he had known peace for a long time. Rarely do I leave this island, but for his crowning I travelled and met his Queen Eleon. And I met Dermott and the false Fainn. Then Conovar took deathly ill, after his son was born and Dermott wrested the throne from Eleon, who threw herself into the sea when Dermott in his rage took the infant by the leg and cast him out.'

Hedda bent to Connor and unclasped the brass pin-brooch. She held it up for them to see, small and round, with five little stars cut into its face.

'The Corona,' Jack whispered.

'Aye,' Hedda said. 'The Sky Crown. And the last time I saw this, it held not rags together, but a cloak of the finest linen.'

Connor listened, agog.

'For this belonged to Eleon, Queen of the Westlands, who leapt from the keep to save her baby son. And save him she did, I think, though she sacrificed her own life in doing so.'

She pinned the brooch back on Connor's shabby tunic.

'When you came up from the chasm, I saw Conovar's face in you. You are your father's son. And the blood of the Dagda, the high king, runs in your veins.'

'Me? A king?' Connor's mouth opened and closed, like a landed haddock. 'No. I can't be. Cripples can't be kings. It's the law.'

Hedda laughed.

'Cripple no more. Whatever damage Dermott did to that infant boy, it has been righted again. An omen of things to come.'

'Wait a minute,' Jack said. 'Remember what the book said? It's all come true.'

He rummaged in his pack and drew the book out again. Once more it flicked itself open and whirred to the page they had read before.

Brave the turning ocean race
Trust in fortune's tight embrace
Take to flight by cockleshell
Face the rip-tide's parlous swell.

The time is close to end of flight
Then journeyman, prepare to fight
For Eirinn and for Eirinn's plight
And turn to battle evil's might

Heroes will return and bring
The harmony that summons spring
To Tara Hill, its song re-born
And with them will a king return

'It told us about the king. And we braved the turning ocean race. And we went by cockleshell, didn't we? So, it *has* to be true.'

'No,' Connor said. 'I'm the least kingly king you ever met. I never had a sword or a crown. And I never rode a horse until Corriwen showed me how. And I've been in rags all my days and a poacher to boot.'

'Those days are done,' Hedda said. 'And the rest of your Rune-book will come to pass. The flight is over and we will prepare to fight. And the harmony? Let me see what you carry.'

Jack reached under the big table and raised Brand's bag. He sat it in front of them, reached inside, and drew out the beautiful golden harp.

'I think this might be what it means.'

It had been a long day and Kerry snored like a tractor on the straw mattress. The giant had draped big woollen blankets over them. Corriwen's red hair gleamed in the faint torchlight. Connor had curled himself into a ball, the way he did when sleeping in the open. He had fallen asleep still protesting that he couldn't possibly be a king, but agreeing that having a horse one day might be a good thing.

Jack couldn't sleep. His mind was in turmoil, and not only because of the sword on Hedda's wall. He had been too stunned then to speak. Now his friends were asleep, this was the time to find Hedda and speak to her about the sword and what she said on the brink of the abyss.

He could wait no longer.

He threw the blanket aside and got up, almost quivering with excitement, slipped out of the chamber and down the passage to the great room.

The fire cast a rosy glow on the weaponry, all of it polished and gleaming as if ready for instant use. Slowly he approached the wall and stood before the Redthorn Sword. He had last seen it riven through Mandrake as they ran for the Homeward Gate, pursued by the monstrous Morrigan.

His hand reached of its own volition, and grasped the hilt. He drew it down from the wall, turned it point-up. It seemed to sing in his hand, as if it were part of him, pulsing with his own heartbeat.

'Made for a man such as you.' Her voice came from behind him.

Jack had somehow known she would be there. He didn't even flinch.

'I knew you would come back,' Hedda said softly. 'The sword called to you.'

They sat together by the warmth of the fire. The light made the whorls and spirals of her tattoos seem to spin and dance on her face and her long red braids coiled about her shoulders.

'I need to know about my father,' Jack said. 'You knew him.'

She nodded. 'A long time ago. But the memory is fresh as a new rose. I met the traveller. Jonathan.'

'Jonathan Cullian Flint.' He held up the penknife the Major had given him. The letters JCF were carved into the bone handle.

She nodded. 'I named him Cullian, as I name all who live the hour by the abyss. In my old tongue, it means Fair Champion. And he was the champion of all worlds. I forged two swords, one he carried, and one you now bear. Swords of great power, made in the heat below these mountains, hilted in faery-glass.'

Hedda bent her head and when she raised it, her eyes were glazed again.

'He was the only man I ever loved, and I know he loved me in his way. As a true friend. But his heart was snared by another and I knew I would not win him. Instead I taught him and together we fought the Fir Bolg and sent them back to the sea. A good and just fight it was and Jonathan Cullian, he saved Eirinn for men.'

She smiled sadly. 'He came back to me at the end.' She got to her feet and crossed to the wall where one blank space showed old stone. Again she touched a carving on the surface and a secret door opened. She reached into darkness and drew something out, then brought it to the fireside for Jack to see.

'The Oaken Club,' she said. 'The third of the Dagda's gifts when he became immortal and went with the Sky Queen.'

It was a massive thing, and hideous too, polished to a gleaming lustre. Solid oak, carved into a skull head, like an ornate mace, with gaping sockets and ferocious teeth. Big spikes studded the skull's head.

'Carved from the first oak,' she said, 'in the far days when the trees could talk. Whoever bears this fears no harm and loses no battle. Jonathan Cullian brought me this for safekeeping, away from the dreams of ambitious men, to hold until such times as Eirinn's need of it returned. As it has now, I believe.'

She placed it on the table where the sockets glared up at Jack.

'Fainn has the Cauldron. You have brought the Harp, but its song is silenced. I must dwell on that.'

Jack was worried that the conversation had taken the wrong direction.

'My father,' he urged her. 'I have been trying to find him.'

'Then your road will be long and hard. You bear the firestone heart, which means he cannot. When he left, it was to go back to the woman who had won his love. Where he went, I cannot say.'

'Can't, or won't?'

'Cannot,' she repeated. 'The Journeyman goes where he is called and will not return until the quest is done. How did you come by the heartstone?'

Jack told her what had happened on the night they had stumbled through the gate in the ring of stones and found themselves in Temair.

'But the Major told me it had been my father's. I think I was brought through the gates as a baby. I had nightmares that things were chasing me and I was being carried. I think they might be memories.'

She nodded, considering this.

'Jonathan Cullian would never have given up the heartstone unless he had to. For your safety or its safeguarding. That can only mean he travelled without it. And now you are the journeyman.'

'But if he is still alive, how can I find him?'

'That I don't know either. You must ask the Sky Queen for help. She will look kindly on one who has risked all for Eirinn.'

Another thought struck Jack right at that moment.

'You said he was in love with someone. Did you know her?'

'I knew *of* her. And that he was the only one for her.'

'Do you think that would have been my mother?'

'Ah, Jack,' she sighed. 'I believe it could have been none other.'

'So what now?'

'We finish the quest and end this sadness in Eirinn. We gird for war.'

They spent a week on the island with Hedda and very skilfully she taught them the secrets of warfare. For Jack it was both amazing and frustrating. He had learned more about his father than he had ever known, and the more he knew, the more he admired a man he had never met.

Yet while emotionally he felt closer to the man known as Jonathan Cullian Flint, his father was still remote. He had vanished as if he had never been, and all Hedda could tell Jack was that he had fallen in love with a woman who must be his mother.

How Jack had come to end up with the Major in the old peninsula house was still a mystery. Where Jonathan Flint had vanished to, nobody had a clue. And his mother? She too was a puzzle yet to be solved.

Were they alive? Were they dead? So far nobody had been able to tell him.

But he was determined to find out, one way or another, even if he had to travel through every gate in the Cromwath Blackwood ring of stones until he found an answer.

Hedda had taken him aside.

'Are you afraid, Journeyman?' she had asked.

'Of course I am,' he said seriously. 'I'm not even fifteen yet.'

'But you have a stout heart and a fine sword. The cause is good. Better to fight the good fight and win your way to TirNanOg.'

'If it's all the same to you, I'd rather not get there any time soon,' Jack said, managing a smile. 'I really want to find my father.'

The broken harp stood between them, its golden surface glittering in the glow of the fire.

'I have been thinking on this,' she said. 'It has lost its harmony and spring fails in Eirinn. 'It must be re-strung.'

'I've got fishing line,' Kerry said. He dug in his pack and brought out a spool of nylon.

Hedda agreed that it might work and he used Corriwen's Swiss Army knife to cut lengths a yard long. He seemed to know what he was doing and quickly tightened up a whole line of strings before he turned to Hedda.

'This is a bit thick for the high notes. Have you anything finer?'

She smiled at him and began to unwind one of her long braids, then cut out a hank of fiery hair. Kerry twisted two or three together to make a fine cord and got to work again. When he had finished the harp looked as if it was playable at least.

Corriwen's nimble fingers turned the keys as she plucked the strings until she thought the harp was in tune. She stroked the strings from top to bottom.

As soon as she did, the heartstone vibrated keenly on its setting. Jack felt it flutter against his chest as if a little jolt of electricity had pulsed through it. In his head, he thought he heard a pure crystalline sound.

The others were intent on the harp, listening to the faint notes fading away.

Hedda said. 'Its power is gone.'

But right at the centre of his brain, Jack could hear whispering words. He cocked his head, eyes fixed on the middle distance. Corriwen ran her fingers down the strings again, harder this time. The faint chord sang out.

Jack heard the sound matched by the heartstone, and underneath that sound, a clear voice.

Take me home to Tara hill
Let me sing to end the ill
End the winter, start the spring
Take me home and let me sing.

'It sang to me,' Jack said in a whisper. The voice was fading away and he wanted to hold on to it, keep its pure note.

He lifted the heartstone and brought it close to the harp. The strings began to hum again and the stone vibrated like a tuning fork.

'It *talked*. It sang to me through the stone.'

'What did it sing?' Hedda asked. She looked unsurprised.

'It wants to go home. To Tara Hill.'

'Then to Tara Hill we go,' she said. 'The end begins.'

Under Hedda's stronghold, Fennel laboured in a deep chamber where a hole in the black rock glowed with intense heat. She was forging new weapons for Connor and Kerry.

'Eirinn's furnace,' she said. In one big hand she held Corriwen's knives, stripped them of the ornate hafts then pushed them into the heat until they went white.

Fennel finally re-hafted the knives which now gleamed with brilliant fire, but instead of the original decoration, she made a simple pair of handles from what looked like snakeskin. When she handed them back to Corriwen, they felt different, and much better balanced.

Hedda undid one of her long braids and plucked a single

hair, holding it up like a copper thread. She let it drop.

'Cut,' she told Corriwen.

The knives flashed. The air sang as they clove, and the fine red hair was first cut in two and then each half split down the middle.

Corriwen looked in amazement as four strands fluttered to the floor.

'A weapon must have power of its own,' Hedda said. 'It draws it from the heart of Eirinn. *Now*, you are the warrior woman Dermott fears.'

THIRTY

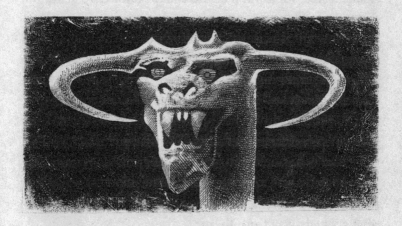

They crossed the chasm together, but this time they walked over a narrow wooden bridge that Fennel laid across its span, and followed the twisting path until they came to the boat with the ferocious dragon's head on its prow.

Fennel busied herself shipping oars made from single trunks of tall trees and helped them climb aboard. Hedda stood in the prow, wearing a tunic of some kind of fish scales that refracted the light into rainbow colour. She was bristling with arms of all kinds and wore an amberhorn bow across her shoulders. Her braided flaming hair hung to her waist.

To Jack, she was the most magnificent person he had ever seen. In the week they had stayed with her, he had come to admire her. And they had learned from her too.

Fennel sat in the stern, and when they were all settled, she heaved at a massive wooden hook that was fixed to a chain pinned to the side of the gulley. There was a grinding creak of protesting wood as the boat began to slip down the slope.

It moved an inch at a time, with Fennel rocking it from side to side to ease its passage. It reached the lip of the gulley . . . and then they were *moving*.

Beneath them the white fog-bank was as flat as a table, studded with those spiny peaks that soared from it like gothic spires. The boat gathered speed in the gulley and they plunged into the mist, faster and faster.

Ahead of them, a hollow booming sound, and Jack remembered the chasm he had almost tumbled into. The mist sucked away from them.

'Fennel!' he turned in the thwarts. As usual Kerry was holding tight with both hands. 'Fennel, there's a great big—'

He never got to finish the sentence. Fennel was smiling at him, unconcerned.

And the boat simply dropped into the hole.

Kerry squawked as the bench fell away from him and for a second he was suspended a foot above it. Fennel's hand clamped on his shoulder and sat him back.

Then they were no longer falling, but screeching down a curve, underneath the mist, heading for a wide clear light.

The boat hit water with an almighty splash and they were out in the open, skipping along on the surface of the sea at such speed that the keel only touched water every few seconds, until they were a clear mile away from the island and it began to slow down.

Kerry whooped in delight. Connor was grinning like an idiot and Corriwen's face was flushed with exhilaration.

'It's the only way to travel,' Kerry said. 'Can we go back up and do it again?'

Now they were powering across the sea, and there was no sign of Dermott's ships.

Connor, standing in the prow, looked entirely different from the ragamuffin they had saved from Dermott's cage. His fair hair streamed behind him and the rags were gone. Fennel had found him a new leather tunic and a plaid cloak. He wore Jack's golden torc which Hedda said was a king's right. Both he and Kerry had new short-swords, Jack had the great sword in a leather scabbard, and his quiver was filled with black arrows, just like the ones he had taken on the last night in the Major's house. He felt as if he was ready to fight.

Fennel steered them closer to the shore when Hedda took a step forward and covered her eyes against the reflections on the water. Jack followed her look and saw a spray of water jet up from the sea.

He moved up to join her. 'Is that a whale?'

'A kelpie, perhaps.'

The water spouted again and a mass of bubbles churned the surface.

'I see something in the water,' Jack said, leaning over the gunwales. A pink shape poked above the waves, then disappeared before another fountain of water sprayed up. Fennel steered towards it.

Jack let out a cry of surprise. What he had thought was a whale, or maybe a walrus was the tip of a big nose, just under the surface. As a wave passed over it, the trough uncovered it and Jack heard a huge suck of air that was cut off by the next wave.

Then, all of a sudden, a huge hand reached up and waved.

'It's Finn!' he cried. 'Finn in the water.'

They all crowded to the side, causing the ship to wallow again. Jack leaned over the gunwales and peered into the depths.

Finn's moon face wavered down there. Both hands reached up and when a wave passed, he managed a mighty gasp before the water covered him again.

'I thought he was gone,' Connor said. 'When the mountain blew up.'

'Must be tougher than we thought,' Kerry said. 'But it looks like he's stuck.'

Fennel uncoiled a rope and made a fast loop. As the boat passed close, she cast it out when Finn's hands appeared again. The loop snared them together. They thrashed the water, but Fennel turned the boat to catch the wind. It sped away for fifty feet, then shuddered violently, almost coming to a complete halt. The wind filled the big sail and it began to move forward again, slowly at first, then a bit faster. All of a sudden there was a sudden jerk and Finn was up on the surface, thrashing about, making huge waves of his own.

Fennel turned the craft about and came alongside him. The giant was spluttering and gasping, coughing gouts of water. He reached the gunwales and hauled himself aboard.

The first person he saw was Jack and he clamped a hand on his shoulder, almost flattening him to the deck.

'I been stuck in that mud and kelp for a week,' he gasped. 'Couldn't get my feet out. It was pure murder every high tide, trying to get a breath.'

'We thought you'd been blown to smithereens,' Kerry said.

'So did I. But I flew like a bird and then dropped like a stone. And I been stuck there ever since, holding my breath at high tide. I haven't eaten for a week and I'm starving to death.'

'I've got food here,' Fennel said and Finn turned.

His eyes widened in surprise. Fennel blushed.

He held out a hand. 'I'm Finn McCuill. Pleased to meet you ... er ... ma'am.'

Corriwen smiled up at him. All of a sudden he sounded so shy that if he hadn't been in a boat he'd be hopping from one foot to foot to the other like a bashful child.

Fennel took his hand. 'Fennel MacNally,' she said, still blushing to the roots.

'That's all we need.' Kerry piped up. 'Love at first sight.'

THIRTY ONE

The boat sped towards the shore under Gerumbel Mountain, where the hulks of two of Dermott's ships lay broken on the rocks. As Fennel steered them towards a shingle beach, Jack recalled the pursuit at sea. Ahead of them, the land was shadowed under dark clouds. It gave Jack a sense of foreboding.

Now the boat ground on the shingle and they stepped onto the mainland. Hedda stalked up the beach, using her lance as a stave. They followed her. Finn held his hand out and helped Fennel step over the gunwale.

'Does anybody know where Tara Hill is?' Kerry asked.

'Hidden from the eyes of men,' Hedda said.

'That's a great help,' Connor said.

'The harp will know,' Jack said simply. He placed it in Corriwen's hands and she strummed softly. The heartstone resonated and Jack spoke the words as they formed within the notes.

> *Sea behind, the hills before*
> *The righteous now march once more*
> *Bearing Eirinn's harmony*
> *Harried now by enemy*
> *Friends beside and foe before*
> *Walk the misty way once more.*
>
> *The end of quest is now at hand*
> *Friends united make a stand*
> *On the way, the wand'ring band*
> *Travels on through shadowland.*
> *To Tara Hill to hear the song*
> *End the winter, right the wrong.*

'Sea behind,' Jack ventured. 'So we head south.'

'Straight for Dermott's lands,' Connor said. 'We'll be walking right into a trap.'

'The misty way,' Corriwen said. 'Where is that?'

Jack considered a moment. 'It's the way Brand took us with the troupe. It was pretty far from here, a long way south. But I think I could find it again.'

'That creepy place?' Kerry interrupted. 'It gave me the heebie-jeebies.'

Jack shrugged. He turned to Hedda. 'What do you think?'

'There will always be enemies. But the Harp sings true.'

'Okay,' Jack said. 'We head south and watch out for the enemies.'

Hedda smiled. 'I will watch, have no fear on that score.'

They walked for two days, through dense forests where weasels and snakes crawled and rustled in the undergrowth, but stayed hidden. They reached the mountains and Hedda remembered a trail from long ago that took them through winding passes and over ridges. Jack was glad they met no more of the fell runners.

Kerry and Connor kept their spirits up, teasing each other along the way. Connor, in his new cloak and bearing a fine sword, had changed radically. Now he *did* look like a young noble.

'You know,' Kerry said, looking ahead at Finn and Fennel who walked close, trampling a decent path through the brush and brambles. 'Beside those two, I feel like a hobbit.'

'What's a hobbit?' Connor asked.

'Sort of little people. On a quest.'

'Like Cluricauns?'

'But with hairy feet. And a magic ring that makes you invisible.'

'Ah, now you're really at the teasing. That's totally made up now, isn't it?'

'No. Really. I saw it in a movie once.'

Connor gave him that blank look again and set Kerry into a fit of laughter.

They tramped on as the south sky grew darker with the threat of storms in the air, but Jack suspected it had more to do with Fainn the Spellbinder. His hand automatically found the hilt of the magnificent twin-bladed sword in its scabbard and for a moment he felt comforted.

The storm wheeled like a dark whirlpool and thunder rolled across the land, bringing cold rain that soon froze to hail that hit like pebbles. They pulled their hoods up and plodded on, heads down.

The horsemen came at breakneck speed along the road.

Hedda heard them long before anyone else and she hurried the group into the trees at the base of the mountains. Hedda stood on the road, lance jammed in the ground, feet braced, her hood pulled right over so that her face was in shadow. The image of a Valkyrie came to Jack: one of the spirit warrior women from Norse legend.

The cavalry troop spurred the horses towards them and pulled up a few yards from where Hedda stood.

'Halt!' a man shouted. 'Who goes there? Where do you think you are going?'

'I *am* halted, as you can see,' Hedda said calmly. Her voice had taken on the rasp Jack had heard when she first came to challenge them. 'What business of yours is my business?'

'Answer fast,' he snorted, 'or suffer the consequences.'

Hedda sighed. A little shiver of anticipation went up Jack's spine.

The man dismounted. Behind him, the riders fanned out, bows drawn. Off to the side, another group came bearing down on them.

'The Lord Dermott hunts thieves and renegades. All travellers face questions at Wolfen Castle.'

269

'Not this traveller,' she retorted.

'Enough,' the man said. 'Take him.'

Jack realised they thought she was a man.

Half a dozen men came forward, swords drawn, while the archers lined up at the ready.

Hedda flipped her hood back. The men gasped and came to an abrupt halt when they saw her face. The ogre's mask, all teeth and horns, glared at them.

Then she moved. Like lightning. Like a red streak. Before they had time to recover she was in amongst them like a fiery tornado. They saw the sword flicker and flash. The big man dropped where he stood without a sound and his head thudded to the ground a split second after him. Blood sprayed scarlet and then she was back where she had stood before, the lance, which had started to fall to the ground, back in her hand.

She stood still as a statue.

One of the men cried out: 'It's killed Captain Gaglan. Murdered him!'

He stood in the saddle. 'Kill the beast now!'

The bowmen let loose a flight, all six of them, and Kerry let out a groan of dismay. Hedda stood stock still. Another sword appeared in her free hand as if by magic, spinning like a propeller.

Pieces of arrow, flights, points, shards of shafts scattered all around in a flurry of shrapnel as the blades cut them to shavings.

'Enough,' Hedda spoke. 'Don't anger me. Go back and tell Dermott his days in Conovar's seat are at an end. Tell him the Scatha comes to meet him.'

'Kill it,' the horseman bawled. 'Send it back to whatever pit it climbed out of.' Beside him more than a dozen archers drew their bows.

Fennel stepped from the trees to stand beside Hedda. The archers got such a fright they took several steps backwards.

'Would you look at the size . . .' one yelped.

'Shoot! Kill them both.'

The horsed archers loosed a volley of arrows. Fennel moved in front of Hedda and turned her body at the last moment and the flight thudded into her thick leather cloak. She brushed the arrows off, as if they were burrs from a dock plant.

But one arrow had caught the side of her neck. She tugged it out. Blood poured down her tunic, though her face showed no pain, nor even irritation.

But when Finn saw the blood, he suddenly went completely berserk.

He gave a furious bellow and crashed out of the trees, grabbing at a pine tree and snapping it off at the bole.

Before the horsemen could turn, he was on them, wielding the tree like a club, smashing men off their horses while the archers at the back shot volley after volley at him until he was so spiked he looked like a mad giant hedgehog.

He waded into them, scattering them across the road, throwing them into trees, batting them skywards. They fell like ninepins. The horsemen at the rear wheeled their mounts and fled.

Finally Finn stopped, wiped his brow, and the red anger faded from his face.

'I'm sorry about that,' he said, somewhat sheepishly,

surveying the carnage. 'I don't know what came over me.'

'Oh, I wouldn't worry,' Fennel said, grinning. Jack saw the delight in her face. Finn had fought because of her. 'They had it coming, be sure of that.'

Hedda turned, sheathed her swords and flicked the grotesque mask off.

'Now we have horses,' she said. 'That should speed us on our way, and save shoe leather besides.'

'What a total *babe*,' Kerry whispered in awe. 'I'm surely awful glad she's on our side.'

THIRTY TWO

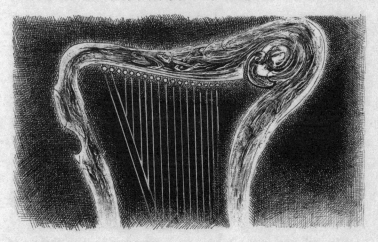

'It was a monster,' the soldier said. He was on one knee, in front of Dermott. 'It came upon us on the road. And there were giants who tore up trees as if they were weeds and laid about us.'

'A monster. And giants.' Dermott bristled. 'Have you been at the ale, man?'

The soldier was visibly shaking. He kept an eye on Dermott's sword hand. It hovered dangerously close to the hilt. 'It is all true. Even arrows were useless against them. One of the men thought it might be a Fir Bolg from the sea.'

'There's been no Fir Bolg in a hundred generations,' Dermott roared.

'But there are giants yet,' Fainn said, leaning in towards the high seat. 'In the lonely places by the sea.'

'Well, we'll soon put an end to them,' Dermott said. 'I won't have giants thwarting me.'

'Indeed not, my lord. But giants are not the concern of the moment.'

Dermott shot him a look, then turned to the soldier.

'Did you see anyone else?'

'Not me, Lord, but a trooper was sure he glimpsed some others. Two or three. And they were small. Like children.'

'Children! Did one have red hair?'

'That I can't say.'

'It's *them*,' Fainn interjected. 'We lost them in the mist and they must have drifted. There is no escape for them now.'

'We will scour the whole of Eirinn for them,' Dermott growled. 'North to south. East to west. Leave no stone or leaf unturned.'

He turned to Fainn. 'And what of this monster creature?'

'A fell runner maybe,' Fainn surmised.

'Well, it's a scrapper. We find it and if we can't make a soldier of it, then we'll burn the damn thing. And those children too. Use all your wiles, Spellbinder, *all* your powers. Drive them to me. I will have them!'

'Indeed you will,' Fainn said.

It was good to be back in the saddle again, although after a hard day's ride, Kerry was beginning to complain.

'My bum is numb,' he told Jack. 'And getting number. It's a bummer.'

Jack laughed. He could always count on Kerry to lower the tone and cajole a smile.

'Better than walking,' Connor said. 'I really like horses. You can go for miles and you can see for miles as well from up here. I think everybody should have a horse.'

They had stopped for the night and Fennel got to work preparing food from her big knapsack. She carried enough to feed a small army, which, Jack thought, was exactly what they were.

'Dermott knows we are coming,' Hedda said as they ate. 'Fainn thinks his storms and hail are driving us to him.'

'The other riders must have reported back,' Jack said.

'And I have seen the outriders,' Hedda said. 'They keep their distance, but they also keep watch.'

'I haven't seen a thing,' said Kerry. 'You must have eyes like a hawk.'

'I thought I saw movement in the distance, but I couldn't be sure,' Corriwen said. 'But if they are only watching and not attacking, then Dermott knows the direction we are taking. He plans an ambush.'

Hedda smiled. 'Well said. That he does. He will draw his forces in and surround us. If he can.'

'Shouldn't we go a different route?' Connor asked. 'I mean if he knows where we are.'

'We go in the direction Jack Flint tells us. And the Harp tells him.'

That was true enough. Every night when they stopped, Corriwen would stroke the strings. The faint noise was nowhere near as loud as a well-strung harp could play, but the aftermath, as the sound faded, whispered words in his head, telling him to keep going south to Tara Hill. So they went south.

Dermott's men kept their distance, but shadowed them all the way, as the weather closed in and fierce winds blew down from the north.

It was close to dawn when Jack saw Hedda move, silent as a shadow, as silent as she had been when she sat, motionless, hardly breathing, always on guard. She touched Fennel lightly and the giantess was awake instantly. By the light of the fire, Jack saw them steal away. He rolled out of his blanket and followed.

They were only a few yards ahead. Despite Fennel's bulk she merged with the shadows and she walked as silently as she could, though Jack could still feel the earth vibrate with every footfall.

He heard a sound, not far off. A snuffling growl, the noise a badger might make as it dug for worms. Something rustled and for an instant Jack felt a shiver of anticipation as he remembered the snakes that had appeared from nowhere as they set out on their search for Corriwen.

Hedda stopped. Her shadow merged with the trunk of a tree and she vanished into it. Fennel parted branches and bent to look down. She reached out slowly. Jack saw her fingers grip something.

A screech rang out. He heard a thrashing sound, branches shaking, twigs snapping. The screech became an angry yammering.

Fennel turned and brought her hand down. Something

squirmed and squawked in her grasp. Hedda stepped out from the shadows, spear at the ready.

'Now would you take your hands off me you clumsy great freak!' The creature in Fennel's hand squirmed and kicked, to no avail. The noise woke Corriwen and the others.

'Can't a fellow enjoy a quiet nap without being waylaid and hoisted forty feet?'

Hedda jammed the lance up against it and the voice cut off.

'You were following us,' she said.

'No I never was,' it protested, still kicking and wriggling. 'I was having forty winks and minding my own business. And anyway, I'm waiting for friends of mine.'

Jack stepped up to where Hedda and Fennel stood. He looked up.

Rune the Cluricaun floated above his head, suspended in mid-air. Fennel's fingers gripped the collar of his jacket. The little fellow was doing his best to get free, but having no success whatsoever.

'Rune!' Jack cried. 'What are you doing here?'

'I told them, I was waiting for you.' He kicked at Fennel's wrist.

'Now put me down or suffer the consequences,' he squawked. 'You're not too big to be taught a lesson.'

'He's a friend,' Jack said. Fennel shrugged and opened her fingers. Rune dropped twelve feet, bounced like a rubber ball and was on his feet, fists up in front of his face, a featherweight ready for a scrap.

'Come on then! Take me in a fair fight.'

Jack clapped him on the shoulder. 'These are friends too.'

'Some friends. Spoiling my beauty sleep without so much as a how'd-ye-do!'

He turned as Hedda stepped forward and he saw her face for the first time.

'Och, it's yourself, Lady Scatha,' he cried. 'Now why didn't you just show yourself and save all this fuss and bother.'

'Master Rune,' Hedda said. 'It's been many a year.'

'Too many,' Rune said. He stuck a diminutive hand out and shook hers vigorously, beaming from ear to ear. His shrewish rage had evaporated instantly.

'Hello Rune,' Fennel said, laughing. 'We heard you snoring. You'd make a truly bad guardsman.'

'Well, you woke me up, for sure. Now do the decent thing and give me something hot to warm my bones. Maybe a keg of porter?'

'I was hoping you'd join this little shebang,' Rune said as he ate. 'I've been waiting here three days for you. There's platoons and brigades marching all over Eirinn. You can hardly get moving on the roads.'

'We met one of them,' Hedda said. 'They lent us their horses.'

'Kind of them,' Rune said, a twinkle in his eye. 'I hope you let a few of them leave on foot.'

Hedda shrugged noncommittally.

'So it's well met by what should be moonlight,' Rune said. 'Except I haven't seen moonlight or sunshine for so long I'm beginning to think I dreamed it. I take it you have a direction?'

'We're going to Tara Hill,' Jack said. 'Wherever that is.'

'Now doesn't that clever book of yours point the way?'

'We've got the Harp,' Corriwen said. 'Kerry re-strung it. It sings to Jack.'

'Ah, that fair music's been gone so long. Its song will be weak for lack of practice. But here we are, on the road. So we might as well travel together and see what transpires.'

'That might be a long, hard road for a little fellow like yourself,' Fennel said kindly. 'And at the end of it, Dermott waits.'

'Dermott's a buffoon. He's never seen what a Cluricaun can do when he's roused.'

'I can't wait,' Kerry murmured and Connor and Jack fell about laughing again.

THIRTY THREE

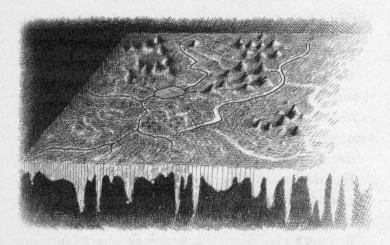

It was snowing when they woke, huddled between Finn and Fennel. The temperature had plummeted. Icy crystals tinkled like bells in the thin branches of trees and hard frost carpeted the couch-grass.

Out in the open, but for the constant wind, it was strangely silent. All the streams had frozen solid. Icicles spiked down where waterfalls had rushed. The ground was hard as rock under the horses' hooves.

They followed the road south, with Rune riding behind Corriwen on a big sturdy warhorse.

'Finest looking girl I've seen ever since I left Skiboreen,' he'd said, making her blush.

'Best looking girl in three worlds,' Kerry whispered to Jack. 'But don't tell her I said that.'

'I think she knows you think that,' Jack said, nudging him in the ribs. 'You can't hide it.'

Kerry went bright red. 'You're kidding me!'

'Of course I am,' Jack grinned. 'Got you good though, didn't I.'

Rune peered from under Corriwen's cape, his white whiskers gathering hoar frost as they travelled. Finn and Fennel took up the rear-guard, and Jack was confident nothing would get past them. He was less confident about what lay ahead.

The horses plodded on, chipping the ice with their great hooves, their breath freezing in the air.

They rode twenty miles or more, and every now and again, Jack would notice a movement on the far flanks. Men on horses were paralleling their journey, but approaching no closer than a mile.

Jack knew the clash would come. He began to scan the land ahead, working out where Dermott's massed men would hide for an ambush.

Finally they came down off the high land, saddle-sore and cold, and entered the rolling foothills of Mid-Eirinn.

The road drove straight for some distance then forked right and left.

'Which way to Tara?' Kerry asked. 'Shouldn't there be a signpost?'

Jack was grateful to get out of the saddle. His legs and hands were frozen and numb. Corriwen took them in hers and rubbed heat back into them. Connor looked like a frosted snowman, but his eyes were bright and clear.

Jack took the Harp from Brand's bag. It gleamed in the frost-light as Corriwen plucked the strings.

It whispered its song to Jack.

> *Choices three, but take the low*
> *Travellers have far to go*
> *Find the way that goes between*
> *Travel on a road unseen.*
> *Now's the time for wand'ring band.*
> *To Voyage on in Shadowland.*
> *Travel where the white road wends*
> *Travail too at journey's end.*
> *Brave of heart and steel of will*
> *Ever on to Tara Hill.*

'It's mentioned Shadowland twice.'

'What's it mean?' Connor asked.

'It's the way we went with the troupe.'

'It comes out at Wolfen Castle,' Kerry said. 'We'd be walking right into a trap.'

'What about the white road?' Corriwen asked. She gestured the land all around them, snow-drifted and frosted. 'It's all white.'

'I could toss a coin,' Rune said.

Jack laughed. 'You disappeared the last time.'

'I'll try it anyway,' Rune said, taking no offence. He held up the gold coin. On one face, the five stars of the Corona twinkled in the frosty light. On the other, a golden harp, exactly like the one safe in Corriwen's hand.

'Stars we go left,' Rune said. 'Harp we go right.'

Jack shrugged. Rune tossed the coin. It sang as it whirred up.

A voice boomed out from behind them, so unexpectedly that Jack almost fell off the horse.

'Rune, you whiskery old son of a toad!'

Brand stood on the wagon buckboard, beside big Score Four-arm who held the reins. Behind them, the small caravan of wagons creaked along the road. Fennel and Finn exchanged glances, as if trying to work out how the newcomers could have sneaked up on them. Jack remembered how Brand's wandering *vaga*band could appear from nowhere.

'Cousin Brand!' Rune cried. He slid off the saddle and lowered himself to the ground. Brand nimbly jumped from the wagon and they came together in a bear-hug in the middle of the road then linked arms and did a quirky little jig.

'You're a long way out of Skiboreen,' Brand said.

'And an even longer way back, to be sure.'

Brand looked about him, taking in the giants and the tall woman on the horse.

'A motley crew,' he observed. 'As motley as my bunch of foundlings. Now is that the Lady Hedda I see?'

'The very same. And here on a matter of serious business.'

'Well then, if it's serious, I suppose we might join you. We're a bit jaded with fun and frolic.'

Score Four-arm sauntered up, Tig and Tag somersaulting together behind, and used all his digits to shake hands. 'Good to see you hale and hearty,' he told

Jack. He turned to Connor. 'And who's this fine upstanding young chief? Surely not the raggedy scoundrel we saved from Wolfen Castle? Man, you could dance a jig and an eightsome reel all night now.'

'Yeah,' Kerry said. 'But can he rock'n'roll?'

'We should get moving,' Jack said. He turned to the crossroads and something glittered as it dropped past his eyes.

Rune's coin tinkled as it hit the ground, rolled towards the edge of the road ... and kept rolling between the two forks.

And as it rolled, the air around it rippled like water, then turned almost opaque, and a new road appeared where before had only been frosted tussock grass. White mist swirled on either side.

'A choice of three,' Jack said. 'The way that goes *between*.'

Corriwen touched him on the shoulder, a gesture he found strangely warming.

'Well, come on, lagabouts,' Brand piped up. 'The way won't be open forever, you know.'

Together, the giants walking behind and Hedda silent on her horse, they followed the wagons into the misty way.

They stayed close as the gauzy tendrils wove around them.

'Don't go off the road,' Kerry told Corriwen and Connor. 'There's weird things in here.'

'It's been nothing but weird since I first met Corriwen,' Connor said, grinning. 'How much weirder can it get?'

He turned and a face swam out of the mist to fix him with wide golden eyes, and he almost fell off his horse.

Jack heard voices that had the frail texture of the mist itself. Shapes swirled, white on white, and swam close, as ethereal and weightless as fog, but strangely powerful in the way their pleas tugged at them.

Once or twice he had to take Connor's reins to prevent him from veering off.

'If you go off the road, you'll never find your way back again,' he said. Kerry had hitched his reins to Corriwen's pommel horn and trailed behind her. He had his eyes tightly shut and his fingers in his ears.

Jack looked behind him and saw Hedda sitting straight in the saddle. If she saw or heard anything, she gave no sign.

Behind her Finn and Fennel strode together, holding hands. They only had eyes for each other.

And behind them the mist closed, offering no way back. They kept moving, hour upon hour, with only those strange whispering voices and the horses' slow hooves breaking the silence.

Fainn was still as a spider, hunched over the long table, staring at its glazed surface.

Ice covered most of the map of Eirinn, a thin frosting he had conjured despite the heat in the smoky room. His hands wove intricate designs in the air and he muttered continuously in his strange tongue.

Some time later, he watched as a thin vapour began to pool in the hollow of the mountains close to where two roads forked. It thickened, crawling into depressions and dells, spreading out until it hid a wide margin from the road to Mid-Eirinn.

He stared a long time, wondering what it was he had conjured here. His spells and incantations had cast a net that would hopefully sniff the fugitives out. But under the thick vapour all was hidden.

Yet ... something tugged at his memory.

The old people, from a time before Fainn himself, had spoken of the *ley*-ways. The hidden roads between places. Old tales maybe, but he remembered how people could vanish into the mist where time and distance held no sway, and emerge far away.

He held his hands over the vapour pools, muttering again.

An image came to him. A golden harp, shrouded in gossamer. It sang faintly, so faint it was like a whisper of grass on a summer day.

And Fainn knew the Harp was coming back.

With it would be the boy with the strange stone, whose power pulled at Fainn like a hook in his dark heart.

He broke his spell and the ice vanished. The misty vapour evaporated and once again, the map of Eirinn was clearly carved on the expanse of old oak.

He turned and hurried up the spiral stairway to the chamber.

Dermott was brooding, fingers tapping the hilt of his sword.

'We have them, Lord Dermott,' Fainn said. 'They are coming to us. And they bring the Harp.'

It was almost dark when they emerged into clear air. Jack shivered, but Kerry seemed happier to be out of the misty way.

Jack looked about them. Ahead some tree-covered hills rose, rolling away into the distance.

'This isn't where we came out last time,' Jack said.

Low hills formed the edges of a wide basin through which a frozen river cut like a winding road. None of them looked high enough or impressive enough to be Tara Hill.

Brand pulled the wagons into a circle and soon they had a fire blazing in the centre. They gathered round and Brand introduced Hedda and the two giants to Thin Doolan and Natterjack.

'Do you know where we are?' Jack asked.

'Where the road takes us,' Brand said, 'is always the right place.'

The heartstone pulsed very gently and Jack pressed it against his chest.

Hedda caught the motion and raised her eyebrows in question.

'Something,' Jack said. 'Something knows we're here.'

'Fainn,' she said. 'Dermott will ride tonight.'

She cupped a hand to Jack's cheek. Despite her ferocity, it was a gentle, motherly touch.

'Rest a while, Cullian's son. We have enough time to prepare. Tonight, eat well, sleep sound. Tomorrow will decide for Eirinn.'

THIRTY FOUR

The sound of horses' hooves and clanking armour told them Dermott had arrived; it was still before dawn and the sky was murky and black.

Hedda came stalking into the camp and sat down beside the fire, scaled armour glinting in the firelight and braids coiled like scarlet snakes.

'Dermott has come in force,' she said softly. 'It seems he really wants the Harp.'

Using the sharp point of her sword, she drew on the ground. 'This is the slope where we are,' she said. 'Dermott has brigades round to the north, the east and west, and more men are coming. They will block the south and encircle us.'

'How many?' Kerry asked.

'Enough for him to think he has us in his hand,' she said, showing no emotion except a hint of exhilaration, or perhaps expectation. 'Dermott himself never came to my island to challenge me. While he thinks he has might, he knows little of war.'

'Neither do we,' Connor said. 'I've been a poacher all my life.'

He swung three smooth stones that he'd tied together to lengths of cord. They clacked in the cold air.

'They will come at first light,' Hedda said. 'On the west side, horses and men. On the east, archers. On the north, foot-soldiers. They will expect us to run, try to escape between them, so they will be ready for that.'

She smiled. In the firelight she seemed even fiercer. 'They will not expect us to take the fight to them.'

The ground shuddered and Finn and Fennel came looming through the ring of wagons.

'After today,' Hedda said, 'I will no longer need an armourer. Finn, I think, needs one more than I do.'

'And what will you do for everything else?' Fennel demanded. 'And that old Gerumbel Mountain of Finn's, it's not hot enough to turn a blade pink. No, I believe I will return home with you to the misty isle and my forge. Finn says he's tired of the headland and wants to try a new fishing ground.'

'He's ever welcome,' Hedda said, smiling.

'And anyway, I need a strong pair of hands to help haul the boat up to the launch,' Fennel said. Finn grinned like a big happy child. Jack hoped he would still be grinning when the day was done.

Fennel hauled her big pannier towards her and delved inside, bringing out a bundle tied in a leather hide. She unrolled it and passed something over to Jack.

'This a gift from the Lady Hedda and myself.' He held it up and saw it was a scaled tunic like Hedda's. It gleamed iridescent.

'Kelpie hide,' Fennel said. 'An orc-whale can't bite through it.'

There was one for each of them and they were grateful to have them, especially after hearing about the companies of archers who surrounded them. Corriwen slipped hers on and drew her cape over it. With her knives and red hair she looked like a miniature Hedda, and for an instant Jack felt his heart beating faster. He looked away quickly before she noticed.

Connor and Kerry donned their tunics and Fennel brought something else out, pulled Connor close and tied it in place. When Connor turned they saw she had set his old brass pin-brooch in a braided leather headband.

'Good style,' Kerry said, nudging him with an elbow. 'You can come to our next Halloween party.'

Brand and his troupe wandered in from his wagon, Rune at their side. Score Four-arm had a thick leather jacket studded with horn plates and in each big hand he carried a curved sword.

'Looks like a combine harvester,' Kerry observed.

Tig and Tag wore no armour, but Natterjack came bumbling along, wearing what looked like a turtle-shell strapped to his broad flat head.

'And *he* looks like a toad-stool,' Connor said and everybody laughed.

'Everything in place?' Hedda asked Finn and the giant nodded.

'We've worked through the night. There's a surprise waiting for them.'

He pointed to the little knoll where the horses were scraping for grass beside a mound of boulders that hadn't been there before, piled twice as tall as a man. Close by, thick spruce trunks, spiked with dead branch stumps, were stacked together. Finn and Fennel had worked hard while Jack and his friends had slept. Neither looked the least bit tired.

'More than one surprise, I promise,' Hedda said, as the day lightened and finally they got a glimpse of the mass of men approaching not half a mile distant. Far beyond them, where Wolfen castle hunched by the sea, lightning flickered and forked and thunder rumbled.

Jack got to his feet and surveyed the land. They were partially protected by a grove of trees. He looked behind, towards the way they had come, out of the mist and through a valley, and his first thought was that they should head back in that direction. Fast. There were just too many men out there, and too few of them here. One fighting woman and two giants, plus a collection of weird circus performers, a girl and three boys.

It didn't look good.

Then as he was turning back, Jack saw something out of the corner of his eye.

In the gulley where they had come through the mist, a low pale line was brighter than the surrounding area.

As he watched, it seemed to writhe towards them. At first

he thought he had imagined it and looked away, but when he turned back again, the line had covered more ground. It meandered out of the gulley, rolling slowly like a carpet, then turned away from them.

'What *is* that?' Jack said to no one in particular.

Corriwen came beside him and followed his gaze.

'More mist? Or is it something Fainn has conjured?'

Hedda noticed and stood. She beckoned to Rune.

It looked like a river, slowly flowing from the gulley, following the contours like water finding its way.

Jack recalled the whispering voice of the Harp.

> *To Voyage on in Shadowland.*
> *Travel where the white road wends*

'It's the White Road,' he whispered. '*Brave of heart and steel of will, ever on to Tara Hill.*

'But where is Tara Hill?' There was no hill near here, except for the low rolling downs.

'Travel where the white road wends,' Rune said.

'I don't understand this,' Jack protested. 'There *is* no hill.'

Hedda nodded. 'Time to follow the road, Jack Flint.'

She beckoned to Fennel, who strode across with a leather wrapping and unfurled it. Hedda held up the great wooden mace.

'The Dagda's oaken club,' she said. 'One of the three treasures. You carry another Journeyman.'

She raised it for them to see and Jack did a double take. The skull had leered at them the first time they had seen it, sockets hollow and dark, teeth clenched. But now eyes as red as fire blazed from the hollows and the mouth was wide open, showing rows of fearsome fangs.

'It hungers for battle,' Hedda said. She gripped Jack's shoulder. You and Kerry, both have speed and you have the finest of swords. Connor is the one to bear the Dagda's club in this fight.'

She touched Connor's forehead. 'Bear this bravely, Eirinn's heir. Now take the Harp home.'

She embraced Kerry and Corriwen.

'Now's the day and now's the hour. Be fast and fleet.'

Hedda took Jack's face between powerful hands and bent to kiss him on the forehead. He felt her warmth and suddenly wanted to hug her tightly.

'Jack Flint, Cullian's son.' There was a slight catch in her voice. 'Your quest is almost done here. The Sky Queen grants a favour to those who would do her work. Do not forget that.'

She kissed him again and once more he thought he saw a glint of a tear in her eye.

'Now take the white road, wherever it leads.'

Jack shouldered Brand's bag with the Harp safely inside, then strung his amberhorn bow before they headed out towards where the pale ribbon snaked down the hill. From the west, a trumpet sounded and a drum rolled, and a squadron of horsemen came galloping towards them.

Hedda reached for her mask, clamped it on and stood tall. Her weapons bristled on her armour and her hair swung every time she moved. On the ends of each long braid was bound a spiked ball like a mace-head.

'Let's take the fight to them,' she said.

Score smiled a savage, hungry smile and whirled his blades so that they whistled in the air. 'Now that sounds like a fine plan.'

Dermott had gathered his men and marched almost as soon as Fainn told him the Harp was on its way.

'But there is something more besides,' Fainn had said.

'Anything important?'

'They are not alone,' Fainn said, 'and I sense destiny at hand. And the return of one seeking vengeance and birthright. There is a force coming together that bodes ill.'

'You've been boding ill as long as I recall,' Dermott snapped. 'I'm not giving up this chance. The whole of Eirinn will be in my hand.' He clenched a mighty fist, as if demonstrating how Eirinn would fare once it *was* in his hand. 'We ride out,' Dermott growled.

'I will remain and ponder,' Fainn said. 'Perhaps I can fathom what moves against us.'

'Nothing I can't crush,' Dermott said. 'Stay and chant for all you're worth, Spellbinder. I'll be busy letting blood and getting my harp back.'

With that he turned and moments later sallied out of Wolfen Castle at the head of an armed column.

Jack and the others were halfway to the winding pale road when the horsemen came charging towards them.

'We're going to have to run for it,' Kerry said. 'We might make it, but Corriwen and Connor, they're not fast enough.'

Jack kept walking, expecting Hedda or the two giants to move to cut off the squad, but they just stood silently. He turned to the white road and saw that it was a continuation of the mist through which they had travelled, but now a low haze, no more than a foot high, and so even at its edges that it could have been a well-laid carpet. It continued down the slope towards the flat land. If it was heading for Tara Hill, they would have a long walk ahead of them, he thought.

And the horsemen were closer, spurring their mounts, and drawing swords.

'I don't like the look of this,' Kerry said. 'Why doesn't Hedda move?'

'Hold! Thieves!' a man shouted, close enough to be heard. He raised his sword high, standing up in the stirrups.

Then, quick as a blink, man and horse vanished.

Behind them, the rest of the cavalry, hurtling at full gallop followed in tight formation.

The ground beneath the hooves just fell away as a deep pit opened under them.

Jack heard their shouts of surprise and sudden fright as the horses plunged headlong, and then they saw the thin branches that had been laid across the trench and disguised with leaves and dry grass.

Now Jack knew where the mound of stones had come from. Fennel and Finn had been even busier than he had thought.

The cavalry troop couldn't stop, so tightly bunched were they, that every one of them plunged over the lip of the pit and the screams of hurt and broken men and horses tore the air.

'Come on,' Jack urged them. 'They've bought us some time.'

'She wasn't kidding about the surprise,' Kerry whooped. 'That had to hurt!'

The white road rolled downslope, gathering speed. They reached it and waded into the mist to follow wherever it led.

In the pit, one man clambered out, limping badly, and dragged himself back to the line. None of his fellow riders managed to get out.

The four walked on for another quarter-mile, when another blare of trumpets sounded, and a mass of archers wheeled towards them.

Then Hedda started down the hill, with Score Four-arm beside her. Jack saw Finn and Fennel tramp up to the great pile of boulders and he turned, walking backwards, to watch.

Hedda's ferocious mask made her look like a demon as she raced downhill at blinding speed, taking the company of archers by surprise. She crossed 500 yards so fast that Score was only halfway there when she crashed into the archers, both swords whirling.

It was as if they had been hit by a tank. Jack saw the lead archer turn and behold a monster bearing down on him. He didn't even have time to draw the arrow back before she was past him and he was falling to one side while his arm and longbow went spinning off to the other.

Then all hell broke out.

The screams came clear on the air as she darted in and out, a ferocious red streak. Her head swung and the spikes at the ends of her long braids clawed and battered the bewildered, terrified bowmen who had no chance of even sighting on a target that moved so fast.

'What a mover!' Kerry murmured in unashamed admiration.

Tig and Tag came somersaulting down the slope, back to back, one nimble creature. They held only a long stave each as they spun towards the milling footsoldiers who were taken completely by surprise. One of them dashed forward, swinging a broadsword in two hands.

The acrobats flicked apart in an instant. The sword clove fresh air, jammed point first into the cold ground. Tig's foot caught the man on the chin and they heard the crack of bone as his head snapped back and he dropped like a sack. Tag peeled away, jammed one end of the long stave in a tussock and next thing she was up at its top end, above head-height. A thin blade appeared in her hand as she spun round the upright pole and razored a swathe around herself, carving a neat circle of falling men.

Somebody roared from behind the gathered army and another company of horse came angling towards where Jack and the others had inadvertently slowed down, fascinated by the action.

'*Uh-oh!*' Kerry tapped Jack's shoulder. 'I think this is where we start to run.'

'No.' Jack unshipped the bow and had an arrow strung

before he even realised it. 'This is where we fight.'

He shrugged off the bag and handed it to Corriwen.

'We can hold them a while,' he said. 'Follow the road. Keep the harp safe.'

'I stand with you,' she said resolutely. He shook his head.

'We'll catch up. I promise. Now go!'

Connor needed no second bidding. He snatched at her cape and pulled her away.

'You up for this?' Jack asked Kerry.

'We beat the Fell Runners, didn't we?'

The cavalry came charging. Jack scanned the ground, hoping for another pit, but saw no evidence. One of the riders unleashed an arrow from the cavalry flank. Kerry blurted a warning, a second too late, and Jack took the full force of it in the centre of the chest. It hit hard enough to knock him down.

Kerry yelled in rage. Jack landed on his backside and bounced to his feet. The arrow fell to the ground in three shattered pieces. There wasn't even a mark on the scaly armour.

'Phew!' Kerry gasped. 'Thought they had you.'

'Me too,' Jack gasped. 'Good old kelpie skin.'

Jack drew back and took the lead rider clean in the neck. He tumbled backwards and his sword flew up and came down, blade first, some way behind the riderless horse. A man screeched and fell, stabbed clean through the shoulder.

Two more black arrows found their mark and then the riders were on them. Somebody swung a long sword. Kerry moved like lightning. He flicked away, turned like a hare and jabbed, once, twice. The new blade went in and out like a hot knife through lard. Jack was on the far side now, running in a circle round the group who bunched together, trying to find a target. He fired three more, running all the while, then drew the Redthorn sword's twin. The horses turned, hooves flashing, trying to stamp them flat, and began to circle them. Jack and Kerry leapt back before they were outflanked. A sword came down and Jack parried it with his own blade, the shock riving up his shoulder, but the soldier's sword broke itself on Hedda's fine-forged steel and scattered shards like shrapnel.

There were too many of them. Jack and Kerry were forced back, away from the white road, desperately hacking and parrying as twenty or more cavalrymen tried to ride them down.

Despite their speed, they were being driven towards Dermott's main force when an almighty snarl ripped the air and suddenly riders and horses were scattering in panic.

Jack rolled out of the way of one panicked horse, got to his knees beside Kerry and saw Connor in the middle of the horsemen. In his hands, the great club was swinging and as it swung, Jack saw the mouth open in a savage gape and a hoarse voice roared:

Feed me flesh, feed me BONE!

Connor was swinging like a boy possessed, as the mighty club roared its battle-cry and men flew out of the saddle and bones crunched like sticks. In a matter of seconds, the tide turned and the ones left in the saddle fled for their lives.

The great club swung one last time and the savage mouth, dripping with blood, closed with a snap. Only now instead of a snarl, it had a vicious grin on its face, as if it was satisfied with its work.

'That was absolutely brilliant,' Kerry cried. 'I never saw anything like it.'

Connor caught his breath. 'I never even thought. The club … it *pulled* me back to help. It wanted to fight.'

'I heard it,' Kerry said. 'It was going pure mental.'

'Just as well for us.' Jack wiped his blade on a fallen man's tunic, not looking at the dead face, and re-sheathed the sword, suddenly struck by the realisation that these were the first humans he had ever had to fight.

Kerry grabbed him by the arm and gave him a shake. He could read Jack like a book.

'Come on, man,' he cried. 'It was them or us. You think they would worry?'

Even so, Jack felt as if he'd swallowed something heavy. It would haunt him a long time.

Kerry turned him round. ' Look. Corriwen's in the clear. We'd better get going.'

Jack turned silently and followed Kerry and Connor away from the pile of men.

Score came charging up to where Hedda was scything men down left and right. He had a curved blade in each hand and followed her into the mêlée. Kerry's description had been spot on. He was like a reaper at harvest-time, but now he was harvesting men.

Dermott the Wolf stood on a little knoll viewing the carnage. He was quivering with rage. He'd just seen half his cavalry destroy itself in a deadfall pit. And the other half had been beaten off by three boys. Three *thieves*! Now his archers and foot soldiers were falling like birds in a duck-hunt. The screams and cries of wounded men echoed over the slaughterfield.

'They're getting away, damn you!' he roared. 'Get after them. Bring them to me, heads or no heads!'

Out in the middle of the armed foot, that monster and the four-armed freak were running amok.

A *juggler*! Dermott fumed. A wandering *juggler*. And he was wading through armed men as if he was an immortal.

Dermott jumped off the knoll and strode towards what was left of the cavalry who were milling in disarray,

'Get back there and bring them to me!' He turned to his bugler. 'There's a company not yet here. Call them in.'

Without pause, Dermott lashed his whip and snared one horseman. He dragged him from the saddle and threw him to the ground. If he'd had time, he'd have sliced the coward in two. But far out he could see the thieves hurrying along the pale road. He wheeled his mount and thundered off in hot pursuit.

On the hill, Finn and Fennel watched this new development.

This was expected. They'd held back while Hedda and Score and the rest of the troupe took the battle to the enemy. They'd watched in awe as Hedda savaged her way through them, moving like quicksilver, faster than the eye could follow.

But it was Natterjack and Thin Doolan and the acrobatic twins who put on a real show.

Tig and Tag used their long staves to vault over the heads of the infantry, catching each other in mid-flight and performing feats of such delicate balance that not a blade nor an arrow caught them.

Natterjack and Thin Doolan stood close together. The squat trouper still wore the curious turtle-shell helmet and it was clear why when he approached the line. A man ran out and slammed Natterjack with a broad axe, right on the crown.

The result was so hilarious that Fennel laughed aloud.

Natterjack collapsed like a deflated bladder, absorbing the heavy blow. Then he seemed to haul a massive breath and swell back to his former shape, swung a heavy mallet and crowned his opponent in return. The man went down like a felled ox.

Thin Doolan didn't move fast. He wasn't armoured and only carried a light sword. A big soldier ran forward, swinging widely. Doolan sucked in his breath, turned sideways, and vanished almost completely. The sword came down, found nothing to slice. Doolan raised his blade and jabbed the man in the eye, then moved on to the next.

Another soldier came dashing in. Natterjack opened his wide mouth and the sword speared inside. Natterjack closed it with a loud snap. His bulging eyes blinked and he made a gruesome, gulping sound. The man staggered off, clutching at the bleeding stump of his wrist.

On the hill, the giants saw Dermott rally a brigade of men and pull them away from the fighting. They swung from east to south, haring after the four small figures.

'Now,' Finn said. He hefted a boulder up to shoulder height, braced his pillar-like legs and shot-putted the stone across the battlefield. It hit the frozen ground with an almighty thud, bounced and smashed into the brigade. Beside him, Fennel set down one of the spruce trunks, gave it a shove and sent it rolling like a juggernaut down the slope, letting its spikes mow down the archers who were trying to get out of the way of Finn's big bouncing stone.

The brigade ran for their lives, while Dermott ranted and raved in blind fury.

'They're getting away!' he roared. 'Damn your eyes, you cowards. I will have your heads for this.'

His men were too busy avoiding the lethal avalanche which Finn and Fennel sent their way to care much about their heads for the moment. They fled.

And along the white road, the four fugitives gained a clear distance.

THIRTY FIVE

The scene was total chaos when Fainn arrived in a coal-black wagon.

He stepped down, cloak fluttering, unhitched the ties and drew back a hide cover.

The great silver cauldron carved with the horned god saw the light of the bleak day. Four men helped Fainn set it on the ground as he shrugged off his black cloak and let the wind kite it away.

Raising his hands to the tumbling sky he began to chant.

Inside the rim, the black surface began to swirl, refracting poisonous shades of orange and purple. Green fumes bubbled from its depths and drifted away on the breeze. Fainn's tattoos began to writhe on his skin before he plunged both hands deep into the ancient cauldron, still chanting, calling to strange gods whose names only he knew.

Jack paused and risked a look behind them. The misty road was wider now and the going more exhausting. Far below, on a big horse, Dermott the Wolf was galloping after them, followed by a small company of armed horse.

Jack began to turn to follow the others when he paused. Then it suddenly struck him.

They had been running on the flat, along the low-mist road. But now Dermott was *below* them.

Ahead of him Connor and Corriwen were labouring, breathing hard. But they weren't just ahead of him and Kerry. They were *above* them. He stopped again, puzzled, and looked back again. The battlefield was still a milling chaos. The clash of arms and the shouts of wounded men came clearly across the distance.

But now, Jack could see it was clearly far below them.

They were on a hill. Impossibly, what had been flat land was now the side of a steep hill.

Jack grabbed Kerry. 'We're climbing!'

'Don't be daft. Just keep running.'

He spun him around. Dermott was still coming towards them, only a couple of furlongs behind. He was roaring unintelligibly and waving a huge axe around his head.

Kerry's mouth gaped. 'How did we get up ...'

'It's the hill, man,' Jack cried. 'We've found it! *Tara Hill!*'

Down on the flat, but close to them, Jack saw Fainn gesticulating over the cauldron. Hedda was moving like a streak, wreaking havoc and on the far knoll, Finn and Fennel hurled great boulders down into the massed enemy. Dermott was closer, urging his horse on and gaining on them.

The heartstone suddenly kicked on his breastbone. Jack realised he had to move.

Long arms closed tight around him.

A sickening sensation of cold, foetid cold, seeped through his skin.

Fainn's voice hissed inside his head.

Too late, strange boy. Too late. Come to meeeee!

No! Jack tried to cry, but there was no air. He felt as if he was falling into darkness while the voice scratched in his brain.

Bring it to me ... boy ... bring me the talisman.

Jack tried to move, but his muscles felt like mud. The darkening world spun dizzily.

Something hit him so hard that for a second he blacked out completely and in the next instant his eyes opened and he was tumbling backwards down the hill with Kerry on top of him, yelling at the top of his voice. They ground to a halt and Jack rolled, just in time to see a dark shape, a *Fainn* shape, waver in the air and then fragment into a cloud of tiny black buzzing particles as if a million flies had suddenly swarmed together. They hissed in the air and exploded in a dry puff.

'What happened?' Jack finally found his voice.

'*Jeez* Jack, I didn't mean to hit you so hard.'

'What was it?'

'I don't know. I turned back and there was this shadow wrapped all around you. You were starting to disappear.'

Kerry helped him to his feet. Corriwen had run down the slope and took his hand.

'Something evil was there,' she said. 'It swarmed around you. Like a black cloud.'

'It was Fainn. He was *there*. He tried to get the heartstone.'

Kerry turned. 'No. He's down there ... *uh-oh*. Come on, that loony's catching up.'

Dermott snarled. One hand swung the big axe around his head. The other lashed out with his whip as they turned to clamber away.

It whistled in the air and then Corriwen tripped. Jack bent to haul her up when she was suddenly dragged back a yard.

'Got you,' Dermott bellowed. 'Come and take what's coming to you.'

He heaved at the whip-handle and Corriwen went skittering down the slope as Dermott backed his horse, adding to the traction. Before either of them could move, he had her under its feet and in one swift move, he leant down, grabbed her by the hair and swung her up.

'Give me my Harp,' he snarled. 'Give it back or I'll twist her head off her neck.'

They froze. Connor was higher up. Behind Dermott the rest of the horsemen were climbing fast.

Jack and Kerry stood paralysed as Dermott's hand closed around Corriwen's neck.

'No!' Connor cried. He was too far away to wield the club. Jack couldn't risk an arrow for fear of hitting Corriwen. Her face was turning dark as Dermott's hand squeezed mercilessly.

Down on the flat, Finn's voice boomed like rock-fall, so loud that for a moment the battle stopped abruptly. He pointed up the hill. Hedda spun and raised her eyes.

She crashed through a line of men, jinking and twisting like a predatory cat, striking anyone who faced her and ignoring those who didn't. She hit the slope so fast that divots threw up behind her.

'Give me my harp!' Dermott raged. 'Or she'll die in agony.'

Jack couldn't move. The Harp was in Brand's bag on his shoulder. They had come so close that he couldn't give it up, not to a beast like Dermott.

Yet he could not stand and watch Corriwen die. His hand reached for the long sword.

Dermott laughed.

Something whirred past Jack's head, so close he felt the wind of its passing.

Three stones whirled around each other on cords and wrapped themselves around the horse's legs. It stumbled, tried to rear, lost its footing and crashed on its side. Dermott was thrown, but he still had his hand round Corriwen's throat. She made a desperate choking sound.

Dermott clambered upright. The horsemen were only twenty yards behind him now.

'You had your chance,' he roared. 'First her, and then you three. I'll skin you alive.'

'*Dermott.*'

The voice barked his name. He spun on one heel. Jack drew the great sword.

Hedda came racing up the slope. She was just behind the mounted men, then in amongst them. Jack saw the swords flicker and flash, heard them sing through the air as she cut through the riders, saw men fall to one side or another and blood spray into the air.

Then she was through them, running, the grotesque mask snarling.

Dermott's axe was over his head, ready to slice down. Corriwen squirmed, managed to get one hand to her knife.

'*Fight me!*'

Hedda stopped twenty feet away. She sheathed one sword and then flipped her mask up and off. Her hair tumbled free, unbraided, a cataract of flame-red flowing to her waist.

Dermott froze.

'Your fate is here and now,' Hedda said. 'Not theirs.'

Dermott's mouth opened, closed, opened again.

'You!' He blurted. 'You are the one foretold? The red-haired warrior woman?'

Hedda stood stock still. Corriwen sensed the moment, kicked hard and spun free just as Jack leapt forward. The blade swung, almost of its own volition, came down on Dermott's right shoulder with a sickening *slice*. The axe tumbled away.

Corriwen's blades flashed. She twisted forward and thrust them deep into Dermott's chest, both of them to the hilt. Dermott gasped and went rigid. Blood bubbled through his breath.

'No!' Corriwen cried. '*I'm* the one. For what you did, it was always going to be me!'

Dermott toppled backwards and hit the ground with a crash. His eyes rolled up to stare at the thunderous sky and he did not move again.

Fainn saw Dermott fall.

He turned his face to the purple sky and howled like a beast, then plunged his hands into the cauldron once more.

Inside, it was darker than night, and he clenched his mad eyes tight, summoning all his power.

A black snake looped from the darkness and oozed over the rim. Another flat head appeared and a slick tongue flickered out. Then another and another, long, scaly snakes with glassy eyes and yellow zig-zags down their backs. First a few, then a dozen, then a hundred.

All around Tara, from burrows and clefts, roots and bushes, came the wild snakes of Eirinn, summoned by the Spellbinder.

Corriwen wiped her blades, sheathed them and looked at Hedda, who still stood impassively. Then Hedda raised her sword, touched her forehead with the bloody blade in salute to a fellow warrior. Corriwen nodded.

She turned, grabbed Jack's arm, pulled his eyes away from the dead man.

She pointed down the slopes of Tara Hill. For an instant Jack thought the ground itself was rippling and then his eyes focused.

A vast swarm of snakes was slithering up towards them, faster than he would have believed possible.

'Fainn!' He muttered.

'Come on,' she said. She pointed behind him up the slope. 'We're almost there.'

Together, the four of them climbed to the top of Tara Hill.

Before them stood a tall stone, made of the same polished glass as the heartstone.

On the side facing them was carved an exact replica of the harp they had stolen from Dermott's castle and carried with them all across Eirinn.

Jack knew what would be carved on the other three sides. They had seen the same carvings when they first fell into this world.

He approached it, looking about him for any other evidence that this really was the place. Somehow he had expected more, something *magical*.

'What do we do now?' Kerry asked.

'Whatever it is, you'd better be quick,' Corriwen said. The slithering sound carried up to them, and the sibilant hiss of thousands and thousands of snakes.

Jack took the harp out of the bag and held it up. The wind caught the makeshift strings and strummed a faint harmonic.

Instantly the heartstone vibrated like glass, in resonant sympathy.

Home on Tara Hill. A sweet voice whispered in Jack's head.

> *Home on Tara Hill*
> *Home and peace I bring*
> *Harmony my song*
> *To summon now the spring.*

'Did you hear it?' Jack asked. Kerry shook his head.

Jack walked forward, bearing the wonderful instrument, suddenly sure of what he should do. He approached the stone and raised the harp in both hands. Above him, lightning forked from one black cloud to another. A vast clap of thunder rolled away over the hills.

He placed the Harp on the flat top of the stone.

Some instinct made him draw the great sword and he found that it too was vibrating in his hand, as if a powerful current was running through it and into him. It keened like a taut string in the wind.

He took one step forward, not knowing what to expect, and raised the sword up to the Harp. The heartstone swung forward and touched the hilt . . .

THIRTY SIX

A shockwave jolted through his whole body. Every nerve quivered and tingled with raw power.

The Harp emitted a pure note of sound, as clear as crystal.

Arcs of energy leapt between the heartstone and the Harp and the sword and all through him. It was as if, in a brief instant, they had each become part of an enchanted whole.

The note strengthened and soared and he watched in amazement as Kerry's fishing line and the fine braids of Hedda's hair began to change colour and take on a gleaming hue. Each string was turning back to pure gold.

The power surged through him and he watched, oblivious to everything around him, as the Harp healed itself.

The sound it made swelled: a single note in the clear, cold air, yet it soared like a heavenly choir; a magical symphony. It sounded like the world wakening. It grew louder and louder until Jack was caught within its vibrations. The world seemed to spin.

Then it emitted a huge blast of power like light and sound and energy and life combined.

The thick bank of cloud that had blanketed Eirinn for so long was blasted outward, a vast ebb-tide in the heavens. The clouds rolled away. They *raced*.

And for the first in a long time, they saw clear sky.

In the far west, it was the deep cobalt blue of almost morning. In its depths the corona stars sparkled like diamonds on velvet, shimmering with their perfect light.

And in the east, the sun began to rise.

A ray of sunlight speared through a distant cleft between two tall mountains, a shaft of gold that lanced across the icy landscape in a burst of brilliance.

In that instant the Harp was ablaze, bathed in the sunlight of this midsummer dawn.

And suddenly, within a pillar of light that soared to the sky, Jack saw *her*.

She stood, crowned in her own aurora, splashed with intense light, spangled with the sun and stars.

The Sky Queen.

She was the most beautiful vision he had ever seen. His heart seemed to stop dead in his chest and time stood still. It was as if everything wonderful and good had been condensed into light, made into female form. Golden hair, fine as silk, tumbled to her ankles. A circlet of stars adorned her head. She turned her eyes on him and for a second he felt such vast power he thought he could die of it.

Then she reached towards him and touched his cheek with a hand as soft as a summer breeze.

'My fair champion.'

The music of the Harp sounded in her voice. It was the voice of a mother. The voice of wisdom and beauty. The voice of life. Of all eternity.

She took the Harp in both hands and lifted it above her head. Radiant beams pulsed from it as it sang.

Like a vast canvas, the land around Tara Hill began to change colour as the light of day washed over them.

The ice and snow melted away and the ground began to turn green again. The scent of flowers wafted like honey on the air.

The green spread out, shading fields and hedgerows, meadows and marshes. Hosts of daffodils appeared in swathes of yellow.

And spring returned to Eirinn.

The lady of light turned and looked down from Tara Hill, still holding the Harp high. Its light swept the slopes below like the beam of a searchlight and instantly the writhing mass of snakes began to lash and coil and then, in a black and yellow tide, they slithered fast down the far side of the hill towards the Western Sea.

In a matter of minutes, the hill was clear and a loathsome line of snakes was disappearing in the distance towards the western sea.

Fainn hovered over the cauldron from which shadowy shapes writhed up like fumes, taking grotesque form. They began to spill out, like the darkness that had oozed from the shadows on that Halloween night when they had stumbled through the first gate.

Inside the creeping darkness, they could see vile faces and yawning mouths, a mass of formless demons spreading across the battlefield.

A ray of light shot from the golden harp into the blue sky. Jack heard a faint moan of wind as a sparkling cloud took form, like icy crystals in winter sun. It slowly spun, descending from the heavens, glittering in the magical light.

Over the harp's pure note he heard a whispering, as if many distant voices were trying to make themselves heard.

The gyrating sparkle came ever lower, still spinning, until it reached the horde of foul things still pouring from the cauldron.

Then Jack saw the faces in the glistening haze. Faint and hazy, faces in gauze.

'The Bogrim!' Connor said. 'From the marshes.'

The circling apparitions spun faster, enveloping the foul entities that Fainn had summoned into being, pressing them back towards the cauldron. The dark things slobbered and howled, helpless against this force of light. And with them, Fainn was forced back, back, towards the cauldron's lip.

There was an unearthly sucking sound as the nightmare shapes were drawn back into its depths, to whichever hell had spawned them, and as they disappeared, a dozen thin arms, glistening like tar, reached from inside and fastened around his neck.

He screamed and the unearthly arms pulled him back and back, in and under. Fainn vanished into the darkness of his own creating. The great cauldron bubbled and heaved for a moment and then as if some tide in its depths began to swirl, it shuddered and rolled onto its side. It was empty.

Fainn was gone. The snakes were banished. And spring had come to Temair.

Jack felt a huge joy expand in his heart.

The end of the quest.

In that moment, he knew that for all the danger, and all the anguish, it had been worth it. He and Kerry and Corriwen and Connor had done it. They had won through.

'Fair champion,' her voice came again.

'Heart of my heart,' she whispered in his mind. 'Soul of my soul. For me and for Eirinn you fought the good fight. As I knew you would.'

Jack tried to open his mouth, but no words came. She placed a finger on his lips.

'You bear the key to all my worlds, and you bear it bravely and well. So young. So fine.'

She smiled down at him and his heart did a low, lazy roll.

'My *Journeyman*. It is a heavy burden and unasked, but once taken up, it will not be put down again. But I will be with you in *all* worlds.'

Suddenly Jack recalled what Hedda had said. *The Sky*

Queen grants a favour to those who would do her work. *Do not forget that.*

He opened his mouth again. But before he could speak she smiled again and he heard that wondrous voice.

'The gift you seek,' she said, touching both soft hands to the top of his head, 'is *here*.'

And Jack Flint *remembered* . . .

THIRTY SEVEN

His mind was in turmoil as they trundled along on Score's wagon. He had an answer, or part of an answer.

She had held his head in her hands and he was suddenly back again in the dark, carried in strong arms.

They were running, running fast, though trees. Big trunks flashed past. He was held tight. He could see black shapes flitting from tree to tree, keeping to the shadows, and huge orange eyes that glared coldly.

They were being hunted.

Feral howls split the night, like wolves, but much worse than wolves.

He began to cry and a hand clamped his face to the shoulder, cutting off the sound.

'Hush now,' a man's voice, breathless and ragged, tried to soothe him, but he was still afraid.

My father! In the middle of the memory, Jack recalled the smell of leather and sweat and the damp forest night.

Then they came to the stones. The baby Jack just saw the great grey shapes as they passed and then the man turned. Something leapt at them between the stones and a sword swung and lopped its screeching head off its shoulders.

The space between the stones shimmered and then he saw daylight and trees crowding beyond.

The man hugged him tight and he felt his father's love.

He looked up into a strong face, dark hair falling over his brow. Dark eyes searching his own, face lined with concern.

His father wrapped him tight in a shawl then stood up, tall as a giant, from where the infant lay on the soft ground. He raised a curved horn and blew it hard, three times. The sound moaned through the trees.

'No time,' he cried, almost snarled it. 'No time at all.'

He knelt down and lifted the baby and hugged him close.

'You'll be safe here. And I'll be back.'

Then he reached up and raised something on a chain and put it round Jack's tiny neck, tucking it into the blanket. He shrugged a satchel from his shoulder and placed it under the baby's head, like a pillow.

His father blew three more blasts on the horn, and this time, there was a reply from somewhere beyond the trees.

'He'll understand,' his father said. 'He'll take you home until I get back. I promise.'

And then he turned, walked between the stones and vanished.

But Jonathan Flint had not come back.

Something had happened, and even the Sky Queen could not tell him.

'Some things,' she said sadly, 'happen in places beyond my light. Where he has gone, I cannot tell you. Your destiny is for you to discover.'

'Your quest here is over, and my heart is ever grateful. You are more special to me than you can imagine, Jack Flint. My *Cullian*.' Her smile was bitter-sweet. 'Now your own quest begins. Harmony returns to Eirinn, but not to your heart, Journeyman. The road will be long and hard and fraught, but you have the heart of a hero, and bear the Heart of Worlds.

'I can tell you this only. Take the door into summer. Then find the door to night. Perhaps there, you will find what you seek.'

The Sky Queen bent and kissed him lightly on the lips, holding him tight for an instant. Jack's eyes squeezed shut.

And then he was outside the light and back in Eirinn's springtime. Jack sank to his knees, totally drained.

Connor was standing as if completely paralysed.

'I heard Eirinn speak to me. The whole land! It sang in my head and welcomed me home.'

'It is done,' Hedda said. 'No one will ever abuse the Harp again.'

Connor held up the club. Its features were placid now, bony but placid. In fact it seemed to have a self-satisfied smile carved on its strange face.

'Wield it as you wish. And always honourably.'

She turned from them and faced across the flat land where the soldiers who had been trying to murder them only moments before had stopped fighting and were looking about themselves at the fresh grass and blooming flowers around their feet.

'Harmony returns to Eirinn,' Hedda called out. Her voice soared across the battlefield, loud and commanding. She beckoned Connor to stand by her.

'The rightful High King of all Eirinn has returned to reclaim his seat.'

She raised Connor's hand, which still bore the great Dagda's club. 'Connor, son of Conovar and Eleon, will rule in peace and honour. The battle is done.'

There was a stunned silence that lasted a long time.

Kerry whispered in Jack's ear. 'You think they're going to buy it?'

'It's been a big waste of time if they don't.'

'I'm glad we saved him.'

'No coincidences,' Jack said.

A man, whom Corriwen recognised as the rider who had tried to skewer both herself and Connor with his lance, strode forward and went down on one knee. He held his sword out flat in both hands.

'For my company of men, I pledge to King Connor.'

Behind him, men started to come forward, heads bowed.

Kerry rolled his eyes and pretended to wipe his brow.

'Phew,' he said. 'Had me worried for a minute.'

Connor had accompanied them, sitting tall on his horse. It had still not sunk in who and what he was. He had a lot to learn.

'So I'm really a knight?' Kerry asked, digging him in the ribs.

'I suppose so. It's all a bit weird.'

'It's always weird when you hang about with Jack. I don't suppose anything's going to change.'

Connor had begged them to stay and help him, but Kerry knew Jack had something else on his mind. He wouldn't rest until he'd found what he was looking for.

'Maybe we can come back and visit. Like at Christmas and New Year,' Kerry suggested. 'Or the summer holidays. You and me, we can go poaching. Take a few fish maybe?'

'That would be …' Connor, began. 'How do you say it? Pure dead brilliant!'

'Fan-freakin'-tastic!'

It was after Hedda had bid them farewell and gone north with Finn and Fennel that Jack had approached Rune.

Hedda had taken both of Jack's hands and wished him a safe journey.

'Where it will end, who knows. But fight the good fight.'

Fennel had embraced Corriwen until her ribs creaked. Finn patted Kerry on the back and sent him flying into a hedge.

He pulled himself out, picking burrs and thorns from his cape. 'Big Finn doesn't know his own strength.'

Jack was torn. He hated farewells. He'd had one friend all his life, apart from the Major, and now there were more. True friends. Yet he was itching to be on his way, on the next step.

He found Rune, sitting with Brand by the fire, each smoking their long pipes and looking as relaxed as any two Cluricauns could be.

'I don't need to read the book,' Jack said. 'You know the way, don't you?'

'Ah, there ye have me, Jack boy. I told you the day we met, I travel all the ways. Of course I know where you want to be going.'

'I thought so. You didn't just turn up by accident, did you?'

Rune chuckled. 'We work in mysterious ways, us Cluricauns. Let's say we were just well met, eh?'

And now they were approaching the end of the misty way. Ahead of them, through the rolling veils, Jack could see the wide moorland where gold and pink flowers bloomed among the purple, turning it into an exotic carpet of colour.

On a hill beside a coppice of birch saplings, stood the two standing stones of the Homeward Gate of Eirinn.

Connor sat on his horse, close to Brand and the raggle-taggle troupe as Rune walked with them towards the ancient stone pillars.

He turned to leave, paused, then came back to stand in front of Jack.

'I almost forgot,' he said, with a twinkle in his eye. He drew his hand from his jacket and flipped a gold coin into the air.

It came twinkling down with a faint metallic ring. This time Jack caught it. He opened his hand and saw the five stars of the corona winking up at him.

He turned to thank Rune, but the little fellow was gone, and the mist had closed at the edge of the moor.

He slipped the coin into his pocket, put his arms round his two best friends on this or any world, and together they walked through the gate.

THIRTY EIGHT

'You don't have to go,' Kerry protested.

'I do. And Corriwen has to get home again. To her own world.'

Tears were running freely down their faces. It was time for goodbye, and the next step, Jack had to take alone.

They were in the ring of stones in Cromwath Blackwood. The heartstone was on the carved rock, nestled in the little niche that had been cut so long ago nobody could remember. Jack knew how to do it now.

He was about to open the gates again.

'It's that way,' he said, pointing to the southernmost opening.

The words of the Lady in the light came back to him. *First find the door into summer.*

That was the first step. And then after that, he had to find another gateway.

He turned the heartstone in the niche.

Moonlight shone behind him. Twilight before him. On his left he could see the rock in Temair where Mandrake had met his gruesome end. The man-shape could still be made out, covered now with lichen and moss.

And to his right, brilliant sunlight and the smell of roses and wild honey sweet on the air.

The door into summer.

He only had minutes. He snatched up the heartstone and looped the chain around his neck. Faint lights sparkled and danced in each doorway. Time was running fast.

He drew them to him, hugged them tight, ignoring his own tears, then without a word he turned and vanished from sight.

Kerry held Corriwen.

'I don't want to go home,' he wailed. 'There's nothing there for me.'

'And Temair doesn't need me. It's lasted a long time without.'

'Oh *freak*! This isn't fair.'

'But he wants to do it alone.'

'No he doesn't. He just thinks it would be dangerous.'

'We've faced danger before. The three of us together.'

'That's right. So we have! We can't let that eejit do it by himself, can we?'

They clasped hands, looked in each other's eyes.

And then they were running fast towards the door into summer.

With special thanks to my exceptional editor Fiona Kennedy at Orion for keeping me on the right lines, and to all of the dedicated Orion team for their efforts on this second *Jack Flint* story. Special thanks too for the talents of Geoff Taylor, who created the marvellous illustrations for this tale.